BOOK TWO – HEROES and MARTYRS

StarPassage

CLARK RICH BURBIDGE

Deep**R**iver
B O O K S

StarPassage: Book Two – Heroes and Martyrs
Copyright © 2017 by Clark Rich Burbidge
Published by Deep River Books
Sisters, Oregon
www.deepriverbooks.com

This is a work of fiction. Names, characters, businesses, places, events, and incidents are either the products of the author's imagination or used in a fictitious manner. Any resemblance to actual persons, living or dead, or actual events is purely coincidental.

ISBN – 13: 9781632694430
Library of Congress: 2017938071

Illustrations by Karl Hepworth
Printed in the USA
Cover design by Karl Hepworth and Robin Black, Inspirio Design

Table of Contents

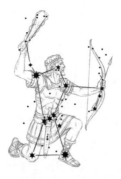

What readers are saying about StarPassage:

"Clark Burbidge weaves an alluring tale of the Carson family as they travel through time with the help of a mysterious relic...I cannot wait to share this book with my students!

"It is a story worth sharing and should be a perfect read aloud for middle grade students. It is a novel suited to discuss the literary element of theme. The clear-cut good vs. evil, faith will see you through, among others, makes it especially appealing...Because of its rich historical content it is particularly appropriate for comparing/contrasting with informational texts about the above mentioned events, a learning standard required as part of the Common Core. And finally, the well-crafted plot lends itself to a study of conflict and the elements of rising action, climax, falling action, and resolution.

"I thoroughly enjoyed Mr. Burbidge's previous series for this age group, Giants in the Land, and it looks like StarPassage promises to be as good or better!"

—TeachersDesk6.blogspot.com

"I loved Tim and Martie. They are upset about where their family is at but through their adventures, which kept me engrossed, they learn about different periods in history. I loved how each trip gave more insight to where the Carson family was with their father's PTSD. It brought them back together. I love how the story approaches PTSD as a serious issue and how they work together with it.

"And of course I loved each adventure through time. That in itself made this book so great. It gave so much more for readers. I think that aspect will help draw kids in and make them want to learn more about the different times Tim and Martie visit. This book is meant for young adults but I also think that older children will really like this book too.

"If you are looking for a great story for all ages look no further. You have all kinds of information and an amazing story."

—JBronderBookReviews.com

"This is great book for pre-teens, teens and even middle school children to learn family values, understanding, tolerance and cooperation. It is a great book for discussion groups to talk about Tim and Martie and what makes them special and how they came to the aid of their parents. It is a great way to explain PTSD and why families need to band together to help someone who comes home from the service and needs support. It would be a great way for a writing teacher to have his/her students create their own adventures for the characters and possibly join in on one holding their own star of passage. Sometimes miracles happen if you believe. Find out what that means when author Clark Rich Burbidge and the Carson family take you back in time to where it all began."

—Fran Lews: Just Reviews/MJ Magazine,
tillie49.wordpress.com

"Our middle school daughters brought the book on a road trip, sharing it and talking about it as we drove. If you are heading out soon, it's worth adding *StarPassage: The Relic* to your packing list...The relic in the book is the device that takes Tim and Martie on their adventures. Of course, any relic that has been used throughout the ages for questionable purposes comes with its own haunted history. This was the part our girls enjoyed the most. They totally bought into the idea that a seemingly ordinary object can have special powers. It fed their imagination and allowed them to go on the adventures with Tim and Martie."

—Shari, TheChicagoMoms.com

Other Books by Clark Rich Burbidge

Gold Medal Award Winning Current Trilogy:

StarPassage: Book One—*The Relic*

Fiction: Gold Medal Award Winning Young Adult Trilogy:

Giants in the Land: Book One—*The Way of Things*
Giants in the Land: Book Two—*The Prodigals*
Giants in the Land: Book Three—*The Cavern of Promise*

Fiction: Gold Medal Award-Winning Family Christmas Story:

A Piece of Silver: A Story of Christ

Non-Fiction:

*Life on the Narrow Path: A Mountain Biker's Guide to Spiritual
Growth in Troubled Times*

Websites:

www.starpassagebook.com
www.giantsintheland.com
www.apieceofsilver.com

Like Clark Rich Burbidge's Facebook page at:

www.facebook.com/clarkrburbidge

DEDICATION

*For Creighton and Lisa Rider, true heroes and a
consummate team inspiring in word and deed.
May the cure you seek be revealed and rest from
your labors be found along the way.*

*"Embrace adversity, never walk away from a challenge...
some...facing adversity think it's the end of the world.
But, by facing it you can see that you can get through it."*
Creighton Rider (August 2015)

*"It's okay to be scared...But you don't run away...
see it through as hard as it's going to be. That doesn't
make it easy...but easy isn't always good."*
Lisa Rider (August 2015)

Author's Note

Writing a series is an interesting challenge. The story must move forward, add fresh ideas, and feel like a new stand-alone adventure. Yet, it must also retain its foundational ties to the roots of history already created. It is important that the story continue and the lives of the characters become richer and deeper.

In Book Two we walk with our characters. They have new adventures and explore internal frontiers. I believe the reader will be inspired anew by the experience. The star, as you know by now, decides the story's direction and chooses the characters with whom it will interact. I am grateful to have been included in such choices so that I may tag along. Like many of the characters, I hold on as directed and can't wait to see what happens next.

I love to write. I have often been asked what makes writing so exhilarating. My answer has always been that I don't write the story. I climb into the pages and live it along with the characters. It is an approach that others may not appreciate and is certainly difficult to express. I write as if I am reading or living it for the first time. Of course, I begin with a rough idea and an outline.

However, when I set my foot on the path, it quickly leads me to meet fascinating people and into desperate adventures I had not imagined. If you have ever read a book so exciting that you have to tear yourself away to engage in regular activities and can't wait to return, you understand what it is like for me when I write. I simply can't wait to get back to the story to discover what is going to happen next or what interesting characters I will meet around the next bend.

The StarPassage series is a labor of love and a personal journey. Book Two continues that journey with its introduction of new characters, challenges, riddles, and adventure.

Whenever history is involved, there is the associated challenge of research and accuracy. While fiction affords the luxury of historical adjustment, I do not engage in this lightly and have attempted to stay true to the basics. I am particularly pleased that readers will have the opportunity to meet an amazing couple, Creighton and Lisa Rider. Their lives have already inspired thousands, and the telling of a small part of their story enriches this book.

The 101st Airborne experience on June 6, 1944, has always intrigued me and been a source of long-standing study. I am frequently surprised when I speak with high school or college-age young adults at how little they know of World War II and other major historical events. I hope a small exposure to history will promote curiosity and my readers will desire to understand better this courageous chapter of our heritage and the regular people who were thrust into it. There are no actual historical characters included, although the situations, units, and locations described are historically accurate and similar circumstances may be found salted throughout literature as well as unit histories. A few particularly excellent examples are included in the references at the end of the book.

The attack on the World Trade Center buildings, the

Pentagon, and the crash into a Pennsylvania field were events I personally witnessed in real time along with millions of others. The horror of that day still haunts many of those who saw it play out live. I remember the initial shock and disbelief. Yet, each succeeding event on that day seemed more incredible and terrible than the worst-case nightmare that preceded it. Having worked in and visited New York City often during my years as an investment banker, I had visited the World Trade Center complex many times. I had walked the offices and underground mall often and stood on the roof of the South Tower observatory on two occasions with members of my family, the last time only a few months prior to the attacks. Such familiarity made the attacks more personal.

I have lived a relatively long life; witnessed assassinations of great American leaders, wars, incredibly destructive acts of nature, moon landings, and space flight tragedies; and endured the threat of nuclear war, the Cold War and its miraculous end, civil strife and riots in the streets, and the creation and demise of entire countries.

However, no other single day or event in my life has been as horrific and tragic as those witnessed on September 11, 2001. I have witnessed many brave acts and been honored to be in the presence of heroes, but none stand taller than the first responders who saved hundreds of lives on that terrible day while in many cases losing their own. I hope that my effort to place fictional characters in this setting is both respectful and appropriate.

William Tyndale is a fascinating historical figure. Much about his life is debated, but his works continue to affect our lives today. I have taken some liberties with fourteenth-century English to allow my story to flow and not bog down the reader. Words, usage, sentence structure, and meanings have changed dramatically over the past 500 years and painstaking accuracy in such speech would certainly have required translation.

Instead, I have chosen to highlight Tyndale's unwavering faith, courage, and sense of being involved in something bigger. His final words quoted herein, "Lord! Open the King of England's eyes!" are widely reported and disputed. I have added a little something to the historical record to tie it into the story that I believe is consistent with Tyndale's writings and life. Remember, my characters' adventures into history always have the possibility of creating small or large changes. It is interesting to note that the King of England did in fact recognize the English translation of the Bible just two years following Tyndale's death. An answer to Tyndale's prayers? You decide.

Individuals like Tyndale stood fast in the face of the mercilessly enforced political correctness of his day. An examination of his defense illustrates that he viewed the oppressive atmosphere in which he lived to be not related to Christianity or religion, rather more a function of the despotic rulers who twisted it to their unrighteous purposes. History calls that tyranny, regardless of the excuse used to exercise it. Such toxic suppression directed against truth and spiritual enlightenment produced at the time an environment where fear, ignorance, and brutal enforcement were the weapons used to control the masses. The fact that the light of truth continued to shine in such darkness is a miracle in itself.

If we know societies by their fruits, then certainly those of Tyndale's day were not desirable. Should the reader choose to learn more about the great fourteenth- and fifteenth-century reformers, they will find striking similarities between attacks on people of faith both in Tyndale's day and today. There has rarely been a time where the practice of true religion and the power of faith had more potential to make a greater difference. Countless souls gave their lives to help raise the world out of a truly dark age, set it back on its feet, and get it moving forward again.

The land and time in which we live, established on the unique ideals of liberty and a transcendent Deity-inspired Constitution, could not have come to be without the sacrifices of the reformers, pilgrims, privates, pioneers, explorers, and artists that helped mankind rediscover light and beauty and a land where it would be tolerated.

I hope you enjoy traveling with the characters through a new and exciting series of StarPassage. Perhaps, if I have done a reasonable job of conveying this adventure, their journeys will inspire the reader to reconsider the heavy spin placed on history and today's reality by those peddling agendas based on past and sometimes ancient error. Modern-day inquisitors attempt to steal from courageous benefactors the terms "progressive," "evolving," and "enlightened." A clearer view of things as they really are reveals it to be a camouflaged dive toward the dark dregs of fear, error, and oppressive enslavement that has been all too frequently the downfall of civility, compassion, and society itself for thousands of years.

This book provides examples of heroes existing around us who masquerade as regular people. It is the greatness we possess within ourselves and that divinely directed potential that, when tapped and released, can raise society up to perform miracles.

PROLOGUE

The Perfect Wave

obby felt the cool Pacific slide beneath his board. His take-off had been flawless. He crouched as he allowed the water to curl overhead and felt the explosion of spray and air as the curl closed, creating a perfect gas chamber. He shot out of the tube just in time to escape its crushing collapse. Executing a sharp cutback toward the top of the breaking wave and a fins-free turn on the shoulder, he dropped back down, pumping his board several times to max out his last ride of the day.

How's that for a sweet show, big bro? He smiled and pointed at a figure standing on the beach, holding a board under his arm. Bobby noticed two others standing just behind the surfer and wondered who else would be out here so early to watch.

Definitely not surfers dressed like that. Tourists. No matter. They're getting the same awesome show.

His older brother Mike had taken a previous wave in. Bobby waited until Mike stood on the Faria Beach shore so he could show off some moves. Mike set his board down and held up both hands with fingers outstretched signifying a score of *10*. Bobby laughed and pumped his fist.

The other two people seemed unimpressed so Bobby decided to end his ride with something they couldn't ignore. His attention returned to the wave, which he sensed was losing energy. He cut toward the shoulder again and launched an adrenalin-fueled Olympic vault over the four-foot liquid mound. He simultaneously performed a backflip in the air and executed a half twist before hitting the water feet first facing the shore and pointing at Mike.

Awesome!

The rush of a solid ride washed over Bobby with the emerald water. He couldn't imagine a better way to start the day. He surfaced, finding the board floating calmly by his side, held by the leash that ran from its tail to his ankle where a double-tongued Velcro wrap held it secure. His wetsuit made a squeegee sound as he slid onto the well-waxed deck for the short paddle in. He checked his dive watch: 7:00 a.m. That gave them just enough time to rush home for breakfast before Dad left for work.

Bobby knew he and his brother Mike weren't the best surfers in a town that considered it a major professional sport, but they could hold their own. They liked to get out two or three mornings a week before sunrise, usually staying closer to Oxnard at Point Hueneme on weekdays so they could make it to school on time. But the surf reports up Pacific Coast Highway were irresistible this morning, and it was Christmas break anyway. A few extra minutes' drive along the two-lane coastal road—also known as Highway 101—delivered them to Faria Beach and the best waves of the holiday.

At fifteen, Bobby had the world at his feet. Already three months into his sophomore year at Santa Clara High School, life was great. Bobby viewed his brother, an eighteen-year-old senior, as a world-class surfer, all-around hero, and best friend.

Grinning, Bobby jogged out of the shallow surf toward

Mike, who wore a broad smile. Mike slapped him on the back. "Hey, buddy, you got some totally awesome air on that bail."

"Yeah, what a great morning." He grabbed a towel to swipe over his head and face. "Hey, who was that with you watching?"

Mike turned and looked around him. "Who're you talking about? Nobody else was on the beach with me."

"I saw them. They were standing right behind you."

"Sorry, kid, we're the only ones out here this early." Mike shoved him on the shoulder. "You must have a little saltwater on the brain."

"Weird. I was sure I saw them right over there." He pointed at the ground just behind where Mike's surfboard lay.

Mike laughed and picked up his board. "That'll make a great haunted beach story when we get back to school. Let's get going. Mom's making breakfast before Dad leaves and I'm starving."

They fast-walked the short distance to the parking lot where Mike had left the car two hours before. They had just finished toweling off when Bobby said, "This has been the best Christmas ever. I hope you paid close attention so you could learn a few of my cool tricks."

Mike looked at him in mock surprise. "So now you're the teacher, huh? We'll see how long that lasts."

"Okay, *you* can be the teacher then." He laughed and purposely let his sentence dangle.

Mike took the bait. "I'll bite. What do I need to teach you *this* time?"

"I brought my wallet." Bobby grinned as they fastened their boards on the improvised roof rack of the junker Toyota Corolla. "I got my learner's permit and I need some practice."

"No, no, no, *compadre*." Mike shook his head at him. "You're not supposed to drive unless you're with someone over twenty-one, like Mom or Dad."

"Ah, come on, bro," he begged. "I won't tell Mom and there's no traffic."

Mike frowned at him for a moment, then shook his head and tossed him the keys with a sigh. "Okay, but we stay off 101 and take the beach road for a while. Then we'll see if I let you drive on the highway. Anyway, when we get close to Ventura we switch."

"Perfect," Bobby said, his brain buzzing with excitement.

He'd never driven with Mike before, and he felt a rush of pride as he belted himself into the driver's seat. He started the car, careful to check his mirrors, trying to do everything perfectly. Backing out awkwardly, Bobby felt relieved there were no cars parked nearby to negotiate around. After moving slowly to the parking lot exit, Bobby stopped smoothly and looked both ways. There were no cars in sight.

"So far so good," Mike said as Bobby made a right turn onto the frontage road that paralleled southbound Highway 101. Bobby loved this stretch of coastline and had always considered it one of the most beautiful in California.

Increasing his speed, he drove past the small Faria colony of beach houses protected by a seawall. The paved two-lane beach road ran along a drop-off to a rocky shore between Faria and the next small beach colony of Dulah. Gazing a moment at the sweet little surfing spot below, his front right tire came a little too close to the edge, and he jerked the wheel back, overcompensating.

"Sorry," he muttered, glancing at Mike.

"Just keep your eyes on the road."

Gripping the wheel, he carefully accelerated to forty miles an hour and then backed off. That's about as fast as he'd ever driven. He swallowed hard. "Thanks for letting me drive."

"Just be careful, Bud," Mike cautioned. "If anything happened to you, Mom would skin me alive."

Bobby remembered they had thrown a few bottles of water in

the backseat. "Mike, could you grab me a water, please? I think they're under the blanket in back."

"You sure you can handle holding a bottle while you're driving, little bro?"

"Yeah, I'm okay. Just need a few sips," he reassured Mike. "Saltwater makes me thirsty."

"Me too." Mike released his seat belt and turned around, reaching over the seat to grab the bottles. "But I don't swallow as much seawater as you do." They both chuckled.

Bobby had some driving experience, having driven about twenty hours with his parents and instructor. However, his unfamiliarity with the beach road made his palms sweat at the narrow spots and curves. But so far, he felt confident.

"Hey bro, you're doing pretty good," Mike encouraged.

But just then a shiver ran up his spine as he remembered what Dad had said the day he came home with his learner's permit. "Driving is a huge responsibility and can be a seductive trap. You may drive in a state of boring sameness for hours, weeks, months, or sometimes even years. You may begin to believe it will always be that way. Then it will happen. Sooner or later you will fight for your life as you experience seconds of pure terror." He shook off the thought just as several things happened at the same time.

Mike unscrewed the cap on the first bottle of water and handed it to him. Then his brother turned to get a second bottle for himself. Bobby took a couple of quick sips and attempted to place the bottle in the center console cup holder. Since he didn't dare take his eyes off the road, he set down the bottle in the cup holder but missed it by three inches. The bottle dropped, landing on the floorboard, and water gurgled out between his legs.

Distracted, he took his eyes off the road for a split second, but it was the wrong second. The car drifted slightly into the oncoming lane, and he never saw the bobtail delivery truck approaching from the other direction until it honked its horn in a long, panicked burst.

Bobby immediately looked up, realized what he had done, and overcorrected by pulling the steering wheel sharply to the right, causing the car to fishtail and head toward the shoulder and the rocks below.

Pure terror gripped him. He swung the wheel back and overcorrected in the other direction. Big mistake. At forty miles an hour, the Toyota did what most cars would do in that situation. Momentum lifted the two left-side tires off the ground and flipped the vehicle into a roll.

Bobby yelled as he helplessly wrestled with the steering wheel and the car began its first cycle. His eyes met Mike's, who gave him a shocked look that suddenly turned to fear. Mike futilely reached toward the steering wheel. Barely missing the oncoming truck, the Toyota rolled twice on the road before tumbling off the steep, rocky embankment onto the beach below.

It came to a stop with an explosion of sand filling the air, causing him to cough and hack. Finally, he wheezed air into his lungs and realized he hung upside down by his seat belt.

He shook his head to clear the confusion and looked at the waves rolling in. *Why are all the windows rolled down?*

His heart raced in an adrenalin-fueled frenzy. Closing his eyes, he tried to slow down his panicked breathing just like his track coach had taught him. He took long, slow breaths in and out.

His coach's voice echoed in his head. *Breathe in and count to six then breathe out and count to six.* It didn't work. Silence except for his breathing and the roar of splashing waves.

What happened? He was sore, bruised, and felt as though he'd been hit by a truck. *The truck!* He closed his eyes as he remembered what happened. *You are in sooooo much trouble!*

He opened his eyes again and struggled to focus. The windows. They weren't rolled down. They must have shattered when the car rolled. He groaned and felt something wet drip in his eyes. He swiped it with his hand. Blood. He looked up and realized dozens of small razor-like cuts covered his body, weeping blood. He closed his eyes again and struggled to unfasten his seat belt.

Mike! His heart thudded in his chest. "Mike, you okay?"

No answer. Still dizzy, he turned his head toward the passenger seat. The door hung open, bent at a strange angle. Mike had disappeared.

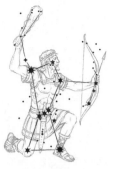

CHAPTER I

The Message

Tim stood in the kitchen doorway as if he had gazed into the eyes of Medusa and turned to stone. Tim's parents, younger sister, and grandma waited for a response, which he seemed powerless to render. Jim and Natalie gave each other a questioning glance and Jim shrugged his shoulders. The Carson family had become used to strange events involving the star, and they'd been in some tough scrapes, but Jim had never seen his son act this way before. Jim stepped over to his son's side, put his arm around him, glanced at the star, and also froze.

"What's going on, Tim," his mom Natalie said from across the kitchen.

"Come on, big bro, spit it out," Martie, his gymnast middle school sister, chided.

"Someone say something," Natalie pleaded impatiently. "What's wrong?"

"There's more writing," Jim said, feeling lightheaded.

"Come on, guys," Martie said. "We just spent a month all over history, risking our lives with that thing. It's not funny."

"What's gotten into you two?" Grandma pleaded. "You're acting like you've never seen this before."

Jim tried to make sense of the words in front of him. The star seemed to glow in Tim's hands. Words were writing themselves across the flat central axis where the points converged. Jim had never seen the writing in progress. Seeing it appear as if penned by some invisible hand was unnerving. He watched until the writing stopped, hesitated, then said, "It knows."

"Dad, you are being way too mysterious," Martie said, furrowing her brow. "What do you mean?"

Jim felt detached as if he were in a trance. His thoughts ran back over Tim and Martie's passages as well as the ones in which he and Natalie had participated. It seemed so long ago, even though it had been less than a month since their family adventures began. George Washington's counsel on hope, the pioneers example of faith, their desperate work together to survive the events that took place on the Britannic, and especially their passage back in history that saved the lives of Kelley, Dilworth, and Alvarez all flashed before him. Slowly, his senses returned to the present. Voices penetrated his thoughts.

"You're both scaring me," Natalie said. "Come on."

"Sorry, babe." Jim combed shaking fingers through his hair. "The star's message triggered a mental review of our recent passages. I guess I got lost in thought for a moment. Reminds me a little of what happened with my PTSD, but this time my thoughts were positive instead of dark."

Natalie put her arm around his waist and let out a whoosh of air. "Glad to have you back, honey. That was a little weird."

"So what does the star say?" Martie said, refocusing him. "You said it knows. What does that mean?"

Tim responded first as he seemed to break out of his stony spell. "The star knows us. I mean it knows our family. The messages have always been personal—just to help *us*."

He held out the star so Natalie and Martie could see the writing. "Here, read it for yourself."

Martie read aloud. *"The family Carson has realigned, another purpose you now must find."*

The writing faded and was replaced with another phrase. She continued reading.

"A soul at school is in great need, upon you rests this hopeful deed."

"Riddles again," Tim groaned. "Why can't it just speak in plain English?"

"Where's your sense of adventure, Tim?" Martie said enthusiastically. "Which one of us has a friend at school in need?"

"I guess we'll just have to keep our eyes open," Tim said. "If someone is in trouble, hopefully we'll notice."

"Maybe the star will give us more detail as you investigate," Natalie suggested.

"Yep, the best adventures start with taking the first step and then seeing what happens next." Almost as excited as his daughter, Jim put his arm around his wife's shoulders and kissed her on the top of her head.

There were no more messages from the star, and Christmas break ended without any further excitement. That was fine with Tim. He didn't need another adventure right now. He looked forward to next semester. Relieved, he sat beside Martie at the kitchen table, eating a bowl of cereal before heading to school.

"Don't forget, the star gave us an assignment." Martie squirmed on her chair, a big grin on her face.

"Yeah, but it might be hard to find the right person," he said. "Don't start bringing home every kid who's having a bad day."

Martie laughed. "You're right. I might have a dozen kids follow me home from school this afternoon. You know how much drama there is in middle school every day."

"Not much better at Santa Clara." He left his spoon in the empty bowl and sighed. "This might be a tough one to solve."

"All we can do is be ready," Martie encouraged.

"I'm not too optimistic," he said. "It's going to be tough finding the right soul in need. Everyone's got problems these days. It'll be like finding a baseball fan at a Yankees-Dodgers game. Finding the right kid, the one the star has in mind, is gonna be tough."

"The rabbit hole awaits, big brother." Martie waved an imaginary wand. "We're gonna find whoever it is. I just know it."

"I get it. Nothing will stop you from diving into another adventure. But you know the danger of trying to force the process. In fact, there's plenty of danger even if we do everything right."

Martie's face turned serious as she nodded her head. "You're right."

Tim pushed back from the table and slung his backpack over one arm. Even if he wasn't as enthusiastic as his sister, he couldn't deny the seductive tug of a new adventure. But it made him very uncomfortable.

Bobby spent the last few days of Christmas break wandering the back alleys in a zombie-like trance. It was midnight. He knew his parents would be worried.

He slumped into a squat next to a restaurant dumpster that reeked of yesterday's discarded food. *School starts again tomorrow and I don't know how to move on.* He felt sick, not because of the overwhelming smell, but rather the terrible crime he felt he had committed. His breathing turned quick and shallow, making his head spin, when he broke into tears and sobbed.

"How can you ever forgive me?" he said and looked at the dark star-studded expanse above. "How can anyone…" His voice trailed off into heart-rending sobs that sounded more like an injured animal than human. Had he looked closer, he would have noticed the constellation Orion with its belt of stars directly over his head.

His outpouring of remorse continued for several minutes until he regained enough composure to stand and shuffle back through the nameless alleys toward home. His feelings drifted through a muddle of confused emotions, but mostly he felt guilty, stupid, and naïve.

His mind slipped downward into dark, accusing thoughts. *It was my fault. If I hadn't begged him…he wouldn't be…it was my idea…selfish…stupid…and Mike is fighting for his life.* Tears again overwhelmed him as he leaned his hands against a cinderblock fence and let them flow.

Five more minutes passed as Bobby hovered on the edge of exhaustion and physical collapse. "Mike had a great life and I've destroyed it," he whispered into the darkness.

Bobby's mind went back over the events of that terrible day the previous week. The delivery truck driver had immediately pulled over and called 9-1-1. By the time the paramedics and police arrived, the driver and a group of surfers had pulled Bobby from the inverted Toyota and laid him on the sand. The paramedics wouldn't let him move until they checked him over and wouldn't answer any questions about Mike.

Only later did he discover that Mike had been thrown from the car during its initial roll before it left the road. The police report said that he appeared to have hit the pavement about thirty feet from where he was ejected, bounced, and then tumbled over the rocky drop-off before coming to a sandy stop on his back.

He was alive, but he had injured his spine, something about the lumbar vertebrae, and couldn't move anything below his waist. Mike had also sustained severe internal injuries and bleeding that were potentially life threatening. It took three days before the doctors upgraded him from critical to serious condition.

The doctors told his parents that he would survive but that spinal injuries were tricky and it was too early to tell if Mike would recover the use of his legs. Bobby loved Mike more than anyone, but he hadn't been to the hospital. He couldn't deal with what he'd done.

Bobby knew his parents could see his struggle. His father tried to reach out. He had sat on the edge of Bobby's bed a few hours before and explained how Mike's condition might respond to therapy.

"I see miracles like that all the time," his dad said, drawing on his experience as a physical therapist. "Mike's a fighter. I've seen it in his eyes the last few days. He's not going to give up. He'll give full recovery a run for its money."

"I'm the reason his life is ruined," Bobby remembered crying out.

His dad had responded calmly. "In my experience, most miracles have a heavy dose of hard work, positive attitude, and family support to go along with faith. Mike has all three going for him. He needs you too, Robert. You can make a difference."

Bobby felt another wave of remorse as he thought back on their conversation. He had lashed out at his dad. "I'm the reason he's in the hospital. It's my fault. Mike doesn't need me. He hates me!"

Bobby hung his head as he remembered stomping toward the door and slamming it as he stalked into the cool December evening full of self-pity.

Six blocks away, Bobby's parents sat at the kitchen table facing each other. Tony's hands were extended holding his wife's hands in his. For several minutes, their heads were bowed in prayer, and then slowly they raised their chins and looked at each other.

"How do we help him?" Bobby's mother pleaded.

"Carla, we can love him and be here for him, but sometimes a child needs to walk their path alone before they're ready to talk. One thing we cannot do is force the matter. If he isn't back soon, I'll go look for him."

"We need to do something, Tony," Carla said. "Robert needs as much help right now as Mike does."

Tony knew she was right. He stared at the ceiling, his gaze dropping out of focus. When he looked at her again, he said, "Carla, a lie cannot effectively be told to another person unless one has already convinced himself. That is Robert's trap right now. Mike doesn't hate him. He loves and needs him. But there is a lot of truth in Robert's sorrow too. He is right about it being his idea and error. He has to grow through this and discover the value in experiencing hard things and learning from them. It's how we gain maturity and prepare to become adults."

"I understand," Carla said. "And it is in the taking of responsibility for our decisions and choices that we empower ourselves and avoid the trap of becoming helpless, hopeless victims. But it is so sad to see them both go through this."

"I suppose God could make it so no one every experiences difficulty in life," Tony said. "But then how would we grow? Adversity is a part of life, and overcoming it is part of His plan for us."

"That doesn't make it any easier," Carla said. "If I had my way, our boys would never have these kinds of trials."

"It will be our most difficult challenge, but we can face it together." Tony stood, moved around the table, and put his arm around Carla's shoulder. "We can do anything together."

"I know," Carla whispered. "We are never alone."

Tony pulled her up against his chest. "Mike and Bobby are Hernandezes. Their great-grandparents learned how to do hard things and make something good from nothing. They came from Mexico to this wonderful country of opportunity. They fought their way to become citizens and make a life that would allow my generation to graduate from college and experience a world they never could have imagined. Our family has sacrificed much. My little sister died in the attack on the World Trade Center before her life even got started. It still hurts, but we have to overcome it and move forward with a commitment to make the world a better place in spite of our loss." Tony felt warmth and security in Carla's arms.

"Thank you…" Carla said, "for giving me hope. I can live on that for a while."

Tony pressed her closer. "They also come from strong Whitney pioneer stock on your side. Your ancestors faced tremendous persecution for their beliefs and were forced out of their homes. They came west and carved new lives out of the wilderness, overcoming impossible odds."

"And we cannot forget Grandpa Robert," Carla added. "He gave his life on D-Day to help preserve our freedoms."

"Yes," Tony said. "Our ancestors walked an impossibly tough road. But they walked it in faith, knowing they were never alone. They faced and overcame their fears and built something great from nothing. We've brought our children up in the light they helped create the best we know how. Our sons are full of courage and their spirits know right from wrong. They know how to make good choices and have the will to hang in there. We must trust them and pray that it is enough."

As Tony's last words echoed in the kitchen, they heard footsteps on the outside stairs. "You see, our prodigal has returned."

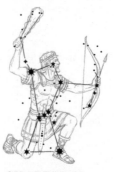

CHAPTER II

Hitting Bottom

B obby said nothing when he returned home after midnight. His parents looked worried and relieved. He wanted to tell them everything, lay all his feelings out, but he just didn't want to talk. Bobby didn't even look up when his mother said, "We love you, dear."

Instead, he continued to his room and crashed onto the bed, falling almost immediately into a deep, fitful sleep.

The first day of school after the break came the next morning. Bobby sat at the kitchen table finishing breakfast. He was running late. School was the last place he wanted to be. Dad had just left for work, and his mom labored to get his little sister organized for second grade.

Taylor squirmed in Mom's arms. "I don't want to go. I want to play with my friends."

His mother responded after taking several deep breaths that gave Bobby the impression she had just about had enough. "Taylor Whitney Hernandez, you will help me get your socks on by sitting still and you will do...it...now!"

Bobby winced. When Mom used their full names, it was the

final warning. Taylor seemed to get the message. She was a smart seven-year-old who knew when she had hit the limit of Mom's patience.

Taylor whimpered. "I'm sorry, mommy, but this was the best Christmas ever and I don't want it to end."

"That's okay, honey, but life goes on. Your things will still be here when you get home. Besides, you and your friends will have fun talking about the great times you had on vacation."

Taylor's face lightened. "Oh yeah!"

"I want to hear all about it when you get home," Mom encouraged his sister.

"Okay," she called as she bounced out the door toward the corner bus stop just one house down the street.

Bobby shook his head. "The best Christmas ever? What planet does she live on?"

Mom smiled, waved at his sister, and then turned to Bobby with a serious look. "We have had some long conversations with Taylor about Mike's condition. She has decided on her own that he is going to be fine."

"He's not fine," Bobby snapped. "Why would you let her believe that?"

"We have tried to help her understand the long road to recovery—the therapy and the possibility that his legs may not be the same again. Even with all that, she has decided to believe he will."

"Good for her," Bobby said sarcastically. "But I live in the real world, and it will never be the same again."

"It may not and it certainly won't be an easy path even if it is," his mom said firmly. "But easy isn't always good."

"Nothing is ever going to be good again," Bobby said, feeling his anger surge. "I made sure of that."

His mother slapped the table, startling him. "You made a big mistake, Robert. It may haunt you for a long time. But at some point, you will have to drag yourself from this pit of remorse and martyrdom and come to grips with the truth."

"So what's the truth?" Bobby snapped.

"Mike wants to see you...he needs to see you."

Bobby froze. His hard shell came close to crumbling as he trembled and his eyes watered. "I can't...I just can't see him right now."

"He loves you. We all do."

"He said he trusted me." Bobby suddenly felt weak.

"There were mistakes made that day and serious errors of judgment by both of you. However, Mike trusting you was not one of them." His mom put her arm around his shoulders and hugged him to her side. "Terrible accidents happen even to trustworthy and wonderful people."

Bobby felt the truth of her statement, but he wasn't yet able to process its implications. He pulled away abruptly. "I gotta go or I'll be late for school."

"I love you, Robert. Have an awesome day."

Bobby grabbed his backpack and bounded down the front steps. He cut across the grass to the driveway, jumped on his used canary-yellow Vespa Sport scooter, and sped down the street. His mom said that every morning. It had never sounded more out of place. *No way would it be an awesome day.* He buzzed the two miles to school with his mind full of dark, remorseful thoughts.

Bobby parked his scooter and headed toward class. He tried unsuccessfully to push thoughts of Mike and the accident to the back of his mind. But the story of his accident had spread like wildfire. By third period, everyone knew.

At first, Bobby responded to the first few well-intentioned comments with a curt "Thanks," but as the day wore on he pushed people away and withdrew into his own self-imposed prison. *If they knew the whole story, they'd hate me too.* By the end of the day, his friends had picked up the vibe and steered clear of him. He felt utterly alone, wallowing in his own accusations and growing bitterness.

After school Bobby barely spoke to his parents. He went straight to his room and didn't bother to reappear for dinner. Later in the evening, a soft knock echoed on his door. Bobby ignored it.

The knock came again, and he heard his mother's voice. "May I come in, dear?"

"I really don't want to talk right now."

"I brought you some dinner...chicken burritos enchilada style with extra cheese and my special hot sauce, guaranteed to make your eyes water and your hair stand on end."

That's not playing fair. She knows that's my favorite.

"Just leave it by the door." He tried to say it in a nicer tone but failed.

"Actually, I'm going to bring it in and set it on your desk," she said firmly. "You're going to have to allow someone back into your life at some point, so why not get food out of it?"

She opened the door without waiting and walked in, set down the tray, and stood smiling as if she were room service waiting for a tip.

"Thanks, really," Bobby managed. "What do you want?"

"Dad and I talked with Mike." She let the words hang in the air. Bobby couldn't resist; he had to respond.

"And...how is he?"

"He sounded positive, and the doctors say he's mending as well as can be expected."

"Except he'll never walk again...or surf."

"Robert, we don't know that," his mom said with pleading in her voice. "There are many possibilities."

Bobby turned away and stared out the window. As far as he was concerned, the conversation was over. However, his mom wasn't done.

"Stuff happens you know," she said.

"Whadaya mean, stuff?"

"Unexpected things, bad things, scary things, things that we could never have imagined...stuff."

"So..."

"This is one of those times. Robert, it isn't about fault. Mistakes were made. Your inexperience and the unlucky timing of the delivery truck all contributed to the accident. It should never have happened to two such wonderful boys. But now it has and we must deal with it, try to learn, grow from it, and continue on."

"Just how am I gonna do that with Mike in a wheelchair the rest of his life, reminding me every day that stuff happened because of me. Just me."

"This is life. Sometimes it can roll along for years without much changing. We get complacent and expect every new day to be the same as the last. Then you wake up one morning and something dramatic happens. You know nothing will ever be the same again. My oldest brother died suddenly of a massive heart attack when I was only twenty. He was larger than life to me—immortal, indestructible. He lay out in the fields for a couple of hours until someone found him. That was one of those days. Yours came last week. I can't explain how we pick up the pieces and reconstruct our lives, we just do. It takes courage and doesn't happen until you stop punishing yourself for whatever role you think you played. Stuff just happens, Robert."

Bobby listened but couldn't open up to the guidance his mother was offering.

"Thanks for bringing dinner up. Really!"

"You're welcome, sweetheart. Dad and I are here when you want to talk. So is Mike. Just don't give up on yourself. We haven't." She retreated and closed the door, and Bobby heard soft steps on the stairway.

He walked to the desk and stared at the food. It looked and smelled great. Bobby shook his head. "Mom never did fight fair. She knew I couldn't ignore it."

When the taste hit his tongue, he realized how hungry he was and devoured everything on the plate almost without taking a breath. When he finished the last bite, he stood up and walked to the mirror.

Why can't you be nice to them? They're only trying to help. It's hard for everyone, and you're making it worse.

His last thought burst the doors open again to the sea of self-pity. He walked to his bed and collapsed, crying himself to sleep.

On the second day back from vacation, Bobby wore earbuds and kept his iTunes turned up so he didn't have to deal with anyone's questions or attempts to be nice. This strategy seemed to work pretty well, so he kept it up.

After a week he noticed the kids simply ignored him and stepped out of his way as if he carried some deadly disease. He had become invisible. His grades began to suffer, and he was called in twice to the counselor. The second time, his parents were there. Bobby put up a wall no one could penetrate.

I don't need anybody, and nobody needs me. Just leave me alone.

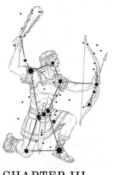

CHAPTER III

Rough Introductions

It had been two weeks, and everyone looked like a candidate. They talked about it most evenings and shared their frustrations. The star had offered no more clues, and Tim felt stuck as he sat in the kitchen.

"No luck again?" his mom said.

"Not really. I never realized before how many people's lives are messed up. If it isn't dating drama, not making a team, or grades, its problems with family or friends."

"It's not that different with adults. Everyone struggles with something," she said. "Too many people think that happiness only comes at the end of something or when you achieve a great goal. But that's not the right place to look. The secret is that happy moments happen along the way and can be found in small things each day."

"I think sometimes people stop looking for it. I still haven't found anyone that seems to fit, and Martie is just as frustrated."

"The right person will come along," Natalie said as she put her hand on Tim's shoulder. "Hang in there."

"Yeah, right," Tim said, sounding more sarcastic than he

intended. He hesitated. "I'm sorry, Mom. I know the star's message is important to someone, but it's such a waste of energy right now. I'm trying to focus on school."

The next morning Tim was running late. Frustrated about the search and the fact he overslept, he jogged across the parking lot, focused on the first bell that had just rung. He saw a couple of friends, called to get their attention, and made it nearly to the sidewalk when a kid on a yellow scooter zoomed by, clipping his leg and spinning him to the ground. His backpack went airborne and crashed onto the sidewalk. Several people ran to help, and two boys yelled at the kid on the scooter, who never even slowed down. Tim stood with some difficulty and brushed himself off.

"You okay?" said one of Tim's friends, named Roger, as he handed Tim his backpack.

"I think so," Tim said. "Who's that kid? Man what a jerk."

"That's Bobby Hernandez," said another boy, named Jake. "He used to be an okay kid, but he changed over the vacation. He's become a real hard case—pushed everyone away."

The last statement caught Tim's attention. "What happened?"

"No one knows," Jake said. "He's spent time in the counselor's office the last two weeks though. Rumor is there was some kind of car accident and someone got hurt really bad."

"His older brother got hurt," Roger added. "I think he's a senior."

"Wait," Tim said. "Mike Hernandez. I've heard his name before."

"Yeah," another friend, named Juan, jumped in. "He's a good guy. Hope it's not serious."

Maybe that's the person they were supposed to help. "What was Bobby like before?"

"A regular kid. Didn't really stand out," Roger said. "Kind of quiet, but he had his share of friends. I know he was on the track team—that's about it."

"It must take something pretty bad to cause that kind of change overnight," Tim said, dusting himself off.

"Yeah, I guess. I'm just glad he didn't take your leg off or something," Jake commented. "Sure you're all right?"

"Yeah, fine," Tim said, smiling. "Thanks for your help, guys. Can't say my day started out boring."

Tim looked around at the crowd and suddenly felt self-conscious. He didn't like being in the spotlight and tried to ease the tension. "Okay, let's move along. Nothing to see here. Just a scratch or two." A chuckle ran through the crowd, and kids drifted off toward the school entrance.

"That's going to be a fun rumor to hear by the end of the day," Juan said.

"Yeah." Jake brightened. "You'll have been run over by a school bus or something by the time the kids finish building it up."

They all laughed as they hurried toward the double doors.

Tim slowed, looked toward the far end of the lot, and saw the kid park his scooter, hop off, and jog toward the doors to the locker room and basketball gym at the rear entrance.

I wonder. In a world of troubled lives, did I just run into the biggest mess?

Earlier that morning Bobby struggled to get up and ready for school. Each day became tougher to face. His brother made progress, still listed as serious but stable. Bobby hadn't gone to see Mike. It wasn't about guilt as much anymore. Now he felt awkward because he hadn't visited sooner. One evening his dad called him into the living room where he waited on the sofa.

"What's up?" Bobby said, not really wanting to know.

"Have a seat, please."

"I'm kinda busy, Dad."

"Well, Robert, this will only take a moment. Please sit down."

"Okay." Bobby reluctantly dropped into one of the chairs next to the couch and positioned himself so he wouldn't have to look at his dad if he didn't want to.

"Mike asked me to give you an update on his condition," his dad began.

Caught by surprise, Bobby looked up. "Mike asked...How's he doing?"

"Mike had several serious injuries, including three broken ribs, which caused internal bleeding. His body got banged around a lot. He shattered his left elbow when he landed. He also had a serious concussion, but the doctors have said he'll fully recover from all that."

Bobby tried but failed to sound supportive. "That's...good to hear."

"The current focus is on his back. Mike had some serious trauma to his L2 and L3 vertebrae. The nerves in that area of the lumbar control parts of the legs. The doctors say he was lucky in that the spinal injuries are 'incomplete,' meaning there's not a complete severance of the ability of the nervous system to send signals to his lower body. There is real hope that with surgery, stabilization, and therapy, he can gain back part of his function."

"That doesn't sound very encouraging," Bobby said.

His dad sighed. "Mike was fortunate. Being thrown from the car like that onto sharp rocky ground could have easily been fatal."

"I'm glad he didn't die," Bobby mumbled. "But at our age, life without your legs is almost the same."

"That's a tough pill to swallow at any age, son. But Mike has a great attitude and is already making plans for a comeback. He knows it'll be tough, but he's committed."

Tony paused and then said, "He really wants to see you. The doctors think it will help. We do too."

"Maybe soon, but I'm not ready yet."

"Robert, you can be an important part of Mike's recovery in spite of how you feel."

"I don't want to talk about it anymore," Bobby said. "I'm just not ready."

He'd never shut his parents out before. He didn't want to. Bobby knew he would be better off talking about it, and they were the right ones to talk to. But not now. He wasn't ready.

"Please think about it," his dad pleaded as Bobby grabbed his pack and headed out the door.

Bobby's mind spun with guilt and concern. He knew his school counselor and teachers were worried. He didn't want to shut them out either, but he couldn't help it. He felt responsible and that maybe losing everything important—his grades, friends, track—might just be the punishment he deserved.

"I don't care," he said as he jumped on his scooter. *I can't care.* He had the scooter fully throttled as he rocketed through the school parking lot, clipping a kid dumb enough not to jump out of the way. It never occurred to him to slow down, and he barely noticed the other kids yelling at him. "It doesn't matter," he told himself. "I don't matter anymore. I've ruined Mike's life. If they knew they'd hate me anyway."

Tim watched for Bobby in between classes and at lunch. He saw him a couple of times in the hallway but couldn't catch up.

The kid seemed to sense his approach and magically melt into the crowd. Tim began to feel like he was wasting his time. He tried running out to stand by the scooter, but Bobby always raced off before he could get there. At lunch Bobby went off campus. The weekend came with no breakthroughs.

"There are plenty of others," Tim said. "This kid is impossible to catch."

"Don't worry," Martie said. "If the star has picked him, it'll work out. Just keep trying."

"But don't stop looking for someone else," Tim told her.

"That's a deal, big bro." Martie gave him a playful punch in the shoulder.

On Monday, Tim saw Bobby once and ran after him. Again Bobby had vanished before he caught up. Angry, Tim shook his head in disgust.

I'm wasting my time on this kid.

He didn't look for Bobby the rest of the day and noticed by the time he got to the parking lot, the scooter was gone...again. Frustrated, Tim decided to walk the longer route home, past the frozen yogurt shop, and indulge himself. He had walked three blocks from campus when he noticed the yellow scooter pulled to the side of the road up ahead. Bobby knelt next to it, looking at the front wheel.

This may be my only chance to make contact, so I can't blow it.

Tim stayed on the sidewalk and kept the scooter between him and Bobby.

"Hey, you need any help?" Tim said, trying to sound friendly and upbeat. Bobby didn't respond.

Tim stepped around the front of the scooter and stood too close to be ignored. "Hi there, is there anything I can do to help?"

There was a long pause, and Tim continued to stand there smiling. Finally, Bobby glanced up and said, "Nope."

Tim noticed the scooter's flat front tire and ignored the brisk, unfriendly response. He knelt down and said, "Looks like you got a flat there. That stinks. You want me to help you push it somewhere?"

Bobby looked at him like he had offered to steal the scooter and said in a rude, gruff voice, "I don't need any help."

Tim felt hurt and had a brief impulse to say something equally rude. He took a couple of deep breaths and decided to ignore the comment. "I know a place where they'll fix that tire for free, and you can get it done without any waiting."

Bobby seemed reluctant to show any interest that would lead to more conversation, but the idea was clearly something he wanted to know more about. "Where's that?"

"One of my classes is auto shop. The teacher, Mr. Vaughn, is always there after school with kids doing extra credit. They'd love to help," Tim said using his best friend voice.

Bobby didn't react for almost a minute. He seemed to be fighting a battle inside and kept tinkering with the tire, trying to get it off. Then he surprised Tim. "Guess that sounds all right."

Tim stepped to the other side of the scooter, grabbed the handlebar, and began to push. It took ten minutes to manhandle the scooter three blocks back to the auto shop. Bobby said nothing the first block, and Tim didn't force a conversation.

Halfway through the second block, Bobby suddenly blurted out, "Why are you doing this?"

"Just being friendly," Tim said. "And you really did need some help."

"Nobody does this kind of stuff for nothing," Bobby said. "What's your angle?"

"No angle."

Bobby stopped pushing and stood to his full height, a couple of inches shorter than Tim. "Don't lie to me, man. Get outta here."

Tim held up both hands as if the words were blows he needed to block. Bobby glared at him as if real punches would come next. "Okay, okay, ya got me." Tim tried to sound serious. "I'm just trying to get to know you so I can get something from you."

Tim didn't say another word. Instead, he pushed the scooter forward by himself and looked straight ahead.

Your move, buddy.

Bobby felt speechless and angry. He watched the older kid struggle to push his scooter toward the next corner.

"You'll never get there by yourself," Bobby blurted out before he could catch himself. Then he moved alongside the scooter and joined in the effort again. They arrived at the corner without another word.

"One more block," the other kid said. "The tire looks okay. I think we're gonna make it."

They crossed the intersection. "So what do you want from me?" Bobby asked. "What's your angle?" He mentally kicked himself for taking the bait to keep the conversation going.

"Something you're gonna fight to keep from giving me."

"Come on. What is this? Some kinda game?" Bobby's anger bubbled to the surface. "I hate games."

"Not a game—more like an adventure."

"This isn't some movie. We're not in the jungle or an amusement park, you freak." Bobby felt the last drop of his patience explode. "This is Oxnard. Nothing interesting ever happens here."

The kid turned for the first time in a block and looked directly into Bobby's eyes. "Oh, but there are amazing adventures going on all around you and you...are...missing...them."

Even if he was helping him, this kid had to be insane. Then Bobby's mind locked up.

The guy shows up out of nowhere. Stops to help. Puts up with my attitude. Why would he do that? It makes no sense.

"Who are you, anyway?"

"Name's Tim Carson," the kid responded. "I'm the one you nearly ran over the other day in the parking lot."

They both stopped pushing at the same time. Bobby didn't know how to accept the revelation the kid had just given him. "You mean a couple of weeks ago?"

"Yep."

"I could have killed you and you're still helping me?"

Tim took a step back. "Your aim was terrible—just a couple of scratches—so why be angry? I've actually been trying to meet you."

"You *are* insane." Bobby went back to pushing the scooter. "Let's get this done so you can go back to whatever planet you came from."

They crossed the street in front of the school and angled through the empty parking lot toward the auto shop's rear doors. Tim banged loudly on the metal doors.

Bobby heard heavy steps and voices inside the building. A tall, thin man in blue grease-covered overalls opened the door. He wore clear safety glasses and had a long wisp of hair between parallel receding hairlines that made him look like a middle-aged Eddie Munster.

"Hi, Mr. Vaughn," Tim said with a smile. "Found some extra credit for your students down the street. My friend Bobby here's got a flat."

Mr. Vaughn gave a deep cheerful laugh that Bobby couldn't deny made him feel a little better. "Hello, Mr. Carson, it seems you have provided a suitable project for us to work on this afternoon. Should only take a few minutes."

The kindness in Mr. Vaughn's voice and the response caught Bobby completely by surprise. He had spent the last month convincing himself that the world wasn't worth his time, nobody cared, and he was worthless. He had decided the isolation resulting from his behavior had been exactly what he deserved. But suddenly, he felt something different.

"Thanks, I'll wait," Bobby said.

"There's a table in the shop you can sit at or you can wait out on the grass. Either way, I'll come get you when we're done."

"That's great, Mr. Vaughn. We'll just hang out on the grass," Tim said before Bobby could speak.

Mr. Vaughn looked at the sky. "Can't blame you. It's a beautiful day." The teacher spun around and disappeared into the shop, pushing the scooter and giving directions to his students.

As they walked over to the grassy hill, Tim asked, "So everybody thinks you've changed. Why's that?"

Tim had crossed a line. Bobby's anger surged, and before he could stop it, his words spewed out like fire. "None of your business! You helped me and so thanks. But I don't owe you anything."

Tim seemed stunned. Bobby knew immediately he had hurt Tim. After all, he was only trying to help. He didn't speak, but he also didn't turn and walk away.

What is it with this kid! Maybe he's just too dumb to get it.

The thought burst into Bobby's consciousness, and he hung his head. "I don't need anyone."

Tim had been struggling to break through Bobby's high walls. He thought trying to help would break the ice, but it had been largely ignored. He had tried everything. Tim was trying not to let loose and beat this obnoxious kid to a pulp, but something kept telling him it was worth it and he needed to stay engaged. So he had. But he felt like giving up. The kid's mean attitude was just too much to take.

Then the words came to him in a flash as if the star's mysterious writing appeared in his own head. He spoke them without hesitating.

"Take one step and then another, or you'll never be able to help your brother."

Bobby looked up at him as if he had been stung by an enormous scorpion and said in a dangerous voice. "What did you just say? Nobody knows about my brother."

"Why don't you tell me," Tim said carefully.

For a moment it seemed that Bobby considered telling his story. His face lightened, then his dark scowl returned. "It's none of your business. Nobody understands what I've done. I don't need anybody."

Bobby refused to say anything else. Tim knew he was close to getting the truth. But Bobby's last words had sounded different. Bobby had said he didn't need anybody, but hidden within the words was a cry for help. What the kid really said was, "I don't deserve anyone."

CHAPTER IV

A New Adventure

Tim shared his experience with Martie when he arrived home. They decided Bobby was the right person to work on and agreed they needed a plan but couldn't come up with anything. A couple of days went by without further progress. Tim saw Bobby in the hallway once, and this time he didn't melt into the crowd and even acknowledged Tim's hello with a nod of the head. However, there were no further conversations.

Martie and Tim sat in the kitchen on Thursday evening doing their homework. Tim had a science test the next day so he was absorbed by a last-minute review.

The doorbell rang and his mom turned to Dad. "Are you expecting anybody?"

"Don't think so," he said as Martie bolted toward the door, disappearing around the corner.

Tim heard the door open. The person at the door said something and Martie replied, "I guess so. I'll get him."

That's curious. Martie usually just yells who it's for.

She came around the corner, her face blank and her mouth wide open. She turned toward Tim still in a mild state of shock, one hand pointing toward the front door. "It's for you—Bobby Hernandez."

Tim raised his eyebrows in surprise. She motioned for Tim to follow and waited for him to get up.

"He's waiting!" she hissed under her breath.

Tim followed her from the kitchen to the closed front door. "You shut the door in his face and left him standing on the front porch?" he whispered back.

She shrugged her shoulders, smiling sheepishly, and swung the door wide. "Come on in."

Bobby stepped through the doorway, stopped, and met Tim's eyes. It was an awkward moment for both of them, Tim suspected, but he recovered first. "How's the scooter working?"

The younger boy shrugged. "Fine, I guess. No more flats anyway."

"Mr. Vaughn will be disappointed," Tim said, and Bobby returned his smile.

Another awkward silence stalled their conversation. Bobby shifted his feet. "You have a minute to talk?"

"Sure," Tim said, having trouble hiding his surprise. "How about coming in?"

Bobby followed him to the living room, where he sat in one of the wingback chairs while Tim eased down onto the love seat. Martie followed them but remained standing. Bobby looked around uncomfortably.

"I probably shouldn't be here," he said. "Maybe I should go."

Martie moved quickly to the side of his chair. "Please, it's all right. We do have something really important to talk about."

"Right." Bobby shook his head as if having second thoughts. "You said you had an angle, that you wanted something I might fight to keep, and that there were adventures everywhere that I was missing. So what am I missing?"

Tim glanced at his beaming sister. "I guess I could answer some questions, but first we will need you to tell us what happened over Christmas."

"Why do you want to know that?" Bobby immediately stood up and took a step toward the door as if to leave.

"Because it's part of what we need to talk to you about," Tim said. "Besides, lots of kids at school have noticed you've become a loner and pushed people away."

"Why do you care?"

"Because we care about you and think we may be able to help," Martie blurted out. "But we can't help if we don't know what's going on, and we don't work based on rumors."

Bobby looked uncomfortable. He hesitated. Tim didn't know if Bobby would say anything or continue toward the door.

The silence stretched, and Tim said, "Okay, I think a quick summary will be enough. You don't have to share any detail you don't want to."

Bobby nodded his head in agreement, sat back in the chair, and briefly explained about going surfing with Mike and his request to drive a little on the way back. He became emotional when he discussed the wreck and Mike's condition.

"That could happen to anyone," Tim said. "That's why it's called an accident."

"That's not the point at all," Bobby said with an edge in his voice. "The point is that Mike nearly died and will never walk again and it's all my fault."

Tim winced at the realization of the heavy burden Bobby carried. The responsibility seemed to be shared at least equally with Mike based on Bobby's story. But that's not how Bobby saw it, and perception could be a big part of reality.

"So you were speeding and driving reckless then?" he asked Bobby.

"Nooo…it was an accident." Bobby stood again and paced, his intensity growing. "I only looked down for a second. But I wouldn't have been driving if I hadn't begged."

"Who's to say it wouldn't have still happened if Mike had been driving?" Martie added. "That's why they're called accidents and not *purposes*."

"But he wasn't," Bobby said, breathing heavily, his voice slightly raised.

Tim knew they had pushed it almost too far. "Yes, I understand. You begged, he agreed, you were being very careful, but it still happened in a split second. I can see why you feel responsible."

"That's right," Bobby said. His body deflated like someone had suddenly let out all his air.

Martie motioned toward the chair, inviting Bobby to sit back down.

"Thanks for sharing that with us," Tim said kindly to the younger kid. "Please sit and we'll tell you our story. It may sound a little crazy, but we know what it feels like to be in a bad place without any clear way out."

Bobby perched on the edge of the chair, and the tense atmosphere eased.

"Everything all right in there?" Natalie said from the kitchen. "It's awfully quiet."

"Martie, would you let Mom and Dad know we're fine and that we just need some space for a few minutes."

"Sure," she said and disappeared around the corner.

Bobby is going to be exposed to enough during the next hour without also being intimidated by adults.

His sister returned and gave a quick nod. Tim knew they would have the space they needed. "Martie, could you please get your shoulder bag?"

"Sure, be back in a sec."

He decided to begin the conversation with a simple question. "Bobby, can you give me the biggest single reason you feel your life is so messed up right now?"

"There are lots of answers to that question," Bobby said.

"I just want to hear the biggest. Only one."

Bobby seemed to think hard about the answer. While he thought, Martie returned with the shoulder bag.

"I guess...if I can only pick one thing...it would be that Mike is in such bad shape and may never be the same again."

"Okay, that works," Tim said. "Let's see what we see."

Martie handed him the bag and backed away, throwing up her hands. "Just like that! This isn't going to go well if we don't give him any prep."

"No different than how we started, Martie."

"What's going on?" Bobby asked in confusion.

"My big bro here wants to take you on a little trip down a rabbit hole," Martie said. "How do you deal with the unexpected?"

"Okay, I guess," Bobby said, sounding irritated. "I'm a little lost though."

"Believe me you're gonna feel a lot more lost in the next few minutes if the star is interested in our direction," Tim cautioned.

"Star?" Bobby said.

"This star," Tim said and withdrew the relic from Martie's shoulder bag.

"What, you mean some stupid Christmas ornament?" Bobby said sarcastically.

"Anything but stupid." Tim handed the star to Martie, keeping his eyes focused on Bobby. "Martie, is there any writing."

"No...wait...you were right, Tim. Here it comes," She angled the star toward Tim and Bobby so they could clearly see the writing appear.

"Whoa...what kind of trick is that," Bobby said, involuntarily pulling back from the star.

"That's no trick, Bobby," Tim countered. "You're gonna get your first message here in a second."

Martie handed the star to Bobby and said, "Here, you read it."

Bobby seemed hesitant to take the star, but finally reached out and drew the star to himself. He read out loud.

"To give your life true angel wings, you must learn to do the hardest things."

Bobby looked up in shock. "What's going on here? Is this some kind of trick?" His hands trembled slightly as he handed the star quickly back to Martie.

"No," Tim responded calmly. "I can't explain it but it isn't some cheap toy like the Magic 8 Ball that tells your fortune."

"We need to do what it says," Martie added. "Then you will understand. You need to remain calm and not freak out."

"I'm already a little freaked out. That writing appeared out of nowhere."

"We're going on a little trip," Tim said.

The middle of the star opened up and a small star that looked like the little brother of the big star sat in the middle. "Look, Tim, it's the Follow Star," Martie said.

He reached over and took the small star out of the compartment, which immediately closed again. The closure was so complete that there were no seams or creases to betray that any compartment existed.

"That probably means all three of us are going, so let's see what the star says next."

New writing appeared and Martie handed the star back to Bobby. "This is your passage, so you should read it."

"That's what we call our trips—StarPassages," Tim clarified.

Bobby waited until the entire message had appeared and read.

"Hold ten and two and side-by-side, you must seek the leader of the ride."

Bobby looked confused and shot a questioning look at him.

"I know, Bobby. I hate riddles, too, but that's how it talks."
Martie spoke quickly, her voice filled with excitement. She
turned the star in Bobby's hands so it stood straight up with the
tree-topper cap at the bottom. "Here we go, guys. It sits on the
tree like this. Think of a clock on the wall. This is the ten o'clock
spike here and the two o'clock spike is here. Bobby, I'll hold it at
ten and you take the two o'clock spike. Tim will follow us because
he is holding the small star called the Follow Star."

Bobby looked like a trapped animal as he reached out and
held the two o'clock point. Tim put his hand on the star in his
pocket just as Martie grasped the star point. The world around
them began to fade.

Bobby almost lost his hold on the star as the world around
him suddenly went out of focus.

"Don't let go," Martie called out.

He felt dizzy. A sick feeling surged in his stomach as refer-
ence points around him went dark gray. He tried to control his
breathing again, as he had after the accident. He focused on the
star and ignored everything else swirling around his confused
senses. It reminded him of being on a roller coaster with sharp
curves and loops. He hated the way it made him feel. Just as
his gag reflex started to kick in, his surroundings came back
into focus. He was not in the Carson living room anymore.

He stood surrounded by a thick pine forest. The trees tow-
ered a hundred feet above his head, and the ground was carpeted by a bed of pine needles, low desert sagebrush, and clumps
of tall, dry grass. Martie stood next to him, holding on to the
star, and Tim had appeared about ten feet in front of them. Tim
faced him and was speaking as his hearing returned.

"...no one can see you, and you can't feel the weather as long as you hold on to the star. One of you must always be in contact with the star or it will return home and leave you both stuck here. Also, remember that even though people can't see you, you are real and physical here, so if a tree falls on you or a car runs you over, you'll be injured or die. Do you understand?"

"I'm not sure I get anything that's happening, Tim," Bobby said in a shaky voice. "But I understand what you just said."

"Follow the rules, and you'll be fine," Tim warned. "This is serious business, so be careful."

"We need to act fast," Martie said as she tugged the star and Bobby along. "I don't want to run into any Trackers this time."

"There are sounds of cars over there," Tim said, pointing. "If we can get to a road, we might learn more about what the star has in mind." As they walked, they heard a strange sound like a cowbell ringing. Tim moved at a fast walk. Martie and Bobby followed closely, weaving through brush and trees.

"What are Trackers?" Bobby asked.

"They're the bad guys," Martie said. "People of all kinds throughout history who lived such terrible lives they're stuck in time. They wander throughout history, unable to do anything about it but watch. They're mean and fierce. Don't let them near you, and especially don't let them touch you. They want the star more than anything so they can be freed from their prison and return to what they call the Present Time."

"Present time?"

"Yeah, the time where we live," Martie said.

"I see, kind of..." Bobby said. But he did not understand and his confusion multiplied.

"When we get back we'll go over the rules of passages with you," Martie said. "It made no sense to do that before your first passage because you wouldn't get them."

CHAPTER V

Creighton's Riders

They broke out of the tree line onto what appeared to be a narrow two-lane mountain road just as a white van pulling a trailer drove by. Martie jerked Bobby back out of the path of the van, which just missed clipping him with its bumper. "Invisible or not, that would have really hurt."

"Thanks," Bobby said. "Where to now?"

Tim walked out into the middle of the road and looked both ways. "That's interesting."

Bobby followed his gaze back the way the van had come from. There were several individuals on bicycles riding along the road at odd intervals. The first one rode past. They wore stretchy racing outfits and padded bike pants, and were riding the fancy kind of bikes he had seen in triathlons and the Tour de France.

"I think we should follow the bike riders," Tim said, pointing. "There's a lot of activity up ahead at that intersection."

The three travelers walked along the road for about two hundred yards, taking care to stay out of the way of the bikers and the half-dozen vehicles that passed. Most of the vehicles had bike racks with additional bikes. When they arrived at the intersection, Bobby spotted an improvised dirt parking lot full of vans, cars, trucks, and recreational vehicles.

Next to the road, the bikers each stopped at a checkpoint and handed what looked like a timing chip to another biker who immediately pedaled back onto the road. Each time a biker would report in, one of the officials rang a cowbell.

"It's a race," Martie said. "That cowbell is getting on my nerves."

Bobby nodded his head. "Yeah, it looks like a relay race and this is an exchange point where one stage ends and the next one begins. I've seen this in cross-country races. Look at all the support vehicles. There must be a couple hundred riders."

"Let's move a little closer so we can hear what's going on," Martie suggested.

Bobby and the other two travelers walked toward the support parking area and stood next to the canopy that seemed to be the center of activity. A biker rode up.

"Number?" the official under the canopy said.

"102-1 Creighton's Riders," the rider answered. Another rider moved forward already on his bike, an S-Works, Specialized Venge with all the wireless gadgets.

"Ready to go," the second rider said. "Pass over the chip." The first rider took a small black object out of the rear pocket of his bike shirt and handed it to the new rider. Once the exchange was made, the new rider pushed off immediately. He rode to the intersection, turned right at a sign indicating US Highway 14, and sped down the road, standing up and pedaling to pick up speed.

They watched him speed away while a couple of people came up and patted the back of the rider that had just finished. "Nice ride, Jason," one of the officials said. "How'd you like the downhill?"

"Well, the climb to get to the downhill was tough, but hitting forty miles an hour coming down? Awesome!"

Bobby listened to the conversations of several riders and

learned that this station marked the end of stage thirteen. There were a total of thirty stages in which ten-man teams were riding over 500 miles from Salt Lake City, Utah, to Las Vegas, Nevada. It seemed to be midsummer, which in this part of the country usually meant 100-degree-plus temperatures during the day and nighttime temperatures in the mid-eighties. Most of the riders wore similar jerseys with a large script CR in a circle and the words Creighton's Riders and Saints to Sinners Relay on it. He wanted to know more.

"If I let go, will I be visible to everyone?"

"Yes," Martie said. "But you won't be able to see me or Tim."

"I want to talk to some of these people," Bobby said.

"I'll go with him," Tim offered. "Martie, you stay close to Bobby in case something happens. Then you can grab his arm and guide his hand back to the correct point on the star."

"Okay, but don't get carried away. The Trackers could show up anytime."

They walked behind one of the larger RVs, where they could appear unobserved. "Let me go first," Tim said. "Then you follow."

Bobby watched as Tim stuffed the small star in his pocket. Tim looked exactly the same, but his hair blew in a breeze he didn't feel. Bobby then let go of the point and Martie disappeared, or he disappeared...he wasn't sure which. He stood frozen, taking in the sudden onslaught of all five senses being exposed to the mountain air, breeze, and temperature. He realized the sun hung low in the sky and the shadows were getting long. The temperature felt cooler than he expected. He shivered.

"Let's do a little mingling," Tim said. "With all these different teams, we can pretend like we're passing through, ask what's going on, and see what we learn."

They walked back to the canopy. They could see several different types of jerseys, but by far the most common was the yellow and blue jersey with the script CR.

Bobby walked up to the rider named Jason they'd seen come in. He wore the distinctive jersey. "We saw a lot of riders with similar jerseys. What does the CR stand for?"

"I'm on one of the Creighton's Riders teams. There are ten of Creighton's teams, with one hundred team members in the race."

"Why the name?" Bobby asked, intrigued.

"We're riding to raise money to find a cure for ALS. Most people know it as Lou Gehrig's disease."

"Don't know much about ALS outside the baseball player's name. Why are there so many of you?"

"It's because of Creighton." He pointed toward a man wearing the same biker jersey, arms at his side, facing the other direction. The man enthusiastically greeted riders as they came into the exchange area. Bobby immediately noticed two things about him. First, he had what appeared to be a metal frame extending out of the neck of his shirt that supported his head, and second, a woman with a similar jersey stood at his side.

"His name is Creighton Rider," Jason explained. "We're all here to support him. He's a tremendous inspiration."

"Can we speak to him?" Tim said.

"Sure, just walk over and say hi. He's not riding this stage so he's cheering us on. He'll answer any questions about the ride or ALS."

"He rides too?" Bobby said.

"Yeah. Creighton is the only person with ALS riding the race. He uses a special tandem bike with his wife Lisa. She's the one standing next to him."

"So they do it together?" Tim said.

"Yes, they're a great team."

"Thanks, we'll check it out," Tim said, then whispered to Bobby. "We need to move this along before the Trackers show up."

They walked through a small crowd of bikes and people to where Creighton Rider stood in his yellow and blue CR jersey.

There were several people talking to him, so Tim waited for a break in the conversation. "Hello, Mr. Rider, can you tell us a little about why you do the race and why there are so many Creighton's Riders?"

Both Creighton and his wife Lisa turned and smiled at the same time.

"Are you passing by or supporting one of the teams?" Lisa said.

"Just traveling through," Bobby said.

"I hope we haven't caused you any difficulty by clogging the mountain roads with bikes and vehicles on a beautiful Friday afternoon," Creighton said in friendly but slightly slurred speech.

Bobby automatically extended his hand and realized only too late that Creighton had lost most of the use of both arms and hands. In response Creighton leveraged his body to swing his hand up to the level of Bobby's, where he weakly grasped it, relying on Bobby's hand to hold and shake it.

"I'm sorry," Bobby said. "I didn't realize..."

"Not a problem," Creighton said cheerfully. "Get it all the time. Keeps me on my toes."

Tim also introduced himself without shaking hands and asked, "So why are so many relays racing as Creighton's Riders?"

Bobby caught a glint of tenderness in the man's eyes as he responded. "It's overwhelming, isn't it? These are my friends. We started riding this race six years ago with twenty people and no support. This year we have over one hundred. Each year we make new friendships and bond as everyone faces their individual fears and discovers they can do it. They're really inspiring."

"But there are so many," Tim continued. "And this appears to be pretty tough terrain. Not your Sunday afternoon stroll."

Creighton smiled at Tim's comment and turned to his wife, who answered, "Doing something really tough teaches us that we can do hard things. There are some sweet and fun times during the race. But there are also some really hard times. We've had four kids go down, flat tires, and all kinds of adversity. But when you cross the finish line it never gets old. All the experiences blend together for a powerful impact on each rider. One of the reasons is because we learn these lessons together and serve each other along the way. That's why it's a relay. Besides, it's so long and crazy hard that very few attempt it alone."

"It's not what you do as much as who you do it with that makes it worthwhile," Creighton added, smiling toward Lisa and winking.

"I hope you will excuse me but..." Bobby said, hesitating, "...these bikers are all in really great shape and you...you have ALS and can't even raise your arms."

Creighton looked hard into Bobby's eyes as if trying to discern the purpose of his question. Then he responded in his deliberate, careful speech. "The Saints to Sinners relay race isn't an ordinary race. It's 517 miles over steep mountains, across bleak deserts, through some of the most beautiful and inhospitable parts of the country during the hottest and worst days of the summer. It runs thirty-plus hours straight, no stops or sleep, along frequently narrow roads often shared with speeding semi-trailer trucks. The legs vary from ten miles through steep mountains to over thirty miles of rolling countryside and desert. It's daunting for anyone to attempt. Why do you think anyone would do this?"

"I have no idea," Bobby responded. "It seems beyond comprehension and possibly insane."

Creighton chuckled and smiled a wide, warm smile that made Bobby feel like he was speaking to a loving uncle. "It is a bit insane, isn't it?" He turned to Lisa and said, "How would you answer that one?"

She responded immediately. "Some of the teams ride the race to win. But our teams ride with a purpose. There are two reasons I can think of, but every rider may have his or her own personal motivation.

"The first is because Creighton is so easy to love. He has learned to allow people to give to him. This is a much tougher lesson than learning how to give to others. He draws you in and allows you to see his determination to never give up. For him it's like a game to find out what the disease throws at him each week or month, then learn how to adapt and continue living and doing the things he wants to and can do.

"It also helps fund research to find a cure for ALS. We're committed to that goal as is everyone you see. Currently, there's no cure for ALS. It's a progressive disease that's always fatal. The life expectancy for someone diagnosed with ALS is three to five years. We are eight years into it, so we feel like we've done quite well and outlived expectations. There is always hope, and that leads us to the next reason. Look around you. What do you see?"

"I see people from their late teens to probably sixties working together for a good cause, I guess," Bobby said.

"Yes, that is true, but it's much more than that," Lisa said, smiling warmly. "This is an impossible task to consider for most people. It's an astounding effort for those involved. They are required to ride at least three stages each. Yet, most will ride more than that because they help pace those with timing chips and provide companionship and drafting. You see, this grueling race is only partly about physical conditioning."

Creighton took up the narrative and continued, "It's really about attitude, hope, and never giving up no matter how your legs and lungs burn or how fatigued or tired you become or the weather or altitude. By tomorrow morning they will have pushed themselves far beyond their limits and will enter a realm of physical and mental performance they could never have comprehended before. That's how we learn to overcome. This is part of a training ground. In it we learn to deal with anything that life throws at us. This is especially important for the younger riders who have yet to face the really tough challenges of life. They learn it's okay to be scared, but you don't run away. You stick to it and see it through."

"And in your case, it's ALS," Tim said.

"You're right," Creighton said. "Although I don't view it as my toughest challenge. It's just part of who I am right now. I see it as my assignment, my test to help me become who I was placed here on earth to be."

"Do you ever get discouraged?" Tim said.

"We all have our good and bad days, of course. But I'm one of the lucky ones. I've had ALS for eight years. At first I was terrified. I just wanted to crawl under the covers and hide. But you adapt. I don't know why my life has been spared, but I can tell you that I try to make it count every day by helping others learn that they can rise above their limitations and reach impossible goals. I don't dwell on the negative. No one can survive that way."

"You're amazing," Bobby said. "I wish I could introduce you to my brother. He was in an accident recently, and the doctors say they don't know if he'll ever walk again."

Suddenly, Creighton became serious and choked up as he continued. "What's your brother's name?"

"Mike. He's in the hospital in Oxnard."

"I understand. Your brother's faith and attitude will make a difference. The doctors tell me that my determination is one reason I've extended my time here on earth. But there's something more you must know. Lisa rides with me the whole way. She's the amazing one. We're a team, committed to living our lives every day and making a difference. We do it together. All these people also support and inspire us, and as a result, I've never felt alone along this difficult path."

"I think I've been too busy having my own pity party to help. It was my fault. I was driving." Bobby dropped his head.

"You can be that support and inspiration for Mike if you don't allow yourself to descend into self-pity and remorse. It's okay to take responsibility, but you do that to empower yourself, not to tear yourself down," Creighton said with a laser focus in his voice. "I would tell you one more thing if I'm not being too preachy."

"Sure, please go on," Bobby encouraged. Creighton's story had opened his eyes.

"To overcome, you must get to know your heavenly Father. The world seems so committed to denying God and telling us we are on our own. I promise you that if you make the effort, you will know He's there just as I stand before you."

"I'm not sure how real God is," Bobby said. "The world is full of such terrible things. How *can* He be real and let that happen, or if He is real, maybe God isn't very interested in us."

"You know the scientific method, don't you?"

"I guess so. You develop a theory or hypothesis, then test it to see if it is true," Bobby said.

"That's close enough. The hypothesis is that God is real and cares and you test it."

"How do I test something that I can't see?"

"Scientists do that all the time. They understand many things they cannot see. You do it by observing their effects on other things. With God you can test His reality in a much more real way. He will answer and you'll hear it or feel it in a very real way. But know this, nobody can do it for you. This is one thing each person must do for themselves."

"I don't know. I guess I can think about it."

"That's good enough for me," Creighton said. "It takes courage. But I can tell you I have tested it and been tested and my questions are fully answered. Yours will be too."

"Is this your secret to dealing with ALS?" Tim interjected.

"Yes, it is. You see, my young friends, I have overcome already for I know that I am never alone and that I, rather than circumstances, luck, or other people, have the power to make the difference. I am not a victim. Neither is your brother, or you. We are not helpless or hopeless. That is the key to empowering your life and knowing you can change your situation, even if all you can do is never give up and keep fighting."

"But you know you're going to lose because there's no cure," Bobby said and immediately regretted the hardness of his comment. "I'm sorry, I didn't mean to..."

"Please don't apologize for stating the facts," Creighton said. "You need to try to understand the full picture. The fact that I will eventually die from ALS is irrelevant. We will all die from something. It's how we live that gives us the victory. How we die is a footnote. We win every day because Lisa and I push the envelope and keep living and loving life and trying to make a difference. Life and happiness are found not just in having a goal, but in the act of overcoming every day along the way to it. You be the support team to your brother he needs and you will overcome together."

"Like the support vehicles in the race?"

"Exactly. You have Mike check out our Facebook page tonight, and I'll post a little shout out to encourage him to hang in there."

They were interrupted as one of the older riders came in and waved to Creighton. "What a great leg. How do you feel?" Creighton said as the rider rolled his bike over.

"Those hills were pretty tough, but I just kept pedaling and here I am," the older rider said with a grin. "It feels great!"

"How are your hips feeling?" Creighton said.

"No problems. I was concerned how they'd do, but no pain at all," the older biker responded. "It's probably good that I didn't know how many climbs there were on that leg. I just kept thinking each one was the last." The two laughed together.

"When's your next ride?"

"Not until six in the morning, so I think I'll get some dinner and a couple of hours' sleep. See you then."

The biker rolled off to speak to some other riders, and Creighton turned back to Bobby. "This is his first time in the race. He is one of the oldest participants but has already ridden two extra stages today to help pace others."

Bobby had a flash of insight. "Are you saying what keeps them going is that they don't just focus on their own performance but they help others too?"

"That's a good point," Creighton said. "You cannot succeed in this race or in life if it is only about you. Sooner or later a selfish focus results in loneliness and depressed discouragement and you drop out. It is compassion and concern for others put into action that allows a person to break through walls and discover the true ability and potential beyond."

A young group of riders rode in and angled toward Creighton. "I think we're going to get interrupted by the young beasts," he said with a grin.

"Thank you for taking time to answer our questions," Tim said. "Bobby, we should probably get going."

"My pleasure. Perhaps you'll join us next year." Creighton flashed his warm smile one last time. "And tell your brother to embrace his adversity and never walk away from a challenge. He will see many over the next year. But it's not as bad as it looks. Some people think adversity is the end of the world. But if you face it head-on, you discover you can get through it. And you can show him how." He looked straight into Bobby's eyes.

Then Creighton Rider was engulfed by the group of young bikers who surrounded him as if he were their father. They flooded him with stories of their ride. Creighton looked back one last time, winked, and mouthed the words, "I believe in you."

Bobby was stunned by this man and the outpouring of love he witnessed. But he was more impressed by the way Creighton took it in stride and gave the credit to his wife and the other riders. "This is amazing!" he said to Tim.

"I hope he doesn't try to find Mike, because this is the past remember. I don't think the accident has happened yet," Tim reminded him.

"That's right." Bobby smiled and nodded his head. "I forgot we were in the past."

Bobby walked toward the intersection, thinking about the conversation with Creighton Rider. He absentmindedly watched a few bikers disappear down the road. Then he heard Tim say, "They're here."

Bobby turned toward Tim, who stared into the forest with a worried expression.

"See something?" Bobby called out, his eyes following Tim's toward the forest.

"Trackers. We have to leave now!"

Bobby looked more carefully and saw what at first he assumed were shadows. But they moved. There were dark figures coming toward them with deliberate, long strides. He turned back toward the road only to see more dark figures approaching from the other direction.

Then he heard one of the shadows say, "So you still ain't learned boy." It was cold and evil. Chills ran down Bobby's spine.

"I told ya, boys, they always comes back till we gets 'em."

Bobby ran toward Tim, about ten yards away.

"Martie, we need you now," Tim called. He put his hand in the pocket where Bobby knew Tim had the Follow Star.

Bobby held out his hands as he approached Tim. "Martie, take my hand and let's get out of here."

The dark figures closed in from both directions. They walked through the middle of the bikers and no one noticed.

"Are they real?" Bobby said. "Nobody else seems to know they're here."

"Oh, they're very real," Tim answered. "But this is the past and nobody from the past can see them unless they have a star."

The Trackers were within ten paces, and the boys began to backpedal. They turned to run but discovered more Trackers coming from behind.

"We're trapped," Bobby yelled.

"Been waiting to get my hands on ya, *Robert*," a Tracker wearing a cowboy hat said.

Bobby looked at Tim like a deer caught in the headlights. "How does he know my name?"

"You been invitin' me into your life for a while, boy," the Tracker answered and laughed with an evil cackle that made Bobby's blood run cold. "Been reachin' out to me, ain't ya? Here I am, *Robert*."

Bobby felt dizzy; the hypnotic moment embraced him. He unconsciously raised his arm as if to reach out to grasp the cowboy's outstretched hand.

"Martie, right now, please," Tim whispered.

The Tracker grabbed hold of Bobby's shirtsleeve. "Got ya, boy."

Then Bobby felt something pull his other hand to the side. He resisted at first, but the brain fog cleared. *It must be Martie.* He let her guide his hand to something that felt cool and hard...the point of the star. Bobby felt the dead cold hand of the Tracker brush against his arm, and the tearing sound of his shirtsleeve echoed in his mind. Then followed a blood-curdling howl that would haunt his sleep for weeks.

Bobby held tight to the star as if trying to crush the metal between his fingers. The scene began to fade into grayness. He noticed his left shirtsleeve had been ripped off, and pain shot up his arm. He felt dizzy and remembered no more.

CHAPTER VI

Bobby's Visit

B obby awoke on Tim's living room floor. His head slowly cleared, and he saw Martie and Tim standing over him. "What happened? My head hurts."

"Seems like you got a little dizzy on the trip back and passed out," Tim said.

"You collapsed when we reappeared and hit your head on the coffee table as you fell," Martie said. "Sorry, tried to catch you but missed."

"How long have I been out?" he said, rubbing a throbbing goose egg near his right ear.

"About five minutes," Martie said.

A woman entered the room. "Is he all right? The first time can be disorienting."

"Who's that?" Bobby said.

"I'm Tim and Martie's mom. Brought you a cool washcloth for your head."

"Thanks, I feel like I have a fever too."

"You're probably okay," Natalie said. "The first passage can be kind of shocking. You'll feel better in a few minutes."

"Did that really happen? Where were we?"

"Yep, that was real," Tim said. "However, it is sometime in the past. By the clothing and vehicles, it looked like the pretty recent past."

"So Creighton Rider is a real person?"

"Of course, he is...or was," Martie said. "But you may have some homework to do."

"What do you mean?"

"Every passage creates an opportunity to learn more," Tim said. "You met a historical figure, and there is always more in the star's purpose than the actual passage. You'll need to understand all you can about this person. It appeared pretty recent, so maybe he's still alive."

"That would be cool," Bobby said. "I guess I can check him out online."

"Like I said, homework."

"Who was that cowboy and how did he know my name?"

"That's a Tracker named Clynt," Tim answered. "We've run into him before."

"I felt something very cold and evil when he spoke. I'm sorry, I just froze."

"That was a close one," Tim said in a serious tone. "You almost lost it. You need to be more prepared if you do this again."

"And don't go wandering away," Martie added.

"I don't like you getting back into this again," Martie's mom said. "I know the star is leading you, but it's so dangerous."

"I don't see that we have much choice," Tim countered.

She faced her son. "What about the rules?"

Tim nodded. "I promised Bobby we would go over the rules before we do it again."

"What rules?" Bobby said.

"We've made a list of the things learned during our passages," Martie said. "I'll go get it and we can talk before we do anything else."

"That sounds like a good plan," her mom said. "I don't need to tell you to be careful. Your dad and I don't want to be chasing you through time again."

"Don't worry, Mom," Martie said and ran out of the room. "Be back in a sec..."

Bobby rose to a sitting position, then stood up. "Before I do any homework, there's something I need to do."

"About Mike?" Tim said.

"Yeah, I haven't gone to see him since the accident. I couldn't deal with everything. Now I know I need to go no matter how bad I feel. We need to talk through it."

"We'll be glad to go with you," Tim said. "I mean if you don't mind."

"That might be a good idea. I better go tonight before I have a chance to think too much about it and back out."

Tim looked at his mom, who nodded and smiled. "Okay," she said. "You can take the car, but bring it back with a full tank of gas."

Martie returned with two sheets of paper in her hand. She laid them down on the coffee table. "Come sit on the couch and we'll go over this."

Bobby sat down next to Martie, and they read through the list together.

Rules for StarPassage

1. *Hold onto the star. It keeps you from being seen or heard.*
2. *Always check the star for new writings.*
3. *Read the writings carefully and follow them exactly.*

4. *While holding onto the star, you don't feel weather or temperature.*
5. *Invisible doesn't mean not physical, so watch out for stuff.*
6. *You return when the purpose of the StarPassage is done.*
7. *Beware. Anything you do may change history.*
8. *You don't get to choose your StarPassage. The star or something else does.*
9. *Watch out for the dark figures. They can see you and want the star. They call themselves Trackers.*
10. *The dark figures move slower than we do but have a strong grip and can use anything, including weapons, that exist in their time.*
11. *They appear to be in every past time and can move between them. But for some reason, they cannot come to the present. They call our time the Present Time.*
12. *There are multiple silver relics of which the star seems to be the most important. The dark figures seek them all and believe that with them they can enter the Present Time. They call the relics Orion's Belt.*
13. *Trackers can't influence history or interact with historical figures. They can only observe.*
14. *Whenever the Star of Passage is used, it will draw Trackers to it.*
15. *Trackers can physically interact with anyone from the Present Time or any historical individual that possesses one of the stars.*
16. *There are at least six stars: the large eight-pointed Star of Passage, two small eight-pointed Follow Stars, two small four-pointed Stars of Tongues, and one small six-pointed Star of Sight.*
17. *The Star of Passage will allow the Trackers to come to the Present Time where they believe they will have*

power to possess the bodies of people and control their minds and acts.

18. *People in the Present Time draw Trackers when they are discouraged or depressed, etc. If people look backward they can be pulled into the realm of the Trackers and be lost. But we have the power always to turn our backs.*

They discussed the rules and gave examples to Bobby of how they had learned a few of them. Martie twirled her pen. "Guys, do you think we should add anything else to the list?"

"Can't think of anything," Tim said.

"Maybe one thing," Bobby said. "When the cowboy, Clynt, got close I felt like his voice had a hypnotic quality. I couldn't move."

"Are you sure it wasn't fear or shock or something?" Martie said.

"Could have been, but it didn't feel natural."

"Let's put it on the list just to be sure," Tim suggested. "I personally hope we don't learn any more about that one."

Martie wrote as Bobby dictated the nineteenth rule:

19. *Trackers may be able to hypnotize you with their voice.*

"That sounds about right," Bobby confirmed.

"We have some work to do then, don't we?" Tim said.

Martie took the paper back to her room and met the boys at the car. She jumped into the backseat while Bobby sat in the front passenger seat. Tim drove the fifteen minutes it took to get to the Ventura County Medical Center.

Bobby didn't feel like talking, and he was thankful the others seemed to respect his desire. He continued trying to absorb an experience that simply could not be comprehended. Tim pulled the car into the parking lot and found a spot near the front.

"Well, here we go." Bobby smiled weakly.

"Hey, we got your back," Tim said. "It'll be fine."

They crossed the warm asphalt and entered the swinging doors to the general reception area. Bobby stood still just inside the doors and looked around.

"You okay?" Martie said.

"Yeah, but I've never been here before. Not sure what the next step is."

"We have some experience with that one," Tim said. "Our dad got injured a year or so ago and we went to see him several times at the VA. It can't be that different."

Tim walked over to the reception desk and said, "Do you have a Mike Hernandez as a patient?"

The receptionist responded casually. "Let me see... I have a Mike Hernandez in room 207 East."

She looked up and smiled. "Just take the main elevators up to the second floor and turn right. Room 207 is just past the nurse's station."

"Thanks," Tim said. They followed the directions and arrived outside 207 East, where Bobby hesitated and looked at Martie and Tim.

"The door's closed. Maybe he can't be disturbed right now."

"Don't worry, Bobby. Just walk in. If it's a bad time they'll send you out." Martie pushed the latch on the door, which swung easily inward.

"You go in and we'll wait here until you tell us it's okay," Tim suggested.

"Sure, I better go in first," Bobby said. "He may not be ready for a big crowd."

Bobby looked into the small hospital room. There was a TV attached to the ceiling on the upper right-hand side. The bathroom blocked the view of most of the room, so he could only see the foot of the bed. Empty chairs stood in front of a window at the far end. *Good, he's alone.* Bobby tentatively entered the room.

He passed the bathroom door and the full room came into view. Mike lay on his back, his eyes closed. He had an IV taped to his right arm and an oxygen clip on his left middle finger. Bobby stopped, trying to deal with what he saw. Mike's bandaged head was swollen and discolored with bruises.

He turned and whispered to Martie and Tim. "He's sleeping. Maybe we should come back later."

Mike's head turned toward them. "I'm not sleeping, just bored." He slowly opened his eyes and focused. Bobby waited.

"Hey, bud, nice to see you," Mike said groggily. "Been worried about how you were doing."

"Hi Mike," Bobby said. "It's been kinda rough the last two weeks."

"For me, too, but we're still here, right?"

Bobby nodded his head and immediately felt embarrassed. *What a stupid thing to say. He's the one who's been in the hospital.*

Mike seemed to read his mind. "The toughest injuries aren't always the obvious ones, bud. You must have had a really hard time."

Bobby moved to the bed and put his hand on Mike's arm. "I'm so sorry. I never should have asked..."

Mike interrupted him. "Hey, I've been thinking a lot about what happened, and we both share the responsibility. Don't you dare take this all on yourself. We were pretty dumb, huh?"

"Yeah, but it still wouldn't have happened if I hadn't brought it up...about driving I mean."

"Okay, that's true, but I could also have just said no." Mike smiled. "But let's not talk about that. What's been going on?"

"A lot actually, but first you tell me how you're doing. I haven't really talked to Mom and Dad much about it."

"They've been worried about you, even more than they have about me I think. I'm a little jealous." Mike gave him a wink.

"I know. I need to visit with them next. But I'm doing better. So what's your status?"

"The doctors say my injuries are healing pretty well. Got bounced around a bit when the door opened. They tell me I'm a pretty lucky guy. In the next week or so they'll be able to start me on some therapy to see where my legs are." Mike laughed. "Didn't mean to make it sound like a joke, but that kind of struck me as funny."

"Have they told you anything about if you will be able to walk again or not?" Bobby said.

Suddenly, Mike's face crumpled, and Bobby knew his brother fought hard to control his emotions. "A little early to tell they say. No feeling yet, although sometimes I think there's something." He hesitated. "But I'm gonna do everything they tell me and work hard. Can't let you be out there in the waves unsupervised."

Tears brimmed in both their eyes. "I'm here to help you. Is that okay, Mike? We're a team, right?"

"You bet we are, little bro. Wouldn't think of having all this fun without you. Heard you talking to someone. Are the nurses hovering again?"

"Nope, I have a couple of friends who've been helping me. Can they come in?"

"Sure, my schedule's not too crowded today."

Bobby motioned to Tim and Martie. They entered the room and stood uncomfortably next to Bobby.

Mike waved his hand toward the chairs. "Hey, take a seat."

After Tim and Martie introduced themselves, Mike cocked his head. "Carson, you look kinda familiar. Do you go to Santa Clara?"

"Yeah," Tim answered. "But I'm a year behind you."

"So how are things at school?" Mike addressed the question to Tim.

"People have heard about the accident, but they don't know the details except that you're in the hospital."

"I've had a few visitors," Mike said. "But the nurses are pretty tough so not too many have snuck through."

Bobby cleared his throat and broke into the conversation. "There's something we need to talk about, Mike."

"About school or Mom and Dad?"

"Neither. Something happened that will be pretty hard to believe," Bobby began carefully. "I'm not gonna tell you that part right now. But there is something you need to do with me."

Mike drew his brows together. "You sound serious. I think I'm doing well enough to hear what you have to say."

Bobby looked at Tim and Martie for help. "It's kind of hard to figure out where to start."

Tim smiled at him. "Just start where your brain takes you, and we'll sort it out."

"Okay, here goes," Bobby said, turning back to look at his brother. "We went on a little trip and ran into someone we think you might like to meet."

"A trip?" Mike said. "Do Mom and Dad know about this?"

"We didn't go anywhere…really…but we kind of did go somewhere." He stammered, struggling for the right words. "But the point is we met this guy who wanted you to know some things. I guess he wanted me to know too."

"Okay, what do we need to know and who is this mysterious guy?"

Tim interrupted. "Bobby, we need to tell him the whole story or it won't make sense."

"I don't know the whole story so maybe you'll have to do that part."

Tim nodded and spoke to Mike. "This is going to sound really strange, but please listen to the whole thing before judging it."

"Okay, I'm not going anywhere. But this sounds a little dramatic."

"Not dramatic, but definitely mysterious," Martie added.

They all sat down and Tim told him about the Carson family's trip to Astoria, Oregon, over four years ago. He explained how they found the eight-pointed star in the back of the shop and the mysterious old lady. He described his dad's injuries and PTSD and the problems their family went through just before Christmas. Mike listened intently and asked several questions about Jim's recovery.

"This is the part that gets a little hard to believe so I'm going to tell it to you straight out," Tim said before continuing.

Tim related the discovery of the star's writing and their first passage. He talked about the homework they gave to his dad and his findings. He then described the second and third passages and finally the passage his parents took by themselves.

Mike lay there stone faced, but listening. Finally, Tim and Bobby together described the most recent passage.

Then Bobby added, "I knew that I had to come to see you and that we had to do the research together."

"This is pretty hard to swallow," Mike said. "I'll need to think about it. But I can certainly do some checking. I have lots of free time."

"So here's the assignment," Bobby said. "I want you to research Creighton's Riders, the Saints to Sinners relay, and Mr. Rider himself and tell us what you find."

"Maybe he's still alive," Martie said.

"Whadaya say, big bro?"

"What you've told me is pretty strange, but...intriguing," Mike said. "I'll do it. Need my computer though."

"I need to talk to Mom and Dad and apologize for my attitude anyway," Bobby said. "I'll ask them to bring it over tomorrow."

"How about bringing it to me tonight? I'd like to get going right away. It's pretty hard to find something interesting and new to do around here."

"Will do," Bobby said.

They talked for another thirty minutes about the passages and answered some of Mike's questions. Mike's eyes began to flutter, and he yawned. "I think I need a little rest before I get into the research."

"We'll be back this evening with the laptop." Bobby stood and gripped Mike's hand. "See you then. Now get some sleep."

"Thanks for coming over," Mike said, his words slow. "Being on a team with my bro is already making a difference."

"Me too," Bobby hadn't felt this good since their surfing trip. They were on a wave together again, and he felt it taking them somewhere.

As they walked down the hall, Bobby said, "It's awesome to see him. This is going to be fun."

Tim shook his head and turned to Martie. "Oh boy, now I have to chaperone two people in wonderland."

She shot a mischievous grin at Tim. "I have a feeling the adventure is just beginning."

"That's what worries me," Tim said, groaning. They broke out laughing as they passed the reception desk, causing several people to give them strange looks. The three adventurers looked at each other and laughed even louder.

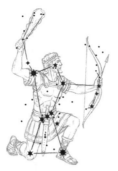

CHAPTER VII

Therapy

Three days passed before Bobby was able to visit and check on Mike's research. Tim and Martie came with him. They entered the room to find Mike propped up on his elevated bed with the computer on a rolling desk extended over his lap. Next to the computer sat a note-covered legal pad with several pages turned.

Bobby smiled at his brother. "Looks like you've been hard at work."

"Yeah, I can tell you all about the relay race," Mike said. "We oughta try it someday."

"Sure, but we need to do a few things first, like get you walking again," Bobby said.

"You're such a spoilsport," Mike said sarcastically.

"So what have you learned, bro?"

"Not only have I learned a lot, but I talked to him."

"To who?"

"Mr. Rider."

"You're kidding. He's still around?"

"Yeah, I asked him if he remembered talking with you during a recent race. He didn't remember at first, but then I told him I'm the brother you mentioned that had been paralyzed in a car accident."

"And he remembered?"

"Yeah. Guess when it was you talked to him?"

"When?"

"During last summer's race." Mike sounded really excited. "He invited me to join him at the finish line next summer. The race is the last week of July."

"That is so cool, Mike." He gave him a high five.

"He invited you to ride if you can get in shape," Mike added.

"Awesome!" Bobby felt elated and then thought about where they were. "That's a great goal so let's work on that one together."

"That's the team spirit, bud," Mike said.

"So what did you learn?"

"I had a bunch of questions that Mr. Rider very patiently answered. I talked to him by speaker phone, and his wife was there too. They gave me three suggestions in dealing with my current situation and getting the most out of it. I wrote them down."

Mike turned the legal pad back one page and handed it to Bobby. "Here, you read it."

Bobby looked at the pad and saw the statements were numbered one through three. He began reading the notes that were in first person as if the Riders were speaking:

"Number one. We were terrified at first. We didn't know what ALS even was. As we learned more, the initial fear threatened to turn to hopelessness. I mean, there is no cure. It usually takes you in three to five years and you usually die by suffocation when your diaphragm stops working. I lost the use of my hands, then my arms over time, and I had to decide how I was going to do things left handed, then with my feet and voice later. The disease throws challenges at you one by one over the weeks, months, and

years. I have to figure out how the rules of the game are chang-
ing and then beat the new challenge. So far we've done well. I'm
in my eighth year, and the doctors think my attitude and ap-
proach to keep fighting has been an important part."

Bobby looked up at Mike, who beamed as if someone had
told him the secret of life.

"Number two. People ask us why we're so involved in biking
and why we do the race. Our answer is because we can. You do
what you can and live your life to the fullest. You never let what
you don't have rob you of what you do have. Best of all, we've
built this weird-looking tandem bike with a bucket seat in the
front so we can both pedal and do it together. Doing things as
a team makes all the difference. We're never alone." Then Lisa
added, *"And it's also because Creighton is an easy guy to love.*
He gives all he can and allows others to give to him. There's no
pride, only compassion."

Bobby had to stop to wipe the gathering moisture from his
eyes. He looked at Mike. "We're a team, too, and neither of us will
ever be alone."

"That's right, and there are others with us. Some seen and
many unseen. Did you know that there were over a hundred
people riding in the Creighton's Rider's relays last summer?"

"It did seem like most of the riders had the same shirt on."

"Go ahead and read number three. It's the best one. I asked
them how they were able to continue to face the challenges
that every day brought."

Bobby read on. *"You need to learn to embrace adversity. Nev-*
er walk away from a challenge. Walk into it and you'll work your
way through. Some people think it's the end of the world, but by
facing it you see that you can get through it." Lisa finished the
thought: *"It's okay to be scared. But you don't run away. You*
stick to it and work through it. That doesn't make it easy. But
easy isn't always good."

Bobby looked up. "That's what she said to me when we met."

"As strange as it sounds, bud, it's true. Your story is true. They remembered you. You really were there."

"Wait a minute," Bobby said. "There's one more thing I forgot to mention."

"About the race?" Mike said.

"Kind of. Mr. Rider said he would do a shout out to you that night on his Facebook page. It struck me as funny at the time because he wrote it before the accident happened."

"Let's check it out," Mike said as he began clicking the keys on his laptop. "I've already been to the Creighton's Riders Facebook page, but I didn't look back at the date. Let me see. It would have been around the end of July last year."

Mike clicked his mouse a few more times, then stopped and read something. He shook his head and looked up at him. "Here it is."

Mike turned the screen so the others could see. There underneath a picture of Creighton and Lisa pedaling their strange tandem bike was a brief caption that read, "This one's for Mike who is in the fight of his life. You can do it!"

"That's *so* cool," Martie said.

"They're the cool ones," Bobby responded.

"I know one thing," Tim said. "That tandem bike looks heavy. I wouldn't want to ride that thing up a very steep hill."

Mike flipped through the hundreds of race pictures included in the gallery. "We definitely have to do this someday."

After several minutes looking at the pictures, Bobby said, "Where do we go from here?"

"Creighton and Lisa gave me their address and email so we could correspond. They want me to keep them up to date on my progress. You see, our team is growing already!"

"Wow, that's amazing! Maybe we can go visit them if you're able."

"*WHEN* I'm able!" Mike said seriously. "I'm gonna fight every day."

"And I'm gonna be there with you." They embraced as the nurse arrived to check Mike's vitals.

"I guess we better get going," Bobby said as he took a step back to allow the nurse access. "See you soon."

Mike gave him a two-fingered salute. "Just remember, this may be tough, but easy isn't always good."

CHAPTER VIII

Whispers in the Dark

D onny Wright was in trouble, but he didn't care. He didn't care about anything. The principal had called him in again today. His mind replayed the meeting; he'd heard it all before. Skipping school, tardiness, bad attitude, fights, disruptive behavior, failing grades. He knew the right things to say to get out of the principal's office. It always worked with the school counselor too. They bought it every time. But he had no desire to change. Life seemed terrible, so why try at all?

His parents had finalized their divorce the previous summer, but that only added to a long trend toward the bottom of the barrel. He lived with his mom, whom he rarely saw because she worked long hours and partied the rest of the time. He didn't hate her; she just wasn't included in much of his thinking. Donny ran his own life and did what he wanted.

Donny didn't want to talk about history or see the bigger picture. In his heart he didn't believe in a bigger picture. His life revolved around how to escape the next couple of hours. He played around with pot and other drugs for several years, but lately he'd started using regularly. His sources included dealers, fringe gang members, and a few friends he hung out with to get a buzz. At first it helped him forget his problems, so he used even more. But in the long term, it sucked out of him the desire to do much of anything except escape. It was easier than living a real life.

Escaping took up most of his time nowadays. He lived a solitary life, using alcohol and drugs mixed with nightly online video gaming that often went until the early hours of the morning. He told himself that he was in charge of his life and his body and he could do what he wanted with it. Besides, he only missed a little sleep time.

But staying up until five in the morning meant he slept until noon. So school rather than sleep became the price of his behavior. He had no interest or energy for anything else. He told his mom and the principal he would work on getting his schedule turned around and that he had friends in the online gaming community so he didn't need any at school. He had argued that his online friendships were even better because they consisted of people all over the world. But he wasn't working on changing his schedule, and he didn't really care about online friendships.

He felt bored and unhappy, but it went deeper than that. His life seemed meaningless. He was going nowhere fast and saw no future. The principal had referred him to a counselor for depression. An appointment was set, but Donny had already forgotten when.

Today, like most days, he slumped in a dingy brown bean bag chair in his basement room with the lights off and the curtains closed. It was depressingly dark even in the middle of the afternoon. He drew in another deep breath of the intoxicating smoke and held it longer in an attempt to get high.

I should feel something, anything—angry, sad, or high—but I don't feel anything at all. "Nothing!" he said out loud in a voice that sounded distant, almost like an echo.

Donny listened and waited, absorbed in his loneliness and self-pity. His mind sank deeper and deeper into the darkness until he heard a faint voice.

"Ya ain't alone, boy."

He opened his eyes and looked around. "Who's there?"

The room was empty, but the voice answered. "We're here. Ya been calling us, and we always come."

Donny's mind engaged slowly. "Who's that?"

"Name's Clynt."

"Where are you, Clynt?"

"Partly in your mind and partly in history just a minute ago."

"History...what?"

"Don't matter now. You'll find out when you need to."

Donny felt confused, disoriented. Did he really hear a voice? "Why are you here?"

"Like I said, ya called so we came."

"Who are you?"

"Yer friends, boy—the only ones who understand," Clynt said.

"No one understands," Donny said to the empty room. "No one cares so why should you?"

"Cause we're where you are—nowhere. We understand."

He pushed himself deeper into the bean bag. Panic crept to the edge of his mind, mixing with anger at being interrupted.

"How could you possibly know what I'm dealing with?"

"You'll be findin' there's one bunch who does. That's us. Join us, boy. We needs yer help."

He sat up, curious about the thought. "My help?"

"Yep, need ya to do somethin' for us. Somethin' only you can do."

"What's that?"

"Just a little matter of getting somethin' for us. It'll be easy, and we'll be friends forever."

Donny thought he heard dark laughter in the distance. It

sent a chill through him. He hesitated, then continued. "I'm listening."

"That's my boy. We knew you'd be helpin' us."

"Okay, maybe. Whatdaya want me to do?"

"We jus' wants a little Christmas bauble. Jus' a little thing."

"A Christmas what?"

"An ornament. Looks like a star. You jus' needs to get it from a kid's house. We knows where it is and can tell ya how to get it."

"I dunno. Why should I? What's in it for me?"

"That's the spirit, boy. Need to look out for number one, eh? We can tell you where to get all the stuff you want and how to beat all the games."

"Now you're talking. I love gaming." Donny warmed to the conversation.

"Ya have my word on it," Clynt said.

"Guess I can do that. What about the police?"

"It's easy. Got a friend who'll help ya. He's an expert he is. Horst'll tell ya how. Then we'll always be here to help. Yep, you'll get what ya deserve."

Another voice joined the conversation. This voice sounded educated with a slight accent Donny couldn't quite place.

"Hello, young man. My name is Horst. I know a few things about getting into places, getting what you want, and getting back out without anyone being the wiser. I will teach you how to become a real spy."

"A spy? That's cool."

"Yes, and you will do an excellent job. In and out without a trace—no evidence, no police."

Donny felt a rush of adrenalin tingle his skin. He listened to Horst explain the plan. In the midst of his drug-induced haze, he decided he liked the idea. He struggled to his feet and walked to the corner of the room where he thought the voices were coming from. Nothing.

I've got nothing in my life, and this is something awesome. Sure it's stealing, but only a small thing nobody cares about... no way to get caught...and a chance to have real friends that understand.

He just needed to find the people who had the star and sneak in. Horst seemed to have heard his thoughts.

"That's correct, my friend. Having something important to do will put you on the path." Wicked laughter echoed in his mind again. But this time he welcomed it and laughed with the voices.

I'm on the path. He fell back into the bean bag and let his mind drift. He didn't care where it led. He'd figure that out later. He had a job to do.

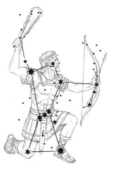

CHAPTER IX

Hanging On

Three weeks passed. Bobby's new resolve fueled his long climb back. Bobby's grades had improved, and most of his friendships slowly returned to normal. He continued to visit Mike as often as possible, at least three times a week. Mike's face looked normal, and the bandages had been removed. He had started his therapy with full leg supports and was working hard.

His big brother struggled to stay optimistic and fought to keep his promise to work hard every day. But Bobby grew increasingly concerned at the fatigue and discouragement that accompanied Mike's lack of progress.

As he rushed to class, Tim stopped him in the hallway. "How's it going this week?"

"School's okay, but Mike isn't making much progress," Bobby answered as they continued to walk toward class.

"Sorry to hear that. How's his attitude doing?"

"Suffering." Bobby lowered his head and shook it sideways. "I can't imagine how hard rehab must be. Doing that every day and feeling like there's no progress. He's hanging in though.

But he really needs to see something happening to keep going. I'm beginning to worry."

"Maybe we can do something to help," Tim said.

"What's on your mind?" Bobby said as they arrived at his classroom door.

"Nothing on mine. But the star seems to have some ideas."

"What do you mean?" Bobby looked up curiously. "It hasn't had anything to say for weeks."

"Well, it did this morning. Can you come by after school?"

"Yeah. I have to visit one of my teachers to make up a test, but then I'll be there."

"Okay, see you later." The bell rang as Bobby stepped through the doorway, his mind a thousand miles away.

There's more writing on the star? Maybe we can show it to Mike too.

Bobby could hardly wait for the end of the day. After his test he ran to the parking lot, jumped on his scooter, and rode straight to the Carson home. He bounded up the steps and raised his hand to knock as Martie pulled the door open.

"Been watching for you," she said. "You're gonna be interested in this."

He closed the door behind him and turned to find Tim holding the star.

"The writing hasn't changed," Tim said, holding out the star. "I think it's for you."

Bobby took the star, his hands trembling slightly with excitement. "How do you know it's for me?"

"Read it and see," Tim said.

Bobby turned the star over and noticed writing in a precise script in the center of the star. He read silently.

"It's time to make a brother's dream, not as impossible as it may seem."

Bobby looked at Tim. "What's the star getting at?"

"Martie and I wondered the same thing. We can't think of any other brother it could be referring to but Mike."

"How can Mike be part of this? You know where he is."

"You see, it's been waiting for you," Martie said, pointing to the star in Bobby's hands. "There's new writing appearing."

Bobby read it aloud.

"Take the star to room 102 so he may travel the path with you."

"I get the message, but it doesn't make any sense," Bobby said. "We need to take the star to the hospital and show it to Mike. But then what?"

"That's how it always is with the star," Martie said. "It gives direction, and you have to follow it before you get more."

"All we can do is take the star to Mike's room and show it to him," Tim added. "He already knows about it so that won't be a big deal. Then we wait and see what happens."

Bobby stayed for dinner and called his parents to let them know he'd be late because he would go visit Mike afterward. His folks asked a few questions, then agreed as long as he got home by ten o'clock.

"Thanks for calling and letting us know," his dad said.

"No prob...see you at ten."

They ate quickly and explained the star's most recent directions to the Carsons. Tim's parents suggested they drive with them to the hospital and stay to see what the star had in mind.

"You know it's good to have someone there to come back to after a passage," Tim's dad reminded them. "You know, just in case."

"Sure, sounds like a plan," Tim agreed.

Bobby felt like dinner and the drive took forever. Then as they parked, he suddenly found it difficult to get out of the car.

"What's wrong?" Martie said. "Having second thoughts?"

"Not really," Bobby answered. "I just can't see how this could possibly be positive for Mike. I mean, he can't go with us because he can't move his legs. It makes no sense to make him feel like he's missing any more than he already is."

"It must be very difficult," Mrs. Carson said as she opened the car door for him. "Mike is already struggling to stay positive. Maybe even beginning to feel it's hopeless. But what else can we do?"

"I don't like it," Bobby said. "I can't think of any way this will end up being helpful."

"So what do you want to do," Mr. Carson said. "It's decision time here."

Bobby sat for another minute going back and forth in his mind until he came to a decision and got out of the car. "It doesn't matter how I feel. We have to do this anyway."

"That's right and probably the only real option at this point," Tim's dad assured him.

They walked together across the lot, into the building, and past the receptionist who barely looked up. They obviously knew where they were going. Passing the elevator, they fast-walked to Mike's new room—102. The door was closed. Bobby hesitated.

Martie stepped forward and handed him the shoulder bag that contained the star. "Here, you'll need this. It's your show this time."

Bobby took the bag. It felt strangely light in his hands. He pushed open the door and walked part way into the room. What he saw threw his mind back into confusion again. His parents were there.

Mike felt discouraged. His ideas and energy had run out. He honestly didn't know how he could face another endless day of the same thing without progress. He felt like a runner in a marathon who had reached his limit.

"Something needs to happen soon to help me feel I'm going somewhere with this," he had said to the therapist after his morning session. He felt the braces were only keeping him from progressing.

His therapist, Kathy, was tough for being so young. At only five foot three and under one hundred and ten pounds, she looked to be in the wrong profession. But her strength and determination were more than enough for them both. Her shoulder-length dark hair was pulled up in a high ponytail, and she wore standard hospital scrubs with brightly colored running shoes.

She's a cute one, Mike thought when he first met her. He might even have been attracted to her had she not been so sickeningly enthusiastic. He really didn't need the constant irritation on top of everything else.

She seemed to enjoy celebrating microscopic, meaningless changes and kept pointing out progress that Mike decided wasn't really happening. He tried not to lose his temper, but it got harder each day, and her relentless energy was getting on his nerves.

During the afternoon session he'd lost it. "Why do you act like this is going so well? It stinks. Nothing's happening!" Kathy had stopped the session and helped him to his wheelchair.

She sat next to him on a bench. "Who exactly is the trained professional here, Mike?" she said sternly.

"You are, of course," Mike snapped back. "But I'm not stupid. I know nothing is happening."

"Actually, you don't know that," she said calmly. "How far did you just walk on the parallel bars?"

"About ten feet."

"And that's about ten feet farther than when we started is it not?"

"Yes, but it's almost all with my hands and arms, not my legs."

"Okay, but almost isn't the same as all," Kathy said smiling.

"Yeah, but..."

She cut him off. "No buts. You are doing more, and in this case more is good. Better will come later."

He had returned to his room frustrated and defeated. Kathy was right. He had to do his part, but he didn't know how long he could keep going.

Donny warmed to his assignment. Over the past week he'd identified the Hernandez kid at school that Clynt said last used the star. He followed Bobby home and watched until he knew where his room was located. Having completed that task, Horst had directed him to the more likely target.

Horst had told him the star was at the Carson home, so he stopped tailing Bobby and focused on Tim Carson. Donny had conversations with Horst over several evenings and reported his progress. Horst informed him that Tim had a sister who kept the star in a shoulder bag in her room.

He rode his BMX bike over to the Carson home several times to check it out. It took two more trips before he saw the girl and another visit to determine which room in the house was hers. He readied his plan. *I'm ready to go as soon as there's a night when everyone is gone.* It wouldn't be fancy. He just needed a ladder to get to the second-floor window and a hammer to break the pane. A quick smash and grab. He'd be in and out in a couple of minutes. He sat in his bedroom considering his plan in a dull drug-induced haze when the voice came again. "Ya ain't bein' smart, boy."

"Clynt, is that you? Whatdaya mean?"

"Yep, kid," he answered. "Ya can't just smash everythin' up. Noise'll attract attention. Ya gots to get in and out quiet like so nobody knows ya been there."

"That means it'll take longer."

Horst's voice answered. "Maybe...maybe not. Check the doors and windows before you do any smashing. You just might find an easy way in."

"Okay, I can do that."

"And be smart about it. Wear gloves and remove your shoes."

Mike had been moved to another part of the hospital which focused on physical therapy and rehabilitation. He was closer to his rehab sessions, but being on the first floor meant his view stunk. *Not much to look at when all there is to see is the side of a building.* Mike's parents stopped by with dinner, but he wasn't in the mood to talk.

"How are you doing, honey?" his mom asked, obviously trying to start a conversation.

"Fine," Mike responded in between bites of homemade lasagna and mashed potatoes.

"That's good to hear, son," his dad said. "I understand Robert has been stopping by. How's he doing?"

"Good," Mike said.

"You know at first he struggled," his mom added. "He felt it was his fault. He pushed away his friends, and his grades suffered. We met twice with the teachers. Everyone was so concerned and tried to help. Then suddenly everything changed the day he came to see you for the first time. Do you know what happened?"

Mike couldn't think of a one-word answer, so he responded, "He met some new friends."

"You mean the Carson kids?" his dad said. "Yes, he told us about them. They sound nice."

"They helped him open up and encouraged him to come see me," Mike said. "Bobby and I had some good talks, and we kind of helped each other."

"I'm so happy to hear you're both working together on this," his mom said.

"But other people can only get me so far. My legs aren't doing their part. It's getting harder to get up for each session."

His parents fell silent and looked concerned. A minute passed until his dad spoke again. "You need to hang in there, son. This is not how your story ends. I know it."

"What can we do to help?" his mom said.

"I don't know. Maybe pray. There isn't much more that can be done. But I appreciate your efforts and support. It does help."

They continued with small talk for a few minutes and Mike began to feel tired. He tried to stay awake but kept drifting off.

"Sorry, the therapy sessions take a lot out of me," he said. "Guess I'm a bit worn out."

"This lasagna is really good," his dad said. "It's your favorite, isn't it?"

Mike brightened. "Yeah, it is. Thanks! You guys are great. I don't know how you do it."

"One step at a time, honey," his mom said. "That's all any of us can do right now."

Their conversation waned while they finished eating and disposed of the paper plates and plasticware.

"How's your homework going?" Mike's dad asked. "The tutors, have they been helpful?"

"They keep me on my toes and have made it as interesting as possible. I'm afraid I've been a little slow getting excited about having school in a hospital room."

They chuckled together and Mike felt a little better. A knock came at the door.

"Must be Bobby," Mike said. "He said he might stop by tonight."

The door opened and Bobby stepped in followed by the entire Carson family. Mike's parents immediately stood and greeted them as Bobby introduced everyone. Mike noticed that Bobby had an unusual shoulder bag under his arm. He wondered if this might be a more significant visit and tried to calm Bobby's surprise.

"Hi, bud! Mom and Dad brought me dinner—lasagna," he said, pretending to make him jealous.

Bobby played along. "Mom, you didn't tell me that's what you were making tonight. You know it's my favorite."

Their mother blushed over the fuss, "Oh, you boys, always teasing. Did you get anything to eat, Robert? I have more in the fridge at home."

"I ate at the Carsons'." Bobby stumbled through the conversation, still appearing off balance. "Sorry I missed dinner, Mom."

"Not to worry, Robert. You called and we knew your plans."

"Robert?" Tim said, looking at Bobby.

"Yeah, that's what they've always called me," Bobby smiled. "I'm named after my great-grandfather who died in the war. A bit formal, but I roll with it."

"This is a pleasant surprise," his dad said. "We've heard a lot about the Carsons and how your children have helped Robert and Mike. Thank you for such kindness during a difficult time."

"We're glad to help," Mrs. Carson responded. "We know what it's like to go through a family crisis."

"And a little about why support from others is so important," Mr. Carson added, putting his arm around his wife's waist.

"Okay, if your heartfelt hellos last any longer, I'll fall asleep," Mike said. "Bobby, what exactly did you have in mind with this crowd?"

Bobby looked uncomfortable. "It's about the star, Mike."

"Oh..." Mike looked at his parents and considered how they might react. "I guess we're at a crossroads here. I say go ahead. Mom and Dad should know."

"Know what?" his dad began, but Bobby cut him short.

"Dad, I think you and Mom should sit down. This is going to be a lot to deal with."

"Let's start with the star," Mike said. "That's what you have in the shoulder bag, isn't it?"

"Yes," Bobby said and pulled it out, laying it on the hospital bed. It was a shiny silver eight-pointed star about the diameter of a smallish car's hubcap. Its mirror-like reflection drew attention to the center where there appeared to be writing.

"We think it's a message for you," Martie said to Mike.

"A message?" His mother sounded confused.

"We'll explain in a few moments," Mrs. Carson said, placing her hand on Carla's arm.

"Read the message so your parents can hear, Mike," Mr. Carson advised.

"Take the star to room 102 so he may travel the path with you."

"Are you saying the star wants me to go on a passage with you? That's ridiculous."

"I know," Bobby said. "That's why we almost didn't come."

"The star always has a way," Martie said. "We just need to roll with it."

"Look, the writing is changing," Mike said in surprise. They all watched as the old writing disappeared and was replaced by a new message.

Mr. Carson moved next to Tony, who scowled at him. "It really isn't a trick in case you were wondering."

"Pretty hard to swallow," Tony said. "I'm not a fan of Magic 8 Balls or hoaxes."

"Believe me, Tony, it's a lot of things but not a trick. It gets harder to swallow than this," Mr. Carson said. "Just trust us and we'll answer all your questions when the star is finished."

"There really is no other way to experience it the first time," Mrs. Carson said to Carla, who had begun to tremble.

Mike read the new writing.

"The path you must follow requires four. Ten, and two will open the door."

The writing immediately changed again.

"Follow stars in the pockets of brothers. Orion's main orb will be used by the others."

"Okay, that's the direction we've been waiting for," Tim said. The center of the star melted away, revealing two small eight-pointed stars. He handed one each to Bobby and Mike. "Here, take these and keep them in your hands."

Mike felt anxious, almost sick. A million questions swirled in his head. *How do I move around? How will they carry me? Why do you need me?*

"What's going on here?" His dad sounded alarmed.

"We're going on a little trip," Bobby said. "We'll be back before the Carsons finish answering your questions."

"Hold on, guys," Tim said as he and Martie grabbed the star by the proper points.

"Wait," Mike felt fear surge through him. "I'm not ready!"

"You'll never be ready for this Mike," Tim said.

"Here we go…" Martie sang.

Mike began to speak again but was distracted by the fading picture of his parents and the hospital room. "What's going on?"

He heard Bobby nearby: "This is how it starts, big bro. Don't let go!"

Mike saw his dad lunge for the bed with his arms wide while his mom covered her eyes and fell sideways into Mrs. Carson's waiting arms. Then all went gray.

CHAPTER X

Screaming Eagles

M ike's senses went blank and gray, and he felt totally alone.
The absolute loneliness of such deprivation pushed him
to the edge of panic.

Fortunately, it only lasted a few seconds before something
began to happen. Shadowy forms slowly came into focus. He expected light or brightness or something. But his surroundings
remained dark. He could tell they were somewhere outside, but
his eyes had trouble adjusting.

Finally, his vision focused. He lay on a dirt path looking up
at a partly cloudy night sky. His first thought was how beautiful and clear the stars appeared.

"Where are we?" he said out loud.

Tim's shadowed figure appeared over him. "We're on a dirt
dike or causeway between two lakes. There's a dirt road that
runs along the top of the dike. Fortunately, there's no traffic
because you're lying right in the middle of it. On the left the
road leads into some woods I think, but I can't make out the
trees very well. The other direction looks like open country."

Bobby's head came into view above him. "Not sure where or when we are yet."

"We're not going to learn sitting here," Tim added. "We'll have to find something to make a stretcher so we can move you. I'll check the woods."

Mike had not attempted to move until Tim stood to head toward the woods with Martie in tow. The idea of the stretcher made him cringe. But when the cringe came it wasn't only from the waist up, he felt it all the way to his toes.

"Wait guys," he called out. "I can feel my legs."

"What," Bobby said surprised.

"I can feel my legs. I mean they feel kind of normal. I'll try to stand up. Can you help me?"

Tim and Bobby helped lift him while Martie supported his back. They raised him to a standing position, and he looked around. "Well, here goes!"

His friends eased their hold and allowed Mike's full body weight to increase slowly until his legs supported him.

"I definitely feel something," he said with excitement.

"We're going to let go now," Tim warned.

"Okay, let 'er rip."

When they removed their hands, he immediately wobbled, stumbled, and fell.

"You okay?" Martie said with concern. "Did you feel anything?"

"Yeah," he said, grinning. "Just a little out of practice. Let's give it another go."

They helped him stand again. This time he wavered and wobbled, but stayed on his feet.

Bobby, Tim, and Martie all hugged him at once and cried.

"It's a miracle," Bobby said, tears streaming down his face.

"It's the star," Tim said. "It must be a rule we didn't know about."

Martie quoted as if she were writing in her list of Rules for StarPassage. "Rule number twenty. Physical handicaps are gone while on a passage."

"Are you sure this isn't permanent?" Bobby said hopefully.

"Could be, but let's not get our hopes up. This certainly solves our current problem though," Tim said.

"I love StarPassages," Mike said loudly and then laughed. "They're awesome!"

"You ready to walk?" Tim asked him. "We should get going."

They began to move toward the woods, and Mike did a little dance to celebrate his ability to walk. He almost stumbled again. "It feels so good."

"Let's take this slowly, guys, until Mike gets his balance and some strength back," Bobby warned.

"Okay," Mike said. "I'll dial it back a bit. But it's pretty hard not to get carried away."

"Wait just a minute," Martie said, snickering. "Mike, we need to find you some different clothes to wear."

He looked down. "Oh man!" He wore only a flimsy hospital gown that tied in the back and the little white socks the nurses had given him to keep his feet warm.

"It's a good thing we're not affected by the weather when we have hold of the star or you'd be freezing right now," his little brother said. "Let's see if we can find something for you to wear."

"It's a good thing it's dark," Martie said. "I might be permanently damaged."

They all broke out in uncontrollable laughter. Finally getting control of themselves, Tim handed his denim jacket to Mike. "Here's a start. Let's find you something else to cover up those lily-white legs."

"Hey, I used to have a pretty good tan, ya know," he said, still trying to control his laughter.

They turned to continue along the path and saw Bobby

standing a few feet in front of them. He seemed frozen. He pointed forward and whispered, "Guys, who are they?"

Mike, Tim, and Martie moved to Bobby's side and immediately sobered. Just ten feet in front of them a platform surrounded with sandbags was dug in on the side of the causeway. Two men sat on a crude bench inside. Mike could not see colors, but he did notice they each wore a steel helmet that caught the starlight. Resting on top of the sandbags, a large machine gun fed with a belt of ammunition stopped him in his tracks.

"They're soldiers of some kind," he whispered. "Where are we?"

"No need to whisper," Tim reminded them. "As long as we hold onto the stars they can't hear or see us."

"But that won't stop the bullets from hitting us if we get in their way, will it?" Bobby said.

"Yeah, that's right," Martie confirmed. "But we're not staying around to test that one. Besides, it seems pretty quiet."

"We need to stay alert," Tim said as they turned to leave. "If this is some kind of war zone, then there could be a lot more where they came from." Then he stopped abruptly and cocked his ear toward the foxhole. "Hold it." The two men were speaking in a foreign language. "I recognize that from the ship, Martie. It's the same language the two spies were speaking."

"They're German? Is this World War I again?" Martie said.

"It could be, or maybe World War II," Tim answered. "Either way, this is not good."

The German soldiers suddenly looked agitated, and both stood up, staring at the sky. One began to speak in excited tones. The other grabbed him by the shoulders and made a shushing sound. They both quieted and moved to the machine gun as if preparing to fire.

"What's going on?" Bobby said.

"Listen," Mike said as he pointed to the sky. "It's the sound of engines—plane engines."

The deep thrumming chorus of dozens—maybe hundreds—of airplane engines caused the ground to vibrate with the noise. The travelers stood spellbound as plane after plane flew over the horizon, blocking out the starlight. Thin lines of light arced into the sky from an infinite number of locations on the ground. Ammunition from larger guns exploded in the air among the planes.

Still the planes continued their forward march. Just then, one of the planes burst into flames and cartwheeled to the ground beyond the tree line. An explosion of white light and flame temporarily blinded them.

They looked again as the planes dodged and jinked to avoid the onslaught from the ground. A second plane caught fire and nosedived toward the ground. Small objects hurtled from the open door of the plane. Two of them appeared to be on fire as they floated toward the earth.

The flashes of numerous explosions revealed something else in the sky. Watching open-mouthed, Mike remembered laying on the ocean floor while scuba diving and looking up through a sea of floating jellyfish. "What in the world...?"

"Parachutes. Hundreds of them," Tim shouted over the noise.

The soldiers in the foxhole yelled in German, pointing as the parachutes came closer. They fired their weapon in deafening staccato bursts of flame and light. Other gunfire erupted around the edges of the lakes. Bullets whizzed by them.

"What's that?" Martie said, ducking. "It sounds like maniac bees."

"Those are bullets from the other guns," Tim warned. "They can travel for miles beyond the target if they miss. We need to run for the woods now or we could be hit."

They started running for the safety of the woods and then, despite their fear, they stopped again, dumbfounded. Soldiers wearing parachutes landed all around them. Most of them hit the water, but a couple landed on the causeway.

Mike watched in shock as a half dozen parachutes with people attached landed in the lake right in front of the machine gun position. Two of the soldiers were immediately riddled with bullets and stopped moving. They watched helplessly as another soldier struggled to loose himself from his tangled cords while trying to keep his head above water. He fought for his life, but disappeared below the surface, pulled under by the weight of his equipment. He fought back to the top of the water and yelled for help, then went under again and never resurfaced.

"They're drowning," Bobby yelled. "Can't we help them?"

"They're also getting shot," Tim said sternly. "We wouldn't last a minute out there."

As Mike and his friends trotted down the path, a huge man fell out of the sky, nearly landing on them, then hit the ground and bounced with a thud.

Lying on his back, he groaned. "What a way to start a war. Those air jockeys panicked and dropped us too low. Nearly broke my back."

The soldier released his parachute, which drifted to the side of the causeway, and struggled to his knees. His young features were hard to distinguish because they were covered with smears of black paint.

"He sounds American," Bobby said as they all moved out of his way and lay down on the side of the hill.

"Look at the patch on his left shoulder," Tim said. "It's the head of an eagle. He's 101st Airborne—the Screaming Eagles."

In one fluid motion, the soldier released his equipment and left it on the road. Then he unfolded the stock of his rifle, placed a magazine in the port, pulled back the slide to push a round into the chamber, and placed several grenades on his straps. "You're not getting any more of my guys," he growled and ran in a low crouch toward the machine-gun nest.

Mike and the others watched him drop to the ground, then crawl the last few yards toward the German position. The staccato light generated by the gun created a strobe-like effect that allowed them to see the action in stop motion. The soldier crept to the other side of the causeway. When he drew even with the foxhole, he crawled onto the road within a few feet of the unsuspecting Germans.

Taking a grenade from his harness, he pulled the pin, waited one count, and tossed it into the nest. The soldier flattened on the road as a blinding flash and explosion ripped the night air. He immediately jumped up and fired his rifle in several rapid three-shot bursts. He stood quietly and slid a new clip into his carbine. The soldier then turned and ran back to where his equipment waited.

Kneeling, the American said, "Thank you, God, for getting me to the ground safely and allowing me to do something. Please protect us so we can make it through the night and get our jobs done."

Without another word, he gathered his equipment, threw a few items to the side, stood, and ran off toward the woods in a crouch. The travelers stood to follow when Mike heard a sound from the water.

Another parachutist struggled in the pond. He put the star in his pocket and climbed down to help the soldier. Bobby followed him to the water's edge.

"Here, buddy, let us help you," Mike said as he and Bobby pulled him onto the bank by his harness.

"Thanks, guys," the dripping soldier said, breathing hard. "Thought I was a goner when I landed in the water. That Kraut gunner gave me a close shave. I owe you for taking him out."

"It wasn't us, but we saw it happen," Bobby said.

"I owe you anyway. I'm so waterlogged I don't know if I could have dragged myself out."

Closing his eyes, the American lay on his back, breathing like he had just finished a marathon.

"What unit are you with?" Mike asked.

"2nd of the 501st," he said. "Fox Company. How 'bout you?"

Bobby looked at Mike for an answer, but he shook his head to warn him not to answer. "We're lost."

The soldier opened his eyes and smiled. "Yeah, we're all lost, Mac. Always looks great on paper but ends up in a big snafu on the ground. That's the Airborne life. But somehow we get the job done, don't we?"

"Sure do," Mike said. "You okay?"

"Will be in a few minutes. Had to cut all my gear off. I lost everything in the water."

"Some more guys will be along soon. We gotta go."

"Currahee...and good hunting," the soldier said. Mike and Bobby climbed back up the bank, and Tim gave them a hand at the top.

"Things are going to get bad real quick," Tim said, holding out the Follow Star. Mike and Bobby grabbed on to it. "Time to head for the trees."

Mike shivered. "And I need to get something on besides this gown."

Mimicking the soldier's tactics, they ran in the same low crouch as bullets flew past, some hitting the ground near their feet, kicking up dirt and rocks. Parachutes filled the sky as far as they could see amidst the gun flashes. Finally, they made it to the trees unharmed and followed the road about a hundred yards before moving off the main path twenty feet to where the terrain opened up into a cultivated field. They sat to catch their breath and get their bearings.

"This is D-Day," Tim said.

"What day?" Martie responded.

"D-Day, the name given the invasion of German-occupied France on June 6, 1944," Tim explained. "That would place us in Normandy, France."

"How can you be so sure, Tim?"

"Because I'm the son of an army officer and history professor. We talk about this stuff all the time."

"But what tipped you off in this case?" Bobby said.

"The Screaming Eagles are the 101st Airborne. They landed behind the Normandy Beach code named Utah. Their job was to secure exit roads from the beach, take bridges, and generally keep the Germans from reinforcing the beach defenses when the Allied forces landed. Paratroopers were spread all over the place because of cloudy weather and their transport planes dodging heavy fire. As quickly as possible the pilots emptied their defenseless planes once they were confused in the dark and enemy fire. Many of the paratroopers were dropped too early or too low or too high or when the planes were going too fast. Resourceful German commanders had flooded much of the low-lying farm land to prevent such an event. American paratroopers now paid with their lives by drowning or as easy targets. It was a mess."

"This is a really dangerous place for us, isn't it?" Martie asked.

"Yeah, it's D-Day morning, and we're caught in the middle of perhaps the most chaotic and desperate battle ever fought. Everyone on both sides is confused. The scattered paratroopers only have a few hours to get themselves together, organized, and take their objectives, or the invasion's success will be at serious risk. The Germans are shooting at anything that moves."

"But it didn't fail," Mike said. "They did their job."

"Yeah, but it ended up being close. We just witnessed one of the countless brave acts, never recorded, that saved lives and made it possible."

"So why did the star bring us here?" Martie said, trying to refocus the conversation.

"We may not know until it's over," Tim said. "What we need to do now is keep moving."

"And keep our eyes open," Bobby added.

"The soldiers were issued toy crickets and passwords to identify each other," Tim said as they stood to leave. "We don't have either, so if you hear any cricket clicks or voices, hit the dirt until we know what's going on."

"Hit the dirt?" Bobby said. "You sound like an old movie."

"Sorry, I meant lay flat on the ground and do it quick," Tim corrected himself. "Oh and by the way, we are in an old movie except everything is deadly and real."

As they stood a tremendous crash came through the trees at the edge of the clearing, causing them to dive to the ground. "What's that?" Martie cried. "Scared me to death."

"Good training," Bobby said smiling. "We hit the dirt pretty fast there."

"Let's check it out," Tim said. They both rose and moved toward the sound. The shadows revealed a large metal box standing on its end with cords draped over it.

"It looks like a coffin connected to a parachute," Mike said. "Is it a bomb?"

Tim walked around the six-foot-long rectangular object. "Looks like a storage container. Let's open it and see what's inside."

"Be careful," Bobby said. "It could be booby-trapped."

"No way," Tim responded. "These are supplies and stuff for the soldiers, dropped by the same airplanes they jumped from."

Tim and Bobby undid the straps that held the container and lifted off the lid. Tim smiled. "You're in luck, Mike. This one has clothing and boots."

"Perfect. Now you can have your jacket back, Tim." Mike rummaged through the container and found a pair of olive-colored pants with pockets and a pair of jump boots and socks. He found an approximate fit and dressed himself, lacing the boots to his mid-calf.

"That's a lot better."

"Dad would call those clothes OD's or Olive Drabs," Tim said. "A nice little souvenir."

Bobby found a set of clothes that fit him and began changing also.

"What are you doing?" Martie asked.

Bobby smiled. "They look durable and will make a nice souvenir. Just ask Tim,"

Martie hushed them and whispered, "Look. A deer."

"Boy, is it in the wrong place," Tim said.

"It's looking straight at us as if it can see us," Martie said. "Do you think it knows we're here?"

"Let's test it and see," Tim raised his hands and yelled. The deer bolted, bounding off into the trees. "Guess we have another rule for your list, Martie."

The teens moved back onto the path. Mike felt uncomfortable being out in the open, but there was no other alternative. They heard gunfire in all directions and were unsure which way to go. Even though they were invisible, none of them knew anything about moving quietly. They made noise like a school class on a field trip. Suddenly, they heard the double click of a cricket.

"Get down," Tim ordered.

They immediately lay flat and froze. The double click came again, a pause, then a subtle rustling of bushes. A soldier appeared at the edge of the road. The soldier stared across intently, directly through Mike, who hugged the ground, imagining the soldier could sense him as had the deer.

A voice came from behind the soldier, deeper in the bushes. "See anything?"

"Nope, must've been another animal scurryin' around."

"We're all a little jumpy. Let's move out."

"Yes, sir," the soldier said and stood up.

Another soldier came into view. "Sorenson...Marks, you two take point. The rest are on me."

A dozen soldiers came through the foliage onto the road. Two of them moved out ahead about twenty yards and the rest followed spaced out on opposite sides of the road. They moved in the direction the travelers had been going.

Tim stood. "Let's follow but give them a little space and try to be quieter. Walk in their footsteps. The star can't help us if one of you steps on a landmine."

They let the soldiers move forward and then followed. "This is going to be a long night," Bobby said.

"Actually," Mike said, "It's referred to in literature as The Longest Day."

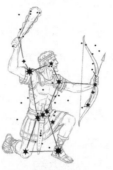

CHAPTER XI

Firefight

They followed the soldiers for about two hundred yards, and the countryside turned from woods to farm fields separated by six- to ten-foot-high walls of dirt and plants.

"Hedge country is not good," Tim said.

"Why?" Martie asked.

"Because the Germans used the narrow roads and high hedges to set up ambushes."

"And our boys up there aren't exactly taking a walk in the park," Mike added. "They're looking for trouble."

The soldiers passed through an opening in one of the hedges. "Sorenson, you check out the field. We'll cover you," the soldier who appeared to be in charge said.

"Yes, sir." Sorensen moved out into the field zig-zagging. The other soldiers took up positions, watching both ways on the road as well as in the field. Sorensen stopped several times as he crossed the field, appeared to listen for something, then continued.

A soldier whispered to the one who had given the order. "Lieutenant, where're we supposed to be going?"

"We missed our drop zone by a couple of miles east as far as I can reckon," the lieutenant said. "We need to get back and hook up with the division. But for now we need to get across this field, so eyes sharp, Morton."

"Yes, sir."

The lone soldier continued in his low crouch and zigzagged across the field of nearly waist-high grass. He reached the other side, knelt stone still for about a minute, then stood and signaled the others to follow.

"Okay, gentlemen, time to go," the lieutenant said and turned to one of the soldiers. "Sargent, you take half to the right, and I'll take the rest left. Marks, you stay here and cover us, then come along when we get across."

They spread out and moved at a quick pace, darting and crouching in an uneven pattern. Marks stood at the opening with his rifle shouldered. The rest of the soldiers had reached the center of the field when suddenly the far corner erupted with machine gun and small arms fire. Hit by the first bullets, Sorensen immediately went down, as did one of the other soldiers crossing the field. The rest immediately disappeared into the tall grass.

Marks remained standing and fired back. Mike and the other travelers stood in the opening behind Marks when the firing started. Tim motioned them to duck quickly behind the hedge. Shots thudded against the hedge, and then Marks flew backward, landing on the road. He didn't move. Bobby and Martie were closest and pulled him out of the line of fire.

Mike checked his pulse and breathing. He tried to give the soldier CPR, but Tim pulled him back. "He's gone, Mike."

Mike felt overwhelmed with emotion. "He's my age. His death seems so random and meaningless."

"Mike, we can't stay here. Grab his carbine and the bandolier of ammunition," Tim said as he pulled the .45 caliber pistol from the dead soldier's belt and stuck it in his waist. "We might need these before it's all over."

"What about the grenade?" Bobby asked.

"Good idea. Let's take one just in case," Tim advised. "Mike, are you comfortable carrying that in your new jacket pocket?"

"No! Do I have a choice?" Confused and disoriented, he hesitated, reaching for the dead man's gun.

"Not really," Tim said and shook Mike by the collar. "Look, all these soldiers are gonna end up the same as him if we don't do something. You've gotta snap out of it. They need someone to help, and we're all there is."

They moved along the road on the opposite side of the hedge until they came to a corner. "If I'm right," Tim continued, "the Germans will be set up down the road to the right with firing holes dug into the sides of the hedge. "Mike, are you up for this?"

"Guess so. We are invisible after all."

"Bobby, you take the star with Martie and give the Follow Star to me," Tim said.

They made the exchange. Mike and Tim turned the corner and dodged from tree to rock to bush down the road toward the sound of gunfire.

"Look, I was right," Tim said. "There they are."

They were twenty yards from the Germans who had dug out the back of the hedge and created a foxhole with a firing port through the field side. There were two soldiers operating a machine gun and two others standing with rifles firing through loop holes. One of the standing soldiers had a scope on his rifle.

"That explains how they got Marks," Tim said.

"There's no way those poor guys in the field can get at them," Mike said.

"That's what I thought, and that's why we're doing this," Tim said. "Okay, here's what we're gonna do. When I throw the grenade at the machine gun nest, you take out the two soldiers with the rifles, starting with the one farthest from the foxhole. Do it before the grenade goes off."

Tim retrieved the grenade from Mike, hung it on his belt, and moved forward with the pistol in one hand and the star in the other. Mike looked at Tim, confused and intimidated.

Tim seemed to read Mike's thoughts. "Look, it's no sweat. Just a couple of things to remember. Keep your finger off the trigger until you're ready to pull it and don't point this at anything you don't intend to shoot."

Mike's eyes were wide. "Okay, got it."

Mike struggled to place a new magazine in the rifle. Actors made it look so easy in the movies. But now that he had been asked to actually shoot someone, it was different. His hands were sweaty and trembling. He pulled the slide back and chambered a round, then moved forward cautiously, trying to get close enough so he couldn't miss.

Mike had never fired a gun before, so he had no idea how much it would kick and only a remote idea of how to aim, so he had tried to get as close as possible to his target and reached an old tree trunk whose flat surface served to hold the rifle steady. He knelt and aimed only ten yards from the two soldiers. *Probably can't miss from this close...but if they turn around I'm done for.* He watched as Tim moved to within ten feet of the foxhole. He turned and gave Mike a thumbs-up, stuffed the pistol in his pants pocket, and took the grenade from his belt.

Mike could see that Tim still had the star in one hand as he pulled the pin, tossed the grenade, and dove to the ground. Mike dropped his star to the ground an instant before the grenade went off, steadied the rifle with both hands, and fired twice at the Germans. A deafening explosion knocked him to the ground. He had no idea if he had hit anything.

Mike was not unconscious, but slow to regain his senses. He had been thrown backward by the concussion. His muffled hearing made everything sound far away, and his ears were ringing. He crawled around until he found the star and cautiously got back to his knees to look over the stump. Nothing moved.

"Tim? Tim are you there?"

"Yeah," came a wobbly answer back. "But I'm not ever going to do that again. That's a little more intense than a few fireworks on the fourth of July."

Mike got to his feet and ran to Tim's side. "Did we get 'em?"

"Looks like it. The foxhole was a direct hit, and it looks like the grenade also took out one of the riflemen. But, Mike, you're a natural sharpshooter. You got the other one."

"I don't feel any better about this than seeing that Marks kid lying dead. These Germans are just kids too," Mike said and lowered his head.

"I know how you feel," Tim said. "There's nothing glorious about this at all. But I hope we saved some lives. Let's get out of here before we get shot by the guys we just saved."

They ran twenty yards down the road, sat in the bushes, and watched. Five minutes passed before the first Screaming Eagle paratrooper came sliding down over the top of the hedge. He landed on his feet and moved quickly toward the former German firing position. After a quick look, he called out, "All clear!"

The other soldiers came through the hedge's opening and gathered around the foxhole. Tim counted only eight.

"Who took 'em out, Lieutenant?" one of the soldiers said.

"Don't know, James," the officer answered. "But we got guys all over the place. They would have killed us all so be grateful for a little help. Lesson number one, the Germans will try to ambush us, so we're not wandering into any more open fields without support."

"It's a miracle," another soldier said.

"You think everything's a miracle," a third countered sarcastically.

"This is *not* the time to question whether God is interested in us, gentlemen," the lieutenant said with authority. "But somebody was in the right place at the exact time to save our lives. It doesn't matter whether the 101st, French partisans, or angels did the job. I for one have no problem if you thank God for the good timing."

They all shook their heads in agreement. Mike watched as the lieutenant sent two soldiers back to check on the four casualties. They were gone for ten minutes, then returned.

"None of them made it," one of the soldiers reported. "But we got their weapons, ammo, and grenades, except Marks. Couldn't find his."

The lieutenant shook his head. "Miracle or not, it cost four good men their lives. Now let's move out. Turk, you take the point. Sargent Lee, you take the right." They fell in on both sides of the road, four less than before, still looking for trouble.

"I think following them is a bad idea," Mike suggested, still shaky from the experience.

"Agreed," Tim said. "We need a little rest anyway."

Martie and Bobby came up. "That was incredibly brave," Martie said.

"It didn't feel brave at all," Tim responded. "Scared to death is more like it."

"Maybe that's how it feels," Mike observed. "Maybe bravery isn't really brave. It's just doing what has to be done in spite of your fear."

"You saved a few lives today, and that's a good thing," Bobby added.

"Yeah, we saved eight by ending four," Tim said sarcastically. "That must be the mathematics of war. I don't like it one bit, and I'm gonna let Dad know when we get back."

CHAPTER XII

The Boy from Twin Falls

They rested for ten minutes, then went back to the intersection and headed the opposite direction. Tim was in the lead and heard an engine. "Something's coming our way. Let's keep moving but be ready to get off the road."

"Not much room to do that," Bobby said.

The sounds grew louder, and Tim felt increasingly worried. After about five minutes he saw dim movement ahead on the road and motioned everyone to press themselves against the earthen banks. As they did, the star's center opened, revealing a small four-point star.

"The Star of Tongues," Tim said. "This will be helpful."

Just as Tim put the small star into his hand, a company of German soldiers and an armored half-track vehicle emerged from the dark. Most of the thirty-plus soldiers were on foot moving cautiously.

He held the star tightly in his free hand and listened. He caught snatches of conversations but learned little. The German soldiers seemed confused. They knew there were enemy troops in the area and had run into some small groups and individuals. But they argued about whether this was the long-anticipated invasion or merely a raid or diversion. Most seemed to believe it was a diversion to draw forces while the main Allied attack happened elsewhere. Supremely confident, they approached their duty like exterminators sent to eliminate some minor infestation. The soldiers passed, and the time travelers could move onto the road again.

"What were they saying?" Mike inquired.

"They have no idea what is going on or the scope of what they're facing," Tim said. "They know enemy paratroopers have landed, and think they're wild men, but so far are unimpressed with the numbers. Nobody is convinced that this is a major operation."

It remained difficult with the hedges and overgrowth for Tim to determine how far they'd traveled. He guessed they'd walked about half a mile with constant pops of small arms fire and occasional explosions in the distance. He felt relieved they had no more encounters with either side. It was still dark, but the clouds had cleared and the moon shone brightly. Passing an opening in one of the hedgerows, Martie pointed to the center of the field and said, "What's that?"

They followed her gaze to a small grouping of tall, ancient-looking trees in the center.

"A bunch of trees," Bobby offered, holding his hands palms upward. "So what?"

"There's something on that tree about halfway up. It looks like a parachute."

They all looked more closely.

"Martie's right," Mike said. "There is something out there. Let's take a look."

"Where there's a chute there might be a person," Martie said.

"What do you want to do?" Mike said to Tim. "Could be a paratrooper."

"How about the two of us check it out," Tim said. "Bobby, you want to change stars again so Mike and I can go out and see?"

"Sure."

Mike still carried the carbine and bandolier, and Tim had the .45 pistol stuffed in his belt. They moved cautiously toward the trees.

"I can't shake the feeling that someone is watching," Tim said uneasily.

As they approached the tree with the chute draped over it, they were impressed with the oak's enormous size.

"This looks like it could have been standing here for hundreds of years," Mike said. "If a tree like this were in our neighborhood, it would have tree houses and kids in it around the clock. It's a great climbing tree."

They looked up into the tangle of thick limbs that supported a thicket of its own dense undergrowth. "Look, do you see that?" Mike said. "About halfway up."

"It looks like a body," Tim said. "Do you think he is alive?"

"Can't tell. No movement."

"We should climb up and check him out," Tim suggested.

"Let me do it," Mike said. "I would like to see if this tree is really as cool to climb as it looks. Besides, I'm the one that needs to exercise his legs."

"This isn't a game in the park, Mike," Tim warned. "There may be people watching and waiting for someone to help this guy."

"Another ambush?"

"Let's assume that's a possibility."

Tim took the carbine and bandolier from Mike. He couldn't shake the feeling of dread about being watched and held tight to the star. He strained his eyes in the dark.

It's useless to try. Can't see anything.

"Okay," Mike said seriously. "I will be careful and quiet."

Tim set the carbine and bandolier against the trunk and

circled the tree, looking for a way to get Mike started. Mike circled with him, then stopped. "What's this?" He reached down and picked up something, holding it out for Tim to see.

"It's a pretty nasty-looking knife. Really sharp too," Tim said as he ran his thumb sideways across the blade. "Someone has sharpened that to a very fine edge."

"Probably dropped from the guy in the tree," Mike said. "I might need that."

He stuffed the blade into one of his pants pockets and put his Follow Star in the other pocket then buttoned both closed. Tim also placed his star in a pocket. They immediately became visible.

"We need to do this fast," Tim said. "It wouldn't do to wake up the enemy."

The cool air and humid, chilling breeze made his cheeks tingle. Mike involuntarily shivered. "It's cold."

"Trust me, this is a walk in the park compared to the temperature at Valley Forge," Tim reassured him. "You sure you can do this? You've only been walking again for a couple of hours."

Mike smiled back. "I got this."

"All right, but I'm not standing around to catch you." Tim made a stirrup with his hands.

"Okay, here goes," Mike whispered as Tim gave him a boost to the lowest branch. The branch seemed thick and sturdy. Mike looked down and realized Tim had vanished again. "Thanks for the hand up, wherever you are, Tim." No response.

He climbed, staying close to the trunk of the tree to avoid snapping a branch under his weight. Moving carefully at first, he tested his legs, but became more confident as he climbed. Mike noticed that the branches naturally circled clockwise around the trunk like a series of crude but sturdy steps. He finally reached a branch level with the paratrooper and realized they were at least thirty feet off the ground. *A fall could do real damage or even be fatal.* The thought sobered Mike as he began to edge his way along the branch toward the body.

Moving to within three feet of the soldier's head, Mike looked him over carefully. The paratrooper was suspended by his right boot, which had jammed into a fork of branches. He hung nearly upside down, hopelessly tangled in the chute cords and smaller limbs. Mike examined the soldier, not sure where or how to begin.

A steel jump helmet with a football chin strap and ski-type goggles made it hard to tell if he was conscious. Even if he was awake, Mike wondered if the paratrooper could move at all with the huge packs attached to his chest. A three-inch-thick strap dangling from his leg must have held something, but the end of the strap appeared to be torn. A carbine like the one Mike had carried was strapped to the man's belly pack. Mike reached out as he spoke. "Buddy, you okay?"

He pushed the paratrooper's shoulder. "Hey," he said louder. "You okay?"

The soldier stirred and slowly became aware. "Hey Mac," he said groggily. "I could use a little help here. Tried to cut myself free but dropped my knife."

"You got yourself in a pretty good fix," Mike said.

The soldier tried to turn his head, but could only manage a sideways look at Mike. He was young. Too young to be involved in this mess.

He couldn't be much older than me.

"I found your knife on the ground," Mike said. "Got it here. What do you want me to do?"

"My foot is stuck pretty tight, but I think I can get it loose if you help me out of these cords. Now I know what a fly feels like in a spider web," he said with a forced smile. His white teeth stood out starkly against his blackout-painted face.

"Okay, I'll cut a few of the cords and see what happens."

Mike cut the cords in ones and twos until about half were gone. "Don't want you to fall. You okay with me cutting the rest?"

"Yeah, gotta do it anyway," the soldier said as he reached out to get a tight hold on the branch below his head. "It's nice to be able to use my hands again. Maybe we outta lighten the load a bit though."

He showed Mike how to release the parachute harness, which was easier to do with less tension from cutting some of the cords. The paratrooper carefully removed his rifle and handed it to Mike. "Hang this over there, will ya, Mac? Don't want that dropping on the ground and breaking. Gonna need it later."

He then asked for the knife and cut loose his chest and belly packs, which crashed to the ground with a loud thrashing and snapping of branches. They froze and waited for an enemy response to the sound. Mike's senses were heightened, and his skin prickled with an adrenalin surge, but he heard nothing.

"That was stupid," the soldier said and shook his head. "But no other way."

"No harm done it appears," Mike said.

The soldier handed the knife back to Mike. "Okay, Mac, let's finish this and get me outta here."

Mike carefully cut the remaining cords. Freed from his nylon straight jacket and heavy weight, the soldier bent upward in an inverted gymnast sit-up. He grasped both sides of the branching "Y" of the tree in which his right foot was wedged. He deftly placed his left foot against the branch and pushed. The angle allowed the boot to move slightly. He pushed again, straining, and with a final grunt, the boot popped free. The soldier uncurled while still holding onto the branch with both hands and easily let himself down next to Mike.

A huge white smile flashed across his face. "Easier than I thought it would be. I always imagined my arrival in France would be a little more glorious than being stuck upside down in a tree." The soldier laughed quietly.

He's a regular guy. We probably could've been good friends had we lived in the same time.

"Let's get down to solid ground," Mike suggested.

"Time to start doing what they sent me here to do," the soldier said, still smiling as he pulled the strap of his carbine over his head.

They climbed down without speaking, then dropped to the ground next to the large base of the tree. Tim reappeared in a crouch on the ground, pointing the rifle at the far edge of the field.

"Hey, there's movement over there," Tim whispered. "We should get out of here before we get pinned down like the other guys we saw."

Sharing the burden of the soldier's equipment, they zig-zagged toward the opening in the hedgerow. A single shot rang out. They dropped into the knee-high grass.

"Sniper...anyone hit?" the soldier called out. Tim and Mike both answered they were okay.

Tim lay with his face in the weeds, prepared to pull out his star. "Mike, time for the star."

"Got it," he heard Mike respond.

"Here's what we're going to do," the soldier said. "I'll get up and run to the right. As soon as he shoots, you guys get out of here and go left."

"Okay," Tim whispered back.

"Now," said the soldier. He rose and sprinted to the right

making one cut left then dove to the earth as another shot rang out. Tim heard some rustling in the grass and assumed the soldier was crawling to change positions. The paratrooper rose again in a different spot than where he had disappeared and zagged left, diving to the ground as another shot kicked up a cloud of dirt near his feet.

Tim and Mike, now invisible, rose with the gear and sprinted straight for the opening in the hedge. Tim saw the soldier rise off to his right at the same time. Mike made the hedge opening first and sprinted through, followed by Tim. The sniper fired again, and Tim felt like he'd been kicked in the back by a horse. The force knocked him through the opening where he face-planted in the road. The star fell from his hand and bounced to the edge of the road. Momentarily dazed, he slowly realized Mike knelt at his side. "You okay?"

"Pretty good shot to hit an invisible runner," Tim said and realized Mike had pocketed his star.

"Yeah, you must've been in line with the soldier."

"Or maybe he just fired at the sounds. We made as much noise as a stampede."

The soldier flew through the opening, diving and summersaulting onto the road, ending in a sitting position next to Tim.

"I guess that's why they wanted us to be in good shape," the soldier said, breathing hard. "That was too close."

He noticed Tim lying flat. "You hit, Mac?"

Tim rolled over. "Felt like someone hit me in the back with a baseball bat."

Mike looked him over and leaned back. "Wow, you must be living right, Tim. You had the paratrooper's belly pack over your shoulder and that's where the bullet struck. The pack stopped the bullet. There's probably a souvenir in there somewhere." Mike lifted the belly pack to show Tim and stuck a finger in a large bullet hole in the center.

Tim recovered and looked at the soldier, who still breathed heavily. "What's your name?"

"Name's Whitney, Robert Whitney, Dog Company, 2nd of the 501st PIR. I owe you one. What unit are you boys with?"

"I'm Mike and this is Tim. We're not with a unit."

Tim realized too late it was a dangerous way to introduce themselves. The soldier stiffened and looked at Mike's olive-colored pants. "Deserters?"

"No, sir," Tim said with authority. "We're actually travelers."

"No Americans are travelers in France in 1944," Robert said. "You better tell me your story quick or you'll be prison-ers." Robert unslung his carbine and pointed it at the boys in a fluid cat-like movement, catching them completely by surprise.

"Okay, the story's a little complex so give us a minute to explain."

Tim's mind raced to find a way to respond when the soldier recoiled in his own surprise. Martie suddenly appeared on the ground in front of him, sitting Indian style.

"We're travelers from the future," Martie said. "From California."

"Come on, Martie," Tim moaned. "You've got to stop with the sudden shocks."

Robert swept the barrel of the rifle back and forth but seemed to realize there was more to the story and slowly relaxed. "You... sound like Americans."

"Stunts like that scare people and in this case could get us shot," Tim said angrily.

"Sorry, big bro, but we are," Martie said. "And we don't have time for discussions. We're on a quest to help two of our friends and their family. You've already met Mike, and this is Bobby."

At the introduction, a young boy appeared sitting next to Martie, causing the soldier to jump back again.

"I think I'd rather have met Krauts."

"Don't worry, you're safe with us. That's my big brother Tim and I'm Martie."

The soldier seemed confused. "I must have hit my head in that tree."

"No, you're fine," Tim said. "It's the story and us that are crazy. And my sister has no tact." He shot a warning look at Martie, who broke into a half smile.

"Look, guys," Tim said, hands extended. "Robert's got a lot on his plate this morning. Martie's right, we've got to make this fast and let him get on his way."

Bobby stared at the soldier. "You said your name was Whitney? Where are you from?"

"A little town in Idaho nobody's heard of."

"Let me guess," Bobby said. "Twin Falls?"

The soldier's eyes grew wide. "Yes, how did you know?"

Bobby leaned back and looked at Mike. "Do you know who this guy is?"

"It couldn't be," Mike said. "But the star does have a purpose. Really?"

"Has to be," Bobby said. He turned to the soldier and held out his hands in a gesture that included himself, the soldier, and Mike.

"Mike, meet Great-Grandpa Robert."

CHAPTER XIII

Meeting the Dead

"W hat? You're nuts," Robert said.

"Not really," Bobby said excitedly. "We're your great-grandsons. You were married during leave just before you shipped out to England, right?"

"Yes."

"And your wife's name is Leah?"

"Yes, but how do you know that?"

"And she's pregnant, isn't she?"

"No, you got that one wrong," Robert said, smiling and visibly relieved. "She gave birth to a healthy boy about four months ago."

"Named Chris," Bobby said.

The soldier seemed stunned. "Yes, his name is Christopher. Got a picture of them both right here." He undid the chin strap and pulled off his helmet. Stuck inside, wrapped in cloth, was a black-and-white picture of a pretty young girl in a flowered dress with a newborn baby boy in her arms.

Bobby looked at the picture in obvious wonder. He shook his head. "Your son, Grandpa Chris—sorry, I mean Christopher—will grow up and become a successful farm equipment dealer in southern Idaho and will have four children, the youngest of which he will name Carla. She will meet a handsome and successful Californian named Tony Hernandez while in college, and they will give you three great-grandchildren, the two of us and a little sister named Taylor."

The soldier shook his head. "Please stop. I don't want to know any more. It's overwhelming, and I have a job to do. You seem to know all about me, but I can't think about this right now. I don't want to know the future."

"We understand," Tim said.

"I'm not saying I buy your story. But can you answer one question."

"Sure, but we agree that it can't be about your future," Mike said.

"Do we win?"

"Win?" Mike said. "You mean is the invasion successful?"

"No, do we win?" Robert said in a deadly serious tone. "The war. Do we beat the Krauts?"

The travelers looked at each other and came to an unspoken agreement. Mike nodded to Tim, who responded, "Yes, you win. In our day, countless books have been written about what we call World War II and the brave generation of people who fought for freedom. Some have referred to you as the Greatest Generation."

Robert bowed his head and was silent for a moment. They heard him say, "Thank you, Lord. I promise I will do all I can."

He remained silent for another minute, then looked up. "Bobby, Mike, please tell me about yourselves. What do you do? What do you like? I can't sit here long but I think I need to hear while I get my gear repacked and sorted out."

"Sure," Mike said. "We love surfing and are both in high school in Oxnard, California. Our parents are great, and we are proud of our heritage of which you are an important part. The reason we know a little about you is that you are a family hero, and Mom loves to do her family history research." The two boys spoke for several minutes as Robert got his gear ready to go.

"Is the world a safe place in your day?"

"Not really," Tim said. "There are always threats. But this one has never returned."

"I guess that'll have to be enough. We do our part, then trust the next generation will carry on."

"Some of our generation have forgotten," Mike said. "They're lost in themselves."

"That's not so different from us," Robert said. "Everyone wanted to forget the War to End All Wars, and because we didn't learn the lesson, we are reliving it. It is a terrible tragedy."

"History calls that war World War I," Tim commented and shook his head. "Of course, you wouldn't have known when you were growing up that it was only act 1 of a two-act play."

"We've known for a long time that there were still problems to be dealt with though."

They looked at each other, sharing a new respect that crossed generations.

"How did you get here?" Robert asked.

"We used an ancient relic that looks like the kind of star that goes on top of a Christmas tree," Tim explained. "It has some kind of consciousness and responds to times of severe need with direction. This direction includes travel to historical times where the star allows us to learn lessons necessary to overcome our own trials."

"It is a gift from God," Robert said.

"It could be, but we aren't really sure," Martie said. "It certainly seems to be a force for good."

"Can I ask one question?" Tim said.

"Of course, I owe you that at least. I might have died in that tree."

Tim thought about how to frame the question. It was a huge

question, and they had almost no time to talk about it. "Why are you doing this? I mean, personally. Why are *you* doing this?"

Robert had just slung his backpack half around his shoulders and was nearly ready to leave. He stopped at the question and stared seriously at Mike, Tim, and their companions. "I'm doing this for you."

"We aren't even born yet," Bobby said. "It can't be for us."

"Look, I'm not much with words. Just a spud farmer from Idaho. But I'm a farm boy that has an opportunity to do something and maybe make a difference. I don't have much time and you need to know what I mean. Maybe that's why you're here."

"Okay, shoot," Mike said.

"I think you want the answer to two questions, and they're both different. *'Why am I doing this?'* and *'Why am I here?'* I've had a year to think about it and that's been the only thing on my mind for the last twenty-four hours. But I think I know the answers to both questions and that makes all the difference."

Robert stopped and held up his hand. He crouched and stared at a spot across the road. A rustling sound came from the dense woods. Robert fluidly shouldered his carbine and froze. A deer broke through the thick undergrowth and moved onto the road, looking at the small group of humans. It seemed to be considering the same questions asked of Robert, hesitated as if waiting for an answer, and then nonchalantly drifted down the road.

Robert breathed a sigh of relief. "Can't stay here long, but I'll give you the short version."

"I'm doing this for my wife, my son, my country, and yes, for you. You are the future, and if we don't stand for something good, we'll get steamrolled by others who stand for something bad. And there's plenty of those people around."

"I understand," said Mike. "What about why *you* are *here*. Jumping out of the sky into occupied France."

"I'm here for them," he said, pointing to the sky.

"Who is them?" Bobby said.

"My buddies. Being a soldier is different than anything I've ever done. I've gone through a nearly impossible experience preparing for this day, and I've grown closer to the men I've shared it with than anyone else in my life. Some of these guys are great, and others I'd never have chosen as friends. But it's all different now. I'm here today because the Screaming Eagles need every one of us."

"But you could die," Martie said.

"Yes, that's possible. Many have already. But I don't want to die. More than anything else I want to live and get back to my family." He stopped for a moment, and his eyes took on a far-away look. "But…if I die in the process of saving some of them, I'd do it without hesitation because they'd do the same thing for me. You see, today all we've got is each other. But our trust and loyalty are complete. Our generation has had to step up. But we've stepped up together. I'm here for them."

"There are critics back home," Tim said.

"Yeah, there will always be 'can't do' or 'don't try' or 'it's not our fight' people, but they don't matter. They are doomed to be forever in the bleachers watching the game. They're not really alive anyway. Life is only lived on the field. Teddy Roosevelt called it the Arena. That's the only place you can make a difference. So I'll try to make a difference as long as I'm granted time to do it."

"But the world has so much bad in it," Bobby said.

"Yeah, we have lots of problems and could do things better. But we're a good and compassionate people that tries to make good choices just because they're good. Because of that goodness we can show others how do make a better world."

"Are you afraid?" Bobby said.

"Are you kidding? I have just been dropped from an airplane flying too fast and too high. My leg strap and pack ripped off immediately and it took ten minutes to descend completely helpless through enemy fire. I drifted miles from the drop zone and landed utterly alone. My war started with me helpless, stuck upside down in a tree with people all around that want to shoot me. I couldn't be more scared. But feeling fear and letting it control you are different things. I'm glad my senses are heightened. I'll need them. I hope I can respond when the time comes."

He held up his carbine. "I hope my training takes over and I don't hesitate."

Robert pulled out the knife Mike used from its scabbard. "Here, you take this. A gift from your great-grandpa."

"But you'll need it. I can't..." Mike stammered.

"I'm a paratrooper. We always have a backup. They crammed over 150 pounds of gear in my packs. I have a trench knife, jump knife, hunting knife, machete, and an entrenching tool. You can keep the jump knife. I'm good. It's got my initials on it so you can prove it to your parents."

"Can I take a picture?" Martie said, pulling out her cell phone.

"That's a camera?" Robert said. "The future must be really cool."

"Mike, you and Bobby stand with Robert," Martie said.

Tim reached out suddenly. "Martie, stop!" But it was too late.

The camera flashed with a blinding white light that lit up the night.

"Oh crap," Robert said as they all hit the dirt and held absolutely still for nearly a minute.

"Martie!" Tim said.

"Sorry, I didn't think of the flash."

Robert froze like a hawk staring into the night for prey. Nobody moved.

"You're a lucky girl," Robert said, flashing a grin.

"Man, what a huge risk, but the picture will be worth it," Mike said. They all smiled.

"Which way are the bad guys," Robert said. "That's where I'm going."

"They're back along that road," Mike said, pointing in the direction they had come. "Saw about thirty heading that way with an armored half-track."

"That's about company size, so I'll be careful until I catch up with some of my buddies."

The travelers watched as the lone paratrooper, a nineteen-year-old father, grandfather, and great-grandfather, walked into the distance. Robert turned once, saluted to the travelers, then disappeared into the darkness.

"What an amazing man," Bobby said.

"Something I'll always remember," Mike added.

"How're we gonna explain this to Mom and Dad?" Bobby said.

"Cross that bridge when we get there, right?" Mike said.

"Got a picture." Martie smiled and held up her phone. "That'll help."

Tim smiled at the thought and had an urge to ask to look at it but realized that would require lighting up the night again. Then he noticed Martie scanning the road in both directions. "What's up, Martie?"

"Why haven't we seen the Trackers yet?"

"Don't know. You're right though. We're really pressing our luck by staying here."

Tim squinted down the road, trying to see movement, then a thought jumped back into his mind and he spun looking at the ground near the hedge opening. "Oh man, this is bad."

"Tim?" Martie said.

"Guys, I dropped my star when I got shot. Did anyone see it?"

"Yep, got it right here. Saw it bounce out of your hand when you did that beautiful dive into the road," Mike said, handing it to him. "Sorry, shoulda said something before, but it was a little distracting meeting our great-grandpa ya know."

"No problem, thanks," Tim said and dropped the small star in his pants pocket. "It wouldn't do to leave that kind of present for the Trackers. Okay, time to go."

Bobby and Martie grasped the large star while Bobby held the carbine in his other hand. They both immediately disappeared. Tim then closed his hand around the Follow Star in his own pocket. Tim realized that Mike remained visible.

"He has a small star," Bobby said. "Why doesn't he use it?"

"Martie, Bobby, hang on for a second," Tim said and let go of the star, reappearing in front of Mike. "You okay?"

Mike appeared to be fingering the star in his pocket. "Not sure I can leave just yet."

"Whatdaya mean?"

"If I go back, I'll be paralyzed again. I know I can't stay here. But meeting Great-Grandpa Robert..."

"Mike, we gotta go...now!"

"I know. Go ahead. I'm coming."

"Okay, but you grab on to your star and follow...promise?"

"Yeah, I know what to do."

"Okay, it's time to go."

Tim's hand closed around the small star. He immediately saw the world beginning to fade and knew they were headed home. He looked for Mike. He wasn't with them. Then his concern turned to shock as, in the fading countryside of 1944 Normandy, Tim saw Mike running down the road after Robert.

CHAPTER XIV

Close Calls

Tim reappeared in the hospital room with Martie, followed by Bobby carrying the carbine.

"Whew, the most awesome trip ever!" Bobby said.

"What happened," his dad asked. "You were only gone about five minutes. What's that?" His father pointed at the rifle.

"Oh, just a little souvenir I picked up."

"Here, unload it and wrap it in my jacket. Not sure the hospital will understand that one." His dad handed a jacket to Bobby. Bobby folded the stock, released the magazine, and pulled back the bolt, ejecting the round in the chamber. He then wrapped the jacket around the carbine and set it on the floor.

"Time is different on a passage—much faster," Martie said.

"Where's Mike?" his mother asked.

"He was right with us," Tim said. "He had the Follow Star. All he had to do was hold it in his hand."

"He must have stayed to be with—" Bobby stopped. "The soldier."

"Where'd you get the weapon?" Tim's dad gestured to the .45 in Tim's waistband.

"In Normandy on D-Day," Tim said.

"Now that's a story worth hearing," his dad said. "No time for that though until Mike is back."

Mike's mom started crying. "I can't imagine what it's like for Mike to lay helpless on some road in a foreign country."

"He can walk on a passage," Martie said.

"What do you mean?" Her mom looked stunned.

"Handicaps are gone on a passage, so Mike used his legs like normal. Another one for the list."

Mike's parents leaned toward each other, clasped hands, and his mom said tearfully, "Maybe he doesn't want to come back and be paralyzed again."

"He can't stay much longer," Tim said. "The Trackers will get him."

Bobby moved to where his parents were seated and rested against the edge of the bed. "There's another reason he may have stayed."

His mom looked up with a pained expression. "Why, Robert?"

"We met Great-Grandpa Whitney. We were there when the Airborne landed on D-Day."

Bobby's parents looked confused. "That's impossible," Carla said. "He never made it to the ground. He landed in a tree and was shot before he could get down. Your Grandpa Chris visited the place in France with your Great-Grandma Leah around the time I was born."

"Maybe history has changed a little," Tim suggested. "You'll have to check that in your family records."

"Tim and Mike rescued him from the tree," Bobby said. "Last we saw him he was headed down the road looking for others."

"As the star brought us back I saw Mike running after Robert," Tim confessed.

"Oh no!" Carla gasped.

"Mike is in great danger," Jim said. "The Trackers will have been drawn by the large star but will sense a lesser pull from the small one and close in."

"We've got to get him back," Natalie said.

"How that happens is in Mike's hands now," Jim said, reaching out a hand toward Natalie, who reached out as well. "All he has to do is hold the Follow Star in his hand. But if he is caught or injured—"

"Then we'll pray if that's all we can do," Mike's mom said and knelt near the bed.

A deathly silence greeted him, as if the house knew it was being violated. It gave him an unearthly standing-on-the-moon feeling. He shivered. Horst was right. Donny had found an unlocked side window and crawled in, careful to remove his shoes before entering. He had given himself five minutes, then he had to leave.

A tide of adrenalin rose within him as he walked through the living room. He couldn't remember the last time he felt so alive. Donny wasted no time finding the stairs and quickly ascended to the girl's room. His senses, which he so often dulled in a foggy mist of drug-induced forgetfulness, were alive with prickly energy. He liked the buzz. He looked under the pillow and in the closet but found nothing. He went through cupboards and drawers, then moved to the boy's room and did the same.

"It's not here," he said angrily.

He searched the kitchen and family room but found no sign of the star. "They must have it with them."

Leaving everything in its place, Donny returned to the window and slipped out onto the grass where his shoes waited like silent watchmen. With nothing more to do, he returned to his basement. Donny spent the remainder of the day and most of the night in a drug-laced haze of gaming. But this time it felt different. His old routine was strangely unsatisfying.

Now he longed to get back to the Carson home. He had a purpose. Bad luck today, but there'd be another chance to get it right. Somewhere in the back of his consciousness, he sensed Clynt smiling.

Mike ran down the dirt road after Robert. "Hey, wait," he called. It was dark and Mike knew he could have gone any direction. He held his hands to his mouth and his lips formed the words again.

Suddenly, someone grabbed him by the arm, roughly pulled him to the side of the road, and slammed him against the hedgerow with a hand over his mouth.

"Are you crazy? You're gonna get us both killed," Robert said. "Assuming you can be killed." Robert slowly removed his hand from Mike's mouth.

"Yeah, I can be killed. Sorry, the others left and I just wanted…" Mike's response stopped dead by the look in Robert's eyes.

"You should not be here. You need to go."

"But I can help," Mike said. "I can fire a rifle. I've already used one today."

"I really appreciate your desire to help," Robert said. "But you are worse than a green recruit. You have no training, no gear, and no common sense. People like you have good intentions, but today all you will do is get yourself and others killed. In spite of what I said earlier, I'd really like to see my wife and son again."

Embarrassed, Mike didn't know what to say.

Robert softened. "Look, Mike, I have a job to do. It is what my generation has to deal with. Your generation will have demands too. You need to survive and be there to make a difference in your time. Nobody else can do what you were placed on this earth for, so go do it."

Mike knew he was right. It hurt, but the truth did sometimes. He tried to change the subject. "It's really weird to call you Great-Grandpa. Can I call you Robert?"

"I am much more comfortable with that too. I'm Bob to my friends, so why don't we do that?"

"Is there anything I can tell the family?"

Robert paused. "I'm not much for words, and this is not the place to get poetic, so I don't know." He had a faraway look in his eyes. "If I make it through this action, I'll write a letter to Leah. I'll put something in it that you will understand."

"Okay, Bob, I'll look for it when I get back."

"Go now, my friend, and remember what we're doing here today," Robert said with a tender tone. He placed his hand on Mike's shoulder. Mike felt as if he really stood in the presence of his wizened great-grandfather rather than a nineteen-year-old kid. "Honor our sacrifice by doing something with the opportunity my generation will give to yours. Make it count for something."

Mike embraced his ancestor and was hugged in return. "I will...I promise."

"Gotta go. Stay here and don't try to follow. I'm very glad we met. I think I understand why the star brought you to me. Remember, I'm doing this for you." A sad expression came over his face when he spoke these final words. He turned, quickly rose, and disappeared into the night.

Mike collapsed against the hedgerow and slumped into a sitting position. He sobbed and forgot he was visible for several minutes.

Something nudged him, then harder. He gradually recovered and looked up. Four soldiers stood in front of him. One with a rifle, the muzzle pointing between his eyes, ordered in a firm voice, *"Holen sie sich bis, schnell!"*

Mike's head spun as he was pulled by the collar to a standing position. These were Germans and *'schnell'* meant fast or something. They made him put his hands behind his head, interlocking his fingers. They did not check his leg pouch or pockets, so they didn't find the knife or the Follow Star.

The soldier jabbed him in the back with the muzzle of his rifle and issued a clear order to get moving. *"Beweg dich."*

He walked in a daze. *How can I get to the star? If I drop my hands to my pocket, they might shoot. I should have listened to Bob. I wouldn't last an hour.* His crisis-induced brain fog lifted as he walked. He wasn't sure how many soldiers were in the group. He could see at least six.

Mike walked in the middle of the road. The soldiers lined up on each side with one directly behind, prodding him along if he moved too slowly. The officer walked immediately in front.

As they moved along the road, he gradually became aware of something else. He discerned dark figures approaching. They materialized from the shadows with outlines that blended into the night. Mike felt both worried and perplexed because they clearly surrounded them but stayed just outside the protective circle of Germans. They were visible to him because they were several shades darker than the night, but the soldiers seemed unaware of their presence.

"Come to us, boy. We're here for ya," a voice whispered.

"Trackers," Mike groaned. "Why don't they just grab me?"

"Ruhig sein!" The soldier to his left whispered and put his index finger to his mouth, gesturing him into silence.

Mike thought about his dilemma and then realized the Trackers had the same problem. *If they make a move for me, the*

Germans will think I'm trying to get away and shoot. If they shoot, the star will return to the present. Mike smiled. *Interesting little problem for the Trackers to solve. They must be biding their time until something happens to distract the soldiers. That's it. Then they'll make their move. I can play that game too.*

The soldiers continued walking, unknowingly surrounded by an ever-growing collection of Trackers. Then the soldiers stopped. Without a word their officer hand-signaled two to move forward to a sharp bend in the road about ten yards in front. As the soldiers approached the bend, Mike heard a distant metallic click. He had already heard this twice since the passage began. It was the pin being pulled from a grenade and the safety band flipping off. The soldier next to him heard it too and looked at him in alarm.

"Granate!"

Before anyone could react, there was a thud in the road like someone had dropped a rock from a tree. The Germans scattered toward the hedges as a deafening explosion and blinding flash split the night air. Mike fell or was knocked to the ground. He wasn't sure which. The Germans began firing at the bend, and flashes came from up ahead indicating someone firing back.

The dark figures immediately moved toward Mike, seemingly immune to the bullets filling the air. They closed in, and he felt his right shoulder turn icy cold. Mike did as he had been practicing mentally. His hand immediately fell to his waist and slipped into his pocket. He found what his hand was searching for and his fingers closed around the star.

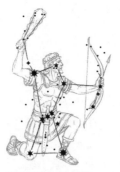

CHAPTER XV

Whispers from the Dead

Mike opened his eyes to the familiar bland hospital room walls. Friendly faces surrounded him, but he felt his heart sink. The air filled with questions assaulting his senses. Mike closed his eyes and held his hands up for quiet. The room fell silent.

He tried to move his legs. Nothing. He fought off intense disappointment and realized he'd need to focus to get back on track with his therapy. He tried again, using Bob's effort to get out of the tree as a point of focus. He grunted.

Wait one moment, kiddo. What's that?

He felt something. It wasn't much, but even something small was good. *No, it's great!* He opened his eyes and saw his mother leaning over him, tears in her eyes. "Are you all right, Michael?"

"I'm great. No, I'm totally awesome!"

"What do you mean, son?" his dad said.

"I felt something," Mike said. "In my legs."

A hush fell over the room.

"You're not kidding?" Bobby said.

"No. It's hard to explain, but there's definitely some feeling."

"That's wonderful," his mom said.

Tim grinned. "One step at a time. That's what Robert and Creighton would both tell you."

Mike smiled at the thought.

His dad's brow furrowed. "What are you wearing and where did that come from?"

"Long story, but I'll just say I got it from a 101st Airborne container. After all, when I arrived all I was wearing a hospital gown." Mike chuckled. "Pretty embarrassing really."

"On D-Day morning, I suppose," Mr. Carson said. "The kids filled us in a little bit but saved the best stuff for when you got back."

"We were really worried," Martie said. "What happened?"

"I wanted to spend a little more time with Bob. He told me he would write a letter with something in it for us."

"Are you referring to Grandpa Robert who died during the war?" his mom asked in surprise. "He never made it to the ground. He died stuck in a tree."

"Yes, we not only met Bob. We got him out of the tree and sent him on his way. He looked in great shape last time I saw him. Look, he gave me this." Mike pulled a military knife out of his pocket. "It has his initials on it."

Mike handed the knife to his dad, who turned it over in his hands. "Right here at the base of the handle. The initials RW. It's well preserved since it has skipped a war and over half a century sitting in a footlocker."

"I can't believe this," his mom said, shaking her head. "It's just too much to take in."

"It's pretty hard to explain what we've just witnessed otherwise," Mike's dad said to her. "But we can call Grandpa Chris and check for the letter."

"We never got any letters from him after D-Day," she said. "I know Great-Grandma Leah was always sad about that."

"What we find may surprise us all," Mike said. "Would you mind if I follow up on this? It will give me something to do. I do have a little extra time lately, and it seems the star had a specific purpose for me anyway."

"Wait," Martie said in excitement. "I almost forgot. I took a picture."

"You what?" her mother said in disbelief.

"I took a picture with my phone."

"But I thought phones didn't work in the past."

"There's no service or GPS back then, but the battery works and the software for the camera is internal," Martie said triumphantly as she navigated to her photo gallery. "Look! Here it is."

Everyone gathered around, straining to see. Martie let each person look and enlarged it with a swipe of her fingers.

"Well, kind of hard to tell with all the paint on his face, but that certainly is Mike and Bobby standing with a soldier," Tony said.

"A Screaming Eagle paratrooper in completely authentic D-Day kit," Mr. Carson added. "Look at the folding stock rifle, the OD's, and the jump boots."

"Wait a minute," Natalie said. "You used a flash?"

"Yeah. Not my smartest move."

"That must have lit up the whole countryside," Jim said. "It's a miracle you didn't get shot by both sides."

"Yeah, Bob was pretty mad at her," Mike said, laughing. "Glad we got the picture though."

"While you're searching for the letter, honey, dig up a few pictures of Grandpa so we can compare it to this one," Carla suggested.

"Sure, Mom," Mike said.

Both sets of parents spent an hour discussing and asking questions about the passage and the kids' conversations with Robert Whitney.

Mike's mom seemed intensely interested and took detailed notes. They didn't leave out any details, including Mike's description of the Trackers.

"Oh, Clynt must've been furious when you disappeared," Tim said with glee.

"What an interesting problem for him," Martie said. She giggled. "Either way he lost."

By the time they finished talking, it was getting late. Carla helped Mike remove his boots and OD pants. Mike kept his new clothing near the bed and decided to wear it during therapy every day. His dad took the knife and the carbine.

"It would be very bad if they found weapons in your hospital room, son."

"I'd like to keep the knife here in the drawer at least," Mike said.

"Okay, but don't be showing it to the staff," Tony warned and placed the knife carefully into the drawer.

"I'll be careful."

Tony nodded and was the last to leave. Mike felt great as everyone filed out of his room, leaving him alone. He had never felt so tired.

Somehow, we're going to make it through this, he thought as he drifted into a deep, sound sleep.

Martie entered her room trying to remember everything she could about the StarPassage. She was tired and couldn't wait to climb into bed. She put the shoulder bag in the closet and changed.

Suddenly, she stopped, turned a full circle, and scanned the room. Everything seemed okay. But it didn't feel right.

Something's wrong.

She opened her dresser drawers and checked under the bed. Nothing.

What is it? Has someone been here?

Backing out of her room, she hurried down the hall and found Tim lying on his bed, still fully clothed, hands behind his head, and staring at the ceiling.

"Tim, gotta second?"

"Pretty tired, but sure, what do you need?"

"Can you come to my room?"

Tim nodded his head yes but didn't move.

"Now?" Martie looked at him with a frown.

"Okay, sis, but then I've got to hit the sack."

They walked the short distance to Martie's room. She led Tim into the center and turned full circle. "Do you notice anything different?"

Tim seemed to catch her serious tone and looked around. "Not really. Why?"

"It feels wrong, like someone's been in my room," Martie said, walking in a circle. "Not family."

"Is there anything you can point to that's out of place or different? Is the window open or something?"

"No, it's just a feeling, and the clothes in my drawers are a little messy."

Tim held up his hands and dropped them to his sides. "Sorry, sis. It's been a long night. I don't know what else to say."

"I think I should be more careful with the star," Martie said.

"That's a good idea, but the rest might be just a little paranoid." Tim smiled.

"Just the same, I'm gonna put the star between my box springs and mattress. That oughta be tougher to find."

"Sounds like a good plan," Tim said. "Now I'm going to bed."

The next week brought progress, excitement, and energy. Mike arrived at each session wearing his OD pants—Olive Drabs as Mr. Carson had told him—and jump boots.

His therapist Kathy laughed the first day. "What in the world are you wearing?"

"I'm using the inspiration of my great-grandpa who fought in World War II."

"Great! If that helps, I'm all for it!"

The nurses didn't mind helping Mike into his ODs and boots each morning if it motivated his effort. Progress seemed slow, but he was definitely getting some feeling back in his legs. His sessions were nothing short of miraculous, as Kathy had told him more than once.

Mike contacted his grandfather Chris in Idaho the day after the StarPassage. He decided not to tell him the weird part of the story, but asked if he would help him on a project.

"The therapists want me to work on something that's important to me," he told Grandpa Chris. "They think it will help me with my recovery."

"Sure, I will do everything I can to help," Grandpa told him. "I've been thinking about you a lot."

"I'm looking for information on Great-Grandpa Robert Whitney and his experiences during the war."

"Hmmm…interesting timing. What kind of information would be helpful?" Grandpa Chris inquired. "I have boxes of stuff from my parents. You know us Whitneys. We're hoarders of history."

"Actually, I'm looking for something specific," Mike said. "The main things I'd like to get are copies of any letters he sent to Great-Grandma Leah or you from the time he landed in Normandy until the end of the war."

There was a brief silence on the other end of the phone. "Grandpa, you there?"

"Yes, I'm here, Mike. Just remembering," he said quietly. "You are aware that my dad didn't come back from the war? I never met him." His voice cracked at the last comment. "I'd give anything to have known him. Mom, bless her soul, did all she could to make him alive in my life. I do love her for that."

"When did he die?"

"He was a paratrooper...jumped into France on D-Day morning. For many years we thought he never made it to the ground. It was reported he hit a large tree and either died on impact or was shot before he could get down. I even visited the place once with Mom in the 1970s. It moved me to tears to stand under the tree, look up, and imagine what happened."

Mike tried to contain his excitement. "We've been told that all our lives by Mom. But you sound like new information has surfaced recently?"

"Yes, it's actually kind of funny you would call with this request now. Just a month ago we were going through some of Mother's old things, and at the bottom of an old jewelry box we found two letters...and something else."

"Really? What did you find?"

"It's kind of strange actually. I meant to call you, but with the holidays and then your accident it slipped my mind. That seems to be happening more often lately."

"I have all the time in the world right now," Mike encouraged.

"Just a moment," Grandpa said. The line went quiet for almost a minute before he returned. "You still there, Mike?"

"Yep. Ready."

"The first letter came from the Department of the Army dated July 1944. It is a commendation and the award of a Silver Star for courage in action. I won't read the full letter, but it speaks of his actions on June 13, 1944, which is referred to in history as D-Day plus 7. Apparently, his company got pinned down in hedgerow country by a group of Germans with an antitank gun and an MG42 machine gun, a particularly deadly weapon. 'Private Robert Whitney with disregard for his own safety,' it says, 'circled behind the gun position and single-handedly killed a dozen Germans, destroying the gun with only his carbine and grenades.'"

"That's amazing!" Mike said. "He was a hero!"

"Yes, and Mom knew but never said anything. There's one more thing you should know. The award was presented posthumously."

"What does that mean?"

"It means 'after death,' son," Grandpa Chris said quietly. "He saved his company but did not survive the action."

Mike couldn't find any words. His eyes watered. "He was a great man. He gave his life for us and to save his buddies."

"Yes, he did. But it has hurt my whole life. Sometimes I wish he'd been a little less of a hero."

"I'm sorry, Grandpa," Mike said. "He did what he had to do. I'm sure his buddies would've done the same for him."

"Yes, you are probably right."

"I came across something of Great-Grandpa's also. I want to show you, but we'll have to wait and do that when I get out of here."

"That's a date," Grandpa said. "But there's something else. I told you there was another letter."

"Okay." Mike suddenly felt nervous. "What does it say?"

"I don't know."

"What do you mean? Just read it."

"It was sealed by your great-grandma with instructions that it could only be opened by you."

"What? I must have been just a kid when she died. What was I, about four?"

"Five actually. Remember I only found out about this a

month or so ago. I can only tell you it was addressed to Mom with the return address from Dad in France. The date on the envelope read June 10, 1944, three days before he was killed in action.

"Mom added a brief note on the front of the envelope. 'This is a private letter to me from Bob. It may not be read by anyone else until after young Mike is old enough to read and appreciate it. Please respect my wishes and do not open the seal.' Quite mysterious really."

"Will you please send me the letter and a copy of the commendation?"

"I'll do better than that, Mike," Grandpa said. "I've been planning to come see how you are doing anyway. I'll make reservations and fly over in a few days. Then we can open it together."

"I'd love that, Grandpa," Mike said. "Could you also bring any pictures you can find of Great-Grandpa?"

"That part's easy. There are only a few."

"Great! See you in a few days. Then we can tell each other the rest of the story."

The night before Grandpa's arrival, Mike had an unexpected visitor. A knock came at the door as he drifted off to sleep. Groggy, he said, "Come in. Nobody ever sleeps in this place."

Martie and her mother entered the room.

"You're the last people I expected this late at night."

"We didn't expect to be here either, but the star gave us a little job to do," Martie said.

"A job?"

"Yeah, I had just added the two new lines to our Rules for StarPassages list."

"Which rules were those?" Mike tried to remember.

"They are numbers twenty and twenty-one. I wrote them like this:

20. *Animals can sense your presence even if you are invisible.*

21. *Severe handicaps we have in the present time may be non-existent on a passage.*

"How could I forget the second one," Mike said cheerfully. "Kind of a big deal."

"Martie, tell him what happened," her mother urged.

"Right. I pulled the star out of the bag just before going to bed as I usually do just to see if anything's changed. It's become part of my end-of-day routine."

"It had some new writing on it?" Mike said.

"It did. The words were pretty simple. They said, *'To pierce the veil, use the Star of Sight, deliver the relic to the hospital tonight.'*"

"The center of the star opened as soon as I read the words, revealing the small six-pointed star." Martie handed it to Mike.

"I've learned when the star speaks it means business, so I got Mom and we came right over."

"What does this do?" Mike said. "It's different than the others."

"It's actually pretty cool," Mrs. Carson said. "But we're only aware of some of its powers."

Martie took up the explanation. "It's called the Star of Sight because it gives the holder the ability to see or perceive beyond one's natural senses. When I used it on the Britannic, I could sense the presence of Trackers. I hope you don't need it for that."

"Me too," Mike agreed. "I'll keep it in the drawer where I can get to it if I need to."

"A doctor we met used it for years to help with his patient care," Martie's mom added.

"So it can be used in a bunch of ways? Interesting..."

"We'll let you get some rest," Mrs. Carson said. "Tomorrow's going to be a big day with your grandpa coming to visit."

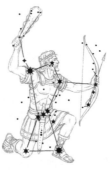

CHAPTER XVI

The Letter

I t had been a week since Mike spoke with Grandpa Chris. He knew Grandpa arrived in town the previous evening, too late to come over. He also knew his mom would have made a special dinner, and the family had planned to bring him up to date on everything except the stuff about the star.

Mike rose early and had a solid, if not spectacular, therapy session. Progress was good, but he grew impatient again. Afterward, the nurse wheeled him back to his room still dressed in his ODs and boots. They turned the corner to find Grandpa Chris standing in the hallway by his room.

In his early seventies, Grandpa wore a flannel lumberjack shirt and a pair of khaki Docker pants. He was fit for his age, although his youngish looking build was betrayed by a balding head with wisps of gray hair and numerous age spots. Grandpa stood six foot two, down a little from his youthful six foot four, but his shoulders were straight and broad and his back unbowed in spite of a life of hard farm labor.

Grandpa moved toward him, his bass voice booming from a face creased with deep crevices of care. "Hello, son. It's nice to see you have the famous Whitney fight. I hear you're doing well."

"Hey, Grandpa. Nobody told me you were here."

"Wanted to watch your session from a distance. Impressive. You'll be surfing again one day. Mark my words."

"I like that idea. Got a little work to do before that though."

"One day and one step at a time, Mike. That's what gets us anywhere worth going."

Grandpa's can-do attitude always raised Mike's spirits. Even when they lost Grandma Chloe to cancer the year before, his faith sustained him and he remained a bright light that uplifted all around him.

"Yeah, I'm doing all right I guess. Wish it could happen faster though."

"That's the trick of life, isn't it," Grandpa said without hesitation. "The tough things seem to take so long to work through, but the wonderful and joyful times flash by like lightning."

"This is one of those long slogging times, I know," Mike said, sounding a little more like Winnie the Pooh's donkey friend Eeyore than he intended.

"Yep, but the funny thing is that the crops always grow faster and more evenly when there's a really good storm. You just don't get the same results by watering." Grandpa smiled. "Yep, you got a doozey of a storm here."

"Thanks for coming. I feel better already."

"Glad to help," Grandpa said.

"Did you bring the letter?"

"I did, and the pictures as well."

"Awesome. Can't wait to see them."

"I feel the same. Got them right here," he said, holding up an old shoe box. "Your mom wanted to stay, but I sent her home. Figured it was a private moment for the two of us."

"That sounds right. We better share it with everyone else later though, or we'll both be in big trouble."

Grandpa laughed a deep cheerful laugh. "You've got that right." He turned his attention to the nurse. "Here, I'll be glad to take over and let you get on to other things."

"I do have a hectic schedule, thank you," she said. "I'll come back and check on you two later."

Grandpa wheeled Mike into the room and helped him into bed. Mike had gotten pretty good at swinging his legs onto the bed.

"Do we need to change you out of your work clothes?"

"Nope, I'll be back in the saddle again this afternoon so I usually keep these on until later."

Alone, Grandpa and Mike looked at each other. Grandpa leaned over and gave him a hug. "You're going to beat this, I know."

"I'm beginning to see some light at the end of this long tunnel too. I don't want to be rude, but what've you got. I'm really excited to see."

"Before you open the letter, I wanted you to have this." He handed Mike a small black box with the words SILVER STAR on the outside and a citation letter from the President of the United States describing the award for Gallantry in Action given to Robert Howard Whitney.

Mike read the one-page letter, which included a paragraph describing Private Whitney's courageous act and stating that numerous lives were saved. It also explained that it took place on July 13, 1944, in the hedgerow country near the French town of Carentan. The German army had counterattacked, trying to retake the town from Allied forces, including elements of the 101st Airborne.

Mike thought about the countryside and hedges he'd seen during his passage. "It must have been an impossibly difficult job to get around the gun position and take it out."

"I can only imagine. When Mom and I visited the area, I was surprised by how high the hedgerows were," Grandpa said. "We tend to think of the little two-foot-high decorative hedges we find in the yards in the US, but these are ten-foot-tall dirt mounds with trees and thick bushes growing on top. They're formidable walls even today."

"I don't know what to say except thanks," Mike said. "It's an overwhelming gift that I'll always treasure."

"Somehow it seems right that you should have it."

Mike carefully lifted the cover off the box. Within, he saw a small, bronzish-gold five-pointed star with its top point attached to a ribbon with a vertical red stripe in the center bounded by two white stripes and on either edge by two blue stripes. Mike also noticed a smaller rectangular ribbon with the same color pattern.

"What's the small ribbon for?"

"That's the one that the soldier wears on his uniform above the pocket with other campaign ribbons and such," Grandpa said. He handed Mike a time-yellowed envelope. "This is for you too."

Mike turned the yellowed letter over in his hands. It had the writing and addresses described by Grandpa Chris during their previous phone call. The envelope was sealed with a round, red wax stamp with the impression of a script capital letter L in the center.

"That's Mother's wax seal," Grandpa explained. "She must have opened and read the letter and then resealed it and written the note to give it to you. It is very curious that she would have chosen you. Do you have any idea why, Mike?"

"I have a good idea, but it's probably best to read the letter together first."

Mike carefully broke the wax seal and lifted the flap. He reached in and pulled out two brittle pages of difficult-to-read handwritten scrawl.

"Great-Grandpa's writing wasn't the best," Mike said, smiling.

Grandpa chuckled. "He probably didn't have a nice desk and ballpoint pen either."

"The letter is dated June 10, 1944, and begins *'My Dearest Sweetheart Leah'.*"

Mike looked up at Grandpa, who pulled several tissues from the box on the nearby table and dabbed his eyes. "Are you ready for me to continue?"

Grandpa, his eyes reddened, said, "Yes, I think so."

Mike unfolded the yellowed pages and slowly read from the letter:

I had hoped to write sooner, but we have been pretty busy here since we landed in France 4 days ago. It was tough to find a stub of pencil and some paper, but I finally did, so here goes. I miss you and little Chris terribly. I love you and want you to know that I feel stronger than ever that we are doing the right thing and that I am where I am supposed to be. I have spent a lot more time on my knees lately and gained a closeness with God and purpose I have not felt before. Life is taken or spared here so randomly. Saints and sinners live or die it seems based on stepping in the wrong spot or simply what place they are at the right or wrong time. I have been very lucky and perhaps blessed so far but have come to realize that such could end at any moment.

I hope what I have said doesn't scare you. Don't worry. I am fine and healthier than I have ever been. The food stinks and your delicious casseroles haunt my dreams. Even the crummy barracks beds sound pretty good right now. There is so much I miss, but I can't allow myself to think about that. I trust you and Chris are well and safe. I haven't received any mail since we were in England so I'll just tell you a little about what's going on.

We landed in the middle of the night. It was a huge mess with our outfit scattered all over the place. We lost a bunch of good men to enemy fire and freak accidents. But we're Airborne and somehow pulled together to achieve our objectives. The Krauts are tough nuts to crack. They make the going very hard. When we push them out they counterattack and we often go through it all over again. But we are winning and they are getting slowly pushed back. The Army won't let us be too detailed in letters home, security you know. But we are going to be making a big push in the next couple of days. Probably the last one before we are pulled out for a little rest.

Something happened the first night I want you to know about. It may seem hard to believe but it is absolutely true. Our transport plane had to take evasive action to avoid being shot down and dropped us too high and way too fast. My stick, sorry I mean the soldiers with me in the plane, was scattered all over the place and each guy has a funny or scary story to tell. In my case I landed upside down in a tree. I know you're laughing and it must have looked pretty funny. I got stuck and couldn't move. I was there for a while. It's hard to keep track of time when you are upside down. I think I passed out or fell asleep. Then someone woke me up and cut me loose of the mad tangle of parachute cords and got me down. There were four of them that helped me. They were Americans, but not soldiers. What comes next is the strange part. They said they were from the future, our future. Yeah, I know, hard to believe. But they knew all about me and you, things they couldn't possibly know unless their wild story was true. I saw them appear and disappear. I don't know how. But here's the real capper...two of them said they were our great-grandsons. They were teenagers. The older one was about my age, named Mike. Yeah, strange to have a great-grandson my same age. He's the one that got me out of the tree. The younger one was named Robert. They called him Bobby. Can you believe that? They told me little Chris would have a great life and four children and that the youngest would be a girl named Carla. They were her two oldest boys. They probably saved my life. Crazy, huh?

I am writing this because I wanted you to know. I will do everything I can to make sure I come back to you. But, as I said, things are pretty random here. Always understand that I know I am doing what our Heavenly Father needs me to do and making a difference.

I love you more than ever. No matter what happens I will always walk by your side and be there to watch over little Chris.

All my love,
Bob

Mike's emotions seemed to fill the entire space of his hospital room. There were no words. He looked at Grandpa Chris, whose head bent in unmoving hands.

Nothing changed for several minutes. The atmosphere seemed thick with memories, and Mike felt a strange sensation, another presence in the room. He remembered when Martie had given him the Star of Sight. She had said, "It'll help you perceive things others cannot."

He slid the drawer open and pulled out the star, letting it rest in his right hand. As soon as he touched it, the room changed. The space around him seemed to gain another dimension. The air became thicker, and the colors and textures ran together like an Impressionist's watercolor painting. Mike closed his eyes and rubbed them as if to see more clearly.

He looked again and saw two individuals standing on either side of Grandpa, each with a hand on his shoulder. He recognized the one on the right. It was Bob, but he no longer wore his military uniform or had his face blackened. He looked slightly older. Bob had regular clothes on, but they were brighter than anything Mike had ever seen. A light seemed to shine from within him. Bob looked at Mike and smiled. He raised his free right hand, giving him a thumbs-up.

On the left side of Grandpa stood a beautiful young woman in a long white dress. She had the same nearly blinding light shining from within her. She looked at him and did not speak but smiled warmly. He felt compassion flow from her like water running over his body. She held out her left hand and gestured for Mike to give the star to Grandpa Chris. Neither of the individuals broke contact with Grandpa's shoulder.

Mike had trouble finding his voice, but finally he managed to mumble, "Grandpa."

He did not immediately answer, so he called him again, "Grandpa, can you hear me?"

Grandpa's head remained bowed. "Yes, son… Sorry… Just thinking."

"Take this and hold it in your hand."

Grandpa's hand reached out unconsciously. Mike handed him the small six-pointed star. To Mike's surprise, the vision did not close even though he no longer held the star.

Suddenly, Grandpa stiffened. His head slowly rose as he glanced left, seeing the figure of the young woman. Mike could see emotion burst from Grandpa's face.

"Mom…how…is…this…possible?"

Grandpa looked long and deep at his mother, whom Mike knew he loved beyond measure and missed terribly. They smiled at each other. He reached out but could not touch the other-worldly being. She gestured to his other shoulder, and Grandpa followed her gaze to Bob. Grandpa's eyes widened, and he began to visibly tremble. He uttered a deep, guttural moan.

"Dad?"

The spectral image of his father nodded with joy etched on his light-filled face.

"I have longed to meet you my whole life."

Mike sensed words in his mind. They came from Bob, without speaking, and were directed at Grandpa.

"My son, your mother and I are so proud of you. We are happy and ever at your side as I promised. You are never alone."

"What do you want me to do?" Grandpa asked.

Bob nodded his head almost imperceptibly. "You have done all you were asked to do. We will embrace one day. There will be joy surpassing anything you have ever known. Watch over your family and especially Mike and Bobby. They will need your guidance and advice."

Grandpa reached for his father's hand but could not grasp it. "I love you, Dad."

Mike heard the words form in his mind again. "I love you too, son, and am so pleased with the life you have lived. I am sorry you and my sweetheart had to do it without me."

"Dad, your example has always been with me, and Mom kept you so alive every day."

The bright beings looked at each other, and Mike sensed a profound depth of love shared that made him feel like he was eavesdropping on something very personal. Grandpa Chris seemed overwhelmed by the feeling and bowed his head again.

Mike felt his great-grandmother's words forming in his mind.

"Michael, because of your kind act Bob's life was extended. It allowed him to make a difference and save others, some of which survived the war and experienced full and joyous lives with their families. Such gifts continue for generations."

Bob's voice came again to his mind. "Such selflessness will bless your life in ways you cannot now comprehend. Never give up."

The vision suddenly ended, leaving Mike and Grandpa in stunned silence. Several minutes passed without conversation. Finally, Grandpa raised his head and gave Mike a hard, questioning stare, one eyebrow raised. He held out the six-pointed star and smiled the biggest toothy smile Mike had ever seen from him.

"I think it's time for me to hear the rest of the story."

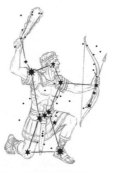

CHAPTER XVII

Second Chance

randpa sat back after Mike had related all he knew about the stars and StarPassages. "Whew! That is a lot to take in all at once."

"It is mind blowing actually," Mike said. "If I hadn't gone on a passage myself I would never believe it."

"Was it hard to come back?" Grandpa said.

"Come back?"

"Yes, from the passage to France where your legs were back to normal?"

Mike stared at Grandpa for a moment, trying to figure out how to respond. Finally, he said, "I'm not sure how I feel about that today. I guess it was hard to get the use of my legs back then lose them again. But it gave me hope."

"Do you think the star would allow me to go on a passage?" Grandpa said.

"The star seems to be the decision maker on that one, Grandpa. Sorry."

Just then a soft knock came at the door. "Come on in," Mike called out.

The door swung open, and in walked Martie, Tim, and Bobby.

"Hi guys, what's up?" Mike said cheerfully.

"Martie drew the star from her shoulder bag and held it out. "New writing appeared this morning. We think you both should read this one."

"Go ahead, Grandpa," Mike said and pushed the star toward him.

Grandpa took the star. "The writing is kind of small," he said sheepishly. "Excuse me while I put on my reading glasses."

He fished a set of narrow glasses from his shirt pocket and placed them on the lower portion of his nose. "Let me see...oh, my goodness."

"What's it say, Grandpa?"

Mike's grandfather read slowly.

"Two generations must journey this time, grandson and grandpa to the start of the climb."

"What does that mean?" Grandpa said.

"Don't look at me," Tim said. "I hate riddles."

"The writing hasn't changed for a while, so we knew we weren't the ones it was trying to speak to," Martie said.

"So it has to be you and Mike," Bobby said.

"Mike, are you okay with this?" Grandpa said.

"Sure, Grandpa. I'd love to do this together. I already have my ODs and boots on so I'm ready to go. Grandpa, you're dressed like a lumberjack as usual so you're probably good no matter where we end up."

"Let's give your grandpa a few tips about passages before you go," Martie suggested. All agreed and they went through some of the more important rules. Ten minutes later Mike said, "I guess we're as ready as we'll ever be."

Grandpa looked a little overwhelmed. Bobby put his hand on Grandpa's shoulder and smiled. "Don't worry, nobody's ever really ready the first time."

They looked at the star again. New writing had appeared.

"Why don't you read it this time, Mike," Grandpa suggested, handing the star to him.

Mike read:

"Take the star at twelve and nine and your past you may have a chance to refine."

"Don't know what that means, but it should be interesting," Mike said. "You ready?"

"I guess so," Grandpa said.

They took hold of the points as directed. The room faded into gray mist. "Is this normal?"

"Happened like this the last time," Mike said to his grandpa. "So I guess the answer is yes."

The gray slowly gave way to outlines and sounds. "We're standing on a beach," Mike said. "Oh no! I know where we are."

They were on a picturesque beach, which jutted out on a point of land. They stood in the early morning shade of the hills behind them. In front of them were the beautiful sounds and sights of a set of perfectly formed waves rolling into shore. A few steps away stood a lone surfer, watching something in the water. Another surfer waited on his board in a perfect spot to catch the building waves.

"That's you!" Grandpa said.

"Yes," Mike said quietly. "And that's Bobby in the water waiting for his last ride."

"Is this the morning…" Grandpa's voice trailed off.

"Yes, the morning of the accident," Mike said. "Why are we here?"

"You appear to have been given an opportunity to change everything," Grandpa said. "This is wonderful."

Mike was stunned by the revelation. "I can change the past. I can make it so the accident never happened?"

"Yes, Mike. Isn't that what you've prayed for?"

"It is. But now that I'm here, I don't know."

They watched Bobby catch the final wave and begin his ride in. Mike noticed Bobby seemed to look right at them. "We're holding the star, right?"

"Yes."

"It looked like Bobby saw us just now," Mike said.

"I suppose anything is possible," Grandpa suggested. "The star is certainly full of surprises."

"That morning when Bobby came in, he asked me who the other two people watching him were," Mike said. "I didn't see anyone, of course, and never thought about it until now."

"We are here, aren't we?" Grandpa said. "It must be for a purpose, and it is pretty obvious."

"Maybe," Mike said. "But we need to let it play out a bit."

Bobby arrived at the beach, placing his board under one arm, and jogged to where the historical figure of Mike stood. Mike and Grandpa listened to the conversation and followed as the boys walked toward the parking lot. They listened as Bobby lobbied Mike to drive home. Mike flinched as his historic self agreed.

Grandpa looked at Mike with concern, "You need to stop it. Why aren't you stopping it?"

"We've got time, Grandpa. Don't worry."

The boys arrived at the car, and the travelers watched as they put their boards on the roof rack. Mike tossed the keys to Bobby and reminded him that they'd change back when they got to town. They both smiled as they jumped into the car and backed out, heading for the coastal road.

Grandpa and Mike walked next to the boys in the car to the stop sign at the parking lot exit. Bobby stopped, looked carefully both ways, and pulled slowly onto the two-lane road that meandered through the numerous coastal beach colonies dotting the landscape between Faria Beach and Oxnard.

"Mike," Grandpa pleaded. "What are you doing? They are gone. You've missed a chance of a lifetime to right a terrible wrong."

Mike asked himself the same question as he watched them drive south. *Why did I let them go?*

But he already knew the answer. He sensed it the moment they appeared on the beach and realized where and when they were and its implications.

"It wouldn't be right, Grandpa."

"Why?" Grandpa pleaded.

"If the accident hadn't happened then, nothing else would have happened either," Mike said.

"What are you trying to say?" Grandpa sniffed back tears.

"I wouldn't have been in the hospital."

"Yes, I thought the point was to avoid that."

"But, Grandpa, if we had just gone home and had breakfast with Mom and Dad, then the accident wouldn't have happened. Bobby never would have been depressed. Tim would never have picked him out of the crowd, and we would never have had any StarPassage experiences."

"Mike, it would have all been worth it to keep you from having to go through this."

"But, Grandpa, you would never have met your dad," Mike said tenderly. "That's worth all the sacrifice."

The last comment stopped Grandpa short. His eyes watered, and his head bowed. Grandpa put his free arm around Mike. "You're too good to have to go through this."

They stood silently for nearly a minute and watched the waves roll toward shore. "I have always believed in a higher power that loves and watches over His children. He must be very pleased with your selfless decision. I feel impressed to tell you that your legs will return to full health again one day."

"I hope you're right," Mike said. "But if not, life isn't over. I know that now. I just keep thinking about how Creighton and Lisa Rider would deal with such a choice."

"You have changed," Grandpa said.

Mike took a half step back. "Yes, this accident and my experiences have changed me. If I can walk again one day, that's great, but I am a better person already."

They stood looking out at the perfect waves curling toward the beach, collapsing and reaching out to its sparkling sandy shores. "You've chosen a very difficult path, son."

"Perhaps that's true, but who knows what twists the other path might have included. Besides, I see things differently now. I think you do too. Maybe the tough times really are also the good times. After all, it's during the trials of life that we experience the most growth. I'm sure God understands that too."

The perfect picture began to fade, and Mike's breathing choked slightly as he heard the distant sound of sirens.

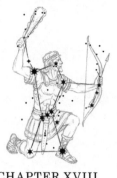

CHAPTER XVIII

Sudden Departure

I t seemed to Bobby that it had only been a few seconds when Mike and Grandpa reappeared. "That was quick. Where'd you go?"

Mike had trouble responding as he lay in his bed. Grandpa put his hand on Bobby's shoulder. "We were on Faria Beach, son."

"On the day of the wreck?" Bobby said, fearing the worst.

Mike nodded his head.

"What did you do," Tim said. "It doesn't look like anything has changed."

Mike looked at Grandpa and closed his eyes, squeezing tears out that ran down the side of his face. "Nothing."

Bobby couldn't comprehend what Mike had said. "What do you mean, nothing?"

Mike shook his head. "I could've stopped it, I guess. I don't know how to help you understand."

"What's to understand?" Bobby said, feeling a hint of anger. "You could have avoided all of this. You could have wiped your injury away in a second."

The comment seemed to have struck a chord in Mike. "That's it, Bobby. I should have jumped at the chance. But then when I was actually there and thought it through, it seemed better for all of us that the accident happened, no matter how hard it's been or how tough it will be in the future."

"You see, son," Grandpa said, "all of us have grown in ways that never could have happened without the wreck."

"That's easy for anyone else to say except Mike," Bobby argued. "He's the one that's paralyzed."

Bobby moved to Mike's bedside and put his hand on Mike's shoulder. "Come on, big bro. We can still go back and make it right. The star will take us."

Mike took Bobby by the arm. "It's already *right*. I promise you I'll be back surfing again even if it takes a while. But the Star-Passages needed to happen for all of us. I'm not glad it happened, but I chose to work through this rather than erase it. It's helping me become someone more than I otherwise would have become."

"Oh, Mike..." Bobby said. "I'm so sorry."

"Apology completely and unconditionally accepted. It happened and the worst part is over," Mike said. "Now we all need to let it go and move forward. We've at least learned that from the passages. Learning from the past is good, but if we dwell on the past, we'll never move forward."

The hospital room grew quiet. Martie admired Mike's decision but felt compassion for the pain Bobby would always feel if Mike didn't fully recover.

"We all have, or will have, heavy burdens to bear in this life," Grandpa said. "It isn't so much the nature of the burden as it is how we bear it. Mike has set an inspirational example we should try to follow."

"The Riders have shown us that the easy way isn't always the right way," Mike said.

Martie picked up the star from the edge of the bed and was putting it in her shoulder bag when she noticed something. "Oh... it can't be."

"What is it, sis?" Tim said.

"There's new writing on the star."

"You're kidding," Mike said. "We just got back. This thing is working overtime."

"Take a look," Martie said. "It seems to be for the three of you guys."

Mike read:

"Three must go where they're short of time. Saving souls depends on an early climb."

"Maybe not," Tim said. "It doesn't say which three."

"Wait a minute," Mike said. "There's more."

"Two must follow and one holds three, boys become men if they all succeed."

The center of the star opened where two small eight-pointed stars waited.

"Okay, guys," Martie said. "That's pretty clear."

"I'll take the big star and you each take a Follow Star," Tim suggested.

"Sounds okay to me," Mike said. "I'd like to team up with Bobby again anyway."

"Me too," Bobby said.

"What's wrong, Martie?" Grandpa said.

"The message sounds like you don't have much time to do what you need to do and there's a climb involved," Martie said. "Sounds like there'll be obstacles to overcome. Be careful."

"We will." Tim smiled. "Mike, you're dressed and ready to

go. We'll go home and change and then we'll call right before I grab the star."

"Okay, see you on the other side," Mike said. "Wait, take this with you."

He handed the Star of Sight to Tim, who placed it in the center opening of the large star and then nodded to Mike. "Yep, never know when we might need that on a passage."

"I think I'll stay here with Mike," Grandpa offered. "He might need my help when he returns."

"Right," Martie agreed. "I'll go with Bobby and Tim and do the same at home."

Tim gave a ride to Bobby and Martie. They stopped first at Bobby's house to get some Levi's and sturdy shoes, then drove to the Carson home. Tim got the star and its shoulder bag, a couple of flashlights, and pocket knives, and they were ready to go.

"Where do we start," Bobby said.

"My room, of course," Martie said. "I'll wait for you there."

They climbed the stairs to Martie's room, and she sat on the bed. Bobby took the small star from his pocket and asked, "Ready?" Everyone nodded yes.

Martie called Mike's hospital room. She waited for an answer, then heard someone pick up. "This is Mike."

"Hi Mike. We're ready here. How about you?"

"All set."

"Okay, Tim. It's time," Martie said. She clenched her teeth. "It's lots harder to be left behind."

"Say a little prayer for us, sis." Tim pulled the large star from the shoulder bag. "Here we go."

He grabbed the star at the three point, immediately faded, and was gone, followed a second later by Bobby.

Martie still held the phone with the line open. "Grandpa? Grandpa Chris...are you there?"

It was quiet for a moment before he spoke. "Yes I am, but Mike is gone."

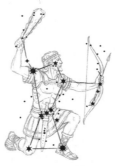

CHAPTER XIX

Underground

Tim and Bobby appeared at the same time. They stood in a long hallway of what looked like a shopping mall. "Where's Mike?" Bobby said.

"There he is. Glad it's not too crowded." Tim pointed to Mike, who lay on his back in the middle of the wide hallway. "He could have been trampled 'cause no one can see him."

Mike faced the other way and had not seen them yet.

"Mike, over here," Bobby called.

He turned and saw Bobby and Tim standing together chuckling as a man dressed in a business suit tripped over his leg, nearly falling. The businessman looked back. Seeing nothing, he shook his head, checked his watch, and continued on.

"Real funny, guys," Mike called out as he got to his feet and walked toward them. "Where are we?"

"Where and when," Tim said. "That's the first thing we need to figure out."

They looked around the mostly empty mall and saw numerous storefronts with the rolling metal bars down and locked. Tim noticed a few people who appeared to be opening their shops for business, rolling up the gates and unlocking the glass double doors.

"Must be morning. The shops are beginning to open," Tim observed.

"Let's put our stars away and find out," Mike suggested.

They moved to the edge of the hallway where they were less likely to be noticed when they appeared. Tim placed the large star in the shoulder bag as Mike and Bobby dropped their stars in their front pockets.

They scanned the hallway. Tim saw a woman opening a shop about forty feet away.

They approached and observed an attractive, athletic woman with dark shoulder-length hair. She lifted up the grating to a shop that sold watches. She wore a long-sleeved, tailored white shirt with the tail untucked, a pair of black slacks, and modest two-inch black heels. A young girl of about five, wearing what looked like a school uniform with a plaid backpack slung over her shoulders, stood close to her.

"Good morning, we're from out of town and a bit lost," Tim said. "Could you please tell us where we are?"

"Sure," the woman said in a pleasant voice. "You tourists?"

"Yep, just arrived in town," Tim said.

"Well, you're in the right place to start," the woman said cheerily. "It's a beautiful day and you'll have a great view."

"Sorry, where are we?" Tim persisted.

The woman looked at him strangely. "The Mall at the World Trade Center...in Manhattan?"

"Thank you," Tim said, smiling. "How do we get to the street?"

She pointed down the hallway. "Better yet, you can get to the observatory in building two if you go that way. It's also called the South Tower. Take your first right. It's pretty hard to miss building two's entrance just before you get to the Marriott Hotel. You picked a good time to beat the crowds."

"It can't be!" Tim mumbled.

"Sorry," the woman said. "I didn't hear that."

"No, just talking to myself," Tim said, shaking his head and patting the shoulder bag. "Our tour director never gives us the full story. We always seem to be learning as we go."

The woman laughed. "Sounds like my life."

She extended her hand. "I'm Donna, and this is my daughter Katherine."

He took her hand. "I'm Tim, and this is Bobby and Mike. We really appreciate your help."

"Can you tell us, what day it is please?" Mike said warmly. "It's hard to keep track when you're in a different city every day."

"Sounds like the economy tour," Donna said, chuckling.

"Yeah, you get what you pay for," Bobby said as they all shared a smile.

"Tuesday," Donna said. "September 11."

Tim's eyes went wide. He looked into the store, searching for and finding a digital wall clock, which read *7:45 a.m.* and the date below *9/11/2001.*

Tim's voice broke. "Excuse us for a moment. Guys, we need to talk right now!" He pulled Mike across the hallway to the grating that covered the Warner Bros. Studio Store. Bobby shrugged at Donna and followed.

"We've never been in a worse place at a worse time," Tim said.

"I've never been interested in visiting New York. No surfing you know." Bobby smiled. "But it's not that bad."

"It's the World Trade Center and it's *9-11,*" Tim said. "The day the buildings were attacked by terrorists who had hijacked commercial jets."

Mike froze. "When does it happen? What time is it now?"

"The clock in the store says 7:45, and the first attack happened about 8:45. I don't remember when the second plane hit or how long it took before the buildings fell," Tim said. He breathed deeply and tried to think.

You've got to get hold of yourself. There's something to do here and not much time.

"What about that nice woman and her daughter?" Bobby said.

Tim turned to look at them, unsure of what to do. Donna and Katherine were in the watch store behind the counter. "We have to do something, but we can't sound threatening or we could be arrested. They've already had a bombing here, so they'll be pretty skittish."

"They're really nice," Bobby said. "We can't leave them here to die."

"What can we say?" Mike said.

Tim struggled, then a thought struck him. "Follow my lead."

Tim walked back to the store. "Donna, we'd love to thank you for your help in some way. Can we buy you a bagel or something?"

"That's nice, but I've got to get the shop ready," she said.

"It'll only take a few minutes, please?" Tim said, trying to sound innocent. "I'll bet there's a cart or shop outside we can grab something? We have a few more touristy questions."

Donna looked at her daughter, raised her eyebrow, and said in a polite voice, "I don't think so. You seem nice, but I don't know you."

"You're right," Tim said. "We could have all kinds of weirdo ideas. Growing up in California can do that to people I guess."

Donna's tension seemed to ease. "That's a pretty good line. Look, I don't want to be rude. But I've got my daughter with me, and there are real crazies around."

"Please…I promise we'll keep our distance," Tim said.

Donna's daughter pulled on her pocket and said, "Momma, I'm hungry, and daddy's always late."

Donna shot a quick warning look at Tim, nodded her head,

and said, "Okay, just a quick bite. There's a little spot we can grab something in the Mall."

"If you don't mind, I'd like to see the sky," Tim said. "It'll help us get our bearings."

Donna hesitated again but Katherine smiled and said, "I want to see the pretty sky too."

"Well, okay, but let's be quick. The Mall opens at eight so I need to get back soon," Donna said. "We can get to the plaza through the South Tower. There's usually a cart on Liberty Street."

"Sounds great, thanks," Tim said.

They all followed Donna, who closed and locked the sliding shop door, then moved at a speed walk to tower two and out onto the plaza. It was a gorgeous fall day.

"This is my favorite time of year in New York," she said.

Tim spied the food cart across the street. "What would you like? It's our treat."

"I think I'll splurge," Donna said smiling. "How about hot chocolate and a bagel for both of us?" Tim looked at Katherine, who nodded her head in enthusiastic agreement. "And don't skimp on the cream cheese," Donna added with a wink at her daughter.

He was glad he had his wallet, even if he may have been using money that wasn't printed yet. Everyone else had small cans of orange juice and a pastry. After paying for their food, the guys returned to the plaza and sat with Donna and Katherine as the hustle and bustle of New York life began another day.

Tim looked at the concern on Mike's face. His eyes scanned the skies. "Mike, you doing okay?"

"Yeah, not used to being in a place with such big buildings all around. We don't get that in Oxnard. Feels like I'm in a man-made Grand Canyon."

Donna laughed. "I hear that a lot."

Mike leaned over to Tim. "Can I talk to you a sec?"

"Sure, excuse us for a minute," Tim said.

Mike pulled Tim a few steps away. "I need to go to the seventy-second floor of the North Tower."

"Are you kidding? It's almost eight o'clock. It's gonna get hit in forty-five minutes."

"My aunt Marie works up there. She's an intern with some investment bank. I've gotta help her."

"I can't let you go," Tim said. "You might never get out."

"Tim, she never made it out that day. I've gotta try," Mike said firmly. "I've got time. I'll use the elevator."

"Okay, but don't mess around," Tim said.

"I'm taking Bobby," Mike said. "He can help if there's difficulty."

"Hurry," Tim ordered. "I'll meet you at the food cart on Liberty Street."

"Right." Mike turned and motioned to Bobby. "Let's go."

"Where to?"

"I'll tell you on the way." They sprinted across the plaza, headed toward the North Tower.

Tim returned and sat down next to Donna and Katherine. "Sorry about that. They have an aunt who works in the North Tower. They wanted to stop by and say hi."

"Everybody in the country seems to have some connection to these two buildings. Did you know that there are over 50,000 people who work at the WTC complex and another 40,000 that pass through every day?"

"It's like a city all by itself," Tim said.

"Well it does have its own zip code." Donna laughed.

Donna is a very cool lady, Tim thought and smiled inwardly. *I'd ask her out if she were ten years younger, not married, and the world wasn't going to blow up in an hour.*

"Is Katherine with you at work every day?" Tim asked.

"No, her dad is picking her up and taking her to school. He has her for the next few days."

"Oh, sorry to pry."

"Not a problem. We're divorced, but we're working hard to make it as normal as possible for her."

"When will he be picking her up?"

"He's supposed to be here at nine, but if he's here fifteen minutes late that would not surprise me. You sure ask a lot of non-touristy questions," Donna said. She glanced at her watch. "Uh oh, five minutes late for opening. Gotta run!"

"There's something I need to tell you," Tim said seriously. His tone seemed to draw Donna's attention immediately.

"O...kay, but this is getting a little strange." She looked around nervously. "Then I've got to run."

"Before I tell you, I need you to look at my driver's license and tell me what you see." Tim pulled out his wallet and flipped it open, revealing his license behind a yellowed plastic sleeve.

Donna hesitated but took the wallet. "You're from Oxnard, California, and are one of those rare people that looks handsome in a mugshot."

Tim smiled. "Thanks. Check out my birthdate."

She squinted for a long moment and then looked up. "Oh, that's really funny. How can the state make that kind of a mistake? It says you're three years old. It also has a funny expiration date—eighteen years in the future."

"It's accurate, Donna."

"Your picture is correct? What's going on?"

Tim opened the shoulder bag and tipped it toward her so she could see its contents. "This brought me and the other two boys you met here. Donna, I'm from the future."

Donna tried to get up. "New York is full of weird people, but that's a new one. Time to go."

Tim rose with her. "Please listen for one minute. Both of you are in grave danger."

She stopped abruptly. "You better talk fast before I decide you're crazy and call the police."

"In my time, September 11, 2001, is as big a day in our life-
times as Pearl Harbor was in our grandparents' lives."

Donna shook her head. "That's today. Why is that?"

"Because in about forty minutes a commercial jet is going
to crash into the North Tower of the World Trade Center."

Donna turned and looked up the vertical face of the North
Tower only fifty yards away. "I don't believe you. That's nuts."

"It doesn't matter if you believe me or not," Tim said. "All I
am asking is when the first plane hits the North Tower, get out
and get as far away from here as you can."

"The first plane? Are there more?"

"Yes."

"An accident?"

"No, a well-coordinated and long-planned terrorist attack."

Katherine pulled on her mother's hand. "Mommy, is a plane
going to crash into the building?"

"You're scaring Kathy, and you're scaring me too."

"I'm not trying to scare you. I'm trying to help you. I'm sorry.
I don't know any other way to say it," Tim said. "There will be
those who say the worst is over after the first crash, but that's
only the beginning. You will think several times today that it is
as bad as it can get, and every time it will get worse."

"I'm not buying this at all. I can't," Donna said. "I thought
you were a nice young man."

"Look, if nothing happens, then chalk it up to another
meeting with a New York crackpot. If something does happen,
be ready to leave."

"I don't know. Should I go back to work?"

"No, you should leave now."

"But I left my cell phone and wallet locked in the shop,"
Donna said. "If this is true, how much time do I have?"

"I don't remember exactly, but it hits around 8:45, so you
have a little time."

"I'm not going back." Katherine pouted, threatening to cry.

"It's okay, Kathy. Mommy's here and we'll be fine."

"I'm sorry if I scared you," Tim said. "I'll go with you. Just in case you need help."

"No, I think you've done enough," Donna said with an edge in her voice. "I'll be ready to get out but that's as far as I'm going with this fantasy."

"May I walk you back to the building at least?"

"I guess so. I'm not saying I believe you," Donna said. "But you are a very nice gentleman for a three-year-old."

The tension eased, but they both scanned the sky as they returned to the stairs that would take Donna and her daughter back to the lower level.

CHAPTER XX

The World at Our Feet

Mike and Bobby entered the North Tower lobby and approached the desk. "We're here to see Marie Hernandez," Mike said. "I think she works on the seventy-second floor."

The desk guard squinted and looked them up and down, then typed her name and checked his screen. "She's with Morgan Stanley. Do you have business with the firm?"

"Not really," Mike said. "We're...relatives from out west—California."

"She's our aunt," Bobby said.

"One moment, please."

The guard dialed his phone, and Mike heard a faint phone ring, then a muffled voice on the other end of the line.

"Sorry to bother you, Ms. Hernandez, but I have two young gentlemen here to see you."

The guard listened for a moment. "Yes, name's Hernandez... relatives from California."

He listened again then hung up. "Please take a visitor badge and lanyard and proceed to the bank of elevators that includes the seventy-second floor. She will be waiting for you when the elevator doors open."

Mike and Bobby placed the lanyards and tag around their necks and fast-walked to the properly numbered elevator bank.

"We did it," Bobby said. "We're in."

"That took too long," Mike said nervously.

The elevator doors opened, and they stepped in with a half-dozen others. There were several stops, but finally they arrived at the seventy-second floor. The doors opened. Marie Hernandez stood before them in a navy-blue business suit and skirt. *She isn't much older than me,* Mike thought.

Marie looked them over with curiosity. "Hello, gentlemen. Relatives, huh? Which side?"

"Your side," Mike said. "But we'd like to tell you the main parts somewhere we can sit down for a moment."

"That's fine," Marie said. "My desk is on an open platform, but it's not too busy yet this morning so we'll have a little privacy."

She led them to an area where they noted a desk that had a name plate on it that said, MARIE HERNANDEZ—FINANCIAL ASSOCIATE.

She walked them to the window, where they could look straight down to the ground. The view to the north of Manhattan Island with the Hudson River on the left was spectacular.

"This is a very cool view," Bobby said. "I can almost see Canada from here."

"Best in the world," Marie said proudly. "Both the view and the firm. The world is literally at our feet."

"You're new here, isn't that right?" Mike said.

"Yes, graduated from Wharton School in June and here I am. Pretty exciting really."

"I'll bet your big brother is really proud," Bobby said.

"Tony? How do you know Tony?"

Mike and Bobby looked at each other and decided they didn't have time to waste. "Because he's our dad."

"Now that's a really bad lie." She reached for her phone.

"I'm Mike and this is Bobby."

"You've done your homework, but Mike is just a toddler and Carla is pregnant with a boy, but I don't know what they will name him."

"They will name me Robert after Grandpa Chris's dad who died in the war," Bobby said before she could object further.

That brought her up short. "Who are you, and how do you know so much about my family?"

"Because we're telling the truth," Mike said, feeling nervous again. "What time is it?"

She checked her watch. It looked a lot like some of the watches in Donna's store in the mall. "It's 8:30. Why?"

"We don't have much time, Mike," Bobby said.

Marie appeared to catch their nervousness. "It's been nice, boys. I don't know who you are, but I think it's time for you to go. I have a lot of work to do."

"Can we buy you some breakfast or something," Mike suggested. "We can chat for a few minutes in the plaza, then take a picture and we'll be off to see the rest of the city."

"Don't think so, but thanks. I have too much work to do this morning to take a break yet. My training starts in the South Tower at 9:30."

"Please do it for a couple of crazy cousins, and we'll leave you alone forever. You know how Grandpa Chris feels about family."

"Tell you what. There's a little lunch room on the other side of those cubicles. It's not fancy, but it usually has fresh doughnuts by now and there's a water cooler and a fridge with some soda. We can chat for a minute, then I have to get back to work."

Bobby glanced at Mike and shook his head slightly. Mike ignored him. "Sure, but I have something to tell you. It's really important that you don't react in a way that draws attention."

Marie gave him a strange look, stopped, and sat back down. "I won't react and draw attention, but you better spit it out right now."

"We really are your nephews, the sons of Tony and Carla Hernandez. That much is true. But we came here from the future to save your life," Mike said without hesitation, looking her directly in the eyes.

Marie leaned back in her chair, rubbed her forehead, and said sarcastically, "Really? What? Am I going to get mugged on the subway or something?"

"No," Mike said, unflinching. "You couldn't comprehend it right now. But in about fifteen minutes you will never be able to get it out of your mind."

"And that's only if you survive," Bobby said.

"Are you saying something is going to happen in fifteen minutes that is so terrible it will change my life forever?"

"That, Aunt Marie, is the best-case scenario," Mike said with authority.

Marie looked as if caught between two impossible choices.

"Please don't call security," Bobby said. "We're not part of anything. We were sent here to help you as crazy as it sounds."

"If nothing happens by 8:45, then we're just two looneys. But if something does, you have a shot at a full life, which in our history, you didn't."

Marie flashed an angry look at them. "I don't know what your game is or who sent you here, but if this is some new trainee prank, it's not funny and I'm done with it. I swear I'll report you. After the 1993 bombing here, the Port Authority takes these things very seriously."

"This is not a joke any more than mom's lasagna," Mike said.

"Lasagna. Carla makes it better than anyone. How did you know that?"

"Because I've eaten it a hundred times for Sunday dinner and still can't get enough," Mike said, trying a little smile.

"We have to go, Mike," Bobby said. "We'll get stuck in the elevator or something."

"What time is it now, Aunt Marie?" Mike asked.

"8:40 by my watch."

"Too late anyway," Mike said. "If anything happens, remember to go down, not up, and don't listen to anyone who says anything else. Get out of the building as fast as you can and don't stop no matter what the building intercom says. Then keep walking and get as far away as you can from the plaza."

Marie gave them an impatient glare and raised her voice slightly. "What's going to happen?"

Mike looked at her, knowing she deserved some kind of answer. *What can I say?* Then it hit him. Simple but clear. He looked into her eyes as a tear broke and rolled down his face.

"War, Aunt Marie! War is going to happen."

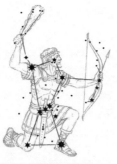

CHAPTER XXI

The North Tower

onna and Katherine had returned to the watch shop to gather their things. Tim let them go at the stairway, waited a few minutes, and couldn't keep from wondering if they took him seriously. Descending the stairs, he walked quickly to the shop and tried unsuccessfully to peek in without being noticed.

"Are you stalking me now?" Donna said, causing Tim to jump.

He struggled to regain his composure. "A...just concerned that you wouldn't take me seriously."

"I don't know how to take you," Donna shot back.

"Look, it's only another six minutes until 8:45. Please could you just walk back up to the plaza with me for a minute and then if nothing happens you can come back?"

"Did you know it's a crime to even talk about these kinds of threats? I could make one call and get you in lots of trouble."

"I know it's a huge risk for me. But for you, walking up to the plaza is zero risk and no trouble."

"Okay, six minutes and that's it." Donna grabbed her purse, shooed them out of the shop, locked the glass doors, and walked the same way back to the plaza with Katherine in tow. They exited the building and walked across the plaza toward the Liberty Street cart. Tim heard the sound of jet engines.

"That sounds way too loud to be an airplane," Donna said.

"What time is it?" Tim said.

Donna glanced at her watch. "About 8:45."

"Run!" Tim yelled and grabbed Katherine, lifting her into his arms. Donna ran with them across Liberty Street as the sound grew louder. Arriving at the far sidewalk, Tim's curiosity took control. He stopped, mesmerized by history unfolding in front of him, turned, and looked up. Donna and Katherine watched with him as a commercial jet approached low and fast, turning slightly and lining up with the north face of the North Tower.

"It's doing that on purpose," Donna yelled.

"Yes, it's a terrorist attack," Tim said.

Tim watched as the jet pierced the center northeast face of the building. His research would later reveal that the jet hit between the ninety-third and ninety-ninth floors at 466 mph. Its momentum caused the plane to disintegrate, and jet fuel filled the building and central shafts with a burst of flame, which set the combustibles in the affected floors on fire, blowing through and out the opposite side of the building in a dramatic fireball. There wasn't sufficient oxygen to ignite all the fuel, so it showered the building and ran down the sides, center stairwells, and elevator shafts, flaring up over time, depending on its ability to find the deadly combination of sufficient heat and adequate oxygen.

The fireball exploded down at least one elevator shaft, bursting onto several lower floors, the worst of which were the seventy-seventh and twenty-second. All floors above the ninety-second were cut off. The crash and explosion had completely eliminated six floors of stairwells. No one above the ninety-second floor survived the next two hours. Those below the impact area had little idea what happened, received conflicting direction, and many succumbed to smoke and fire or the ultimate collapse of the building, which occurred an hour and forty-two minutes later, at 10:28 a.m. eastern time.

Tim, Donna, and Katherine joined dozens of others thrown to the ground by the violent explosion that sent shock waves down the building, shaking the plaza like an earthquake. Unrecognizable pieces of metal, furniture, and parts of the airplane rained down. There were also pieces of something else mixed in with the debris that Tim's mind refused to comprehend. Random bystanders in the plaza were struck and killed instantly, while others in shock wandered around, dazed in a blizzard of paper blown out of the building by the impact.

Bobby and Mike sat facing Marie across her desk. "Which direction are we looking?" Mike asked.

"This is the north face of the building, so we are facing roughly northeast," Marie said.

"We need to step to the center of the building, now," Mike said and pointed.

Marie turned. "That's strange. I've never seen a jet flying that low along the Hudson."

"It's turning toward us," Bobby said. "It's really gonna happen."

They stood and backed toward the center of the building as the jet roared toward them. Mike saw its underbelly disappear as it hit the building with a deafening boom, collapsing the roof tiles and metal supports and tossing the contents, including chairs, desks, partitions, and copiers, in the air like Legos.

Mike, Marie, and Bobby were thrown to the ground and showered by debris.

"It hit right above us," Marie screamed.

The stench of burning plastic, fuel, and smoke began to fill the floor. "We've got to get out of here now," Mike said. "Where are the stairwells?"

"Near the elevators...center of the building," Marie said, sounding disoriented.

"Where's Bobby," Mike said. "Bobby!"

"Over here," came a weak, muffled answer from beneath a pile of collapsed Sheetrock.

Marie and Mike pulled the Sheetrock, twisted metal, and debris off and helped Bobby stand. He nearly collapsed. "What's wrong, bro?"

"My leg," Bobby said, pulling up his pant leg to reveal a long gash.

"We need to stop the bleeding," Mike said.

"Here, try this," Marie said, offering her scarf.

"At least it's a clean slice," Mike said. "And not too deep."

Mike tied his aunt's scarf tightly around Bobby's leg, and they began to move toward the stairwells with a half-dozen other people. Mike pulled at the first door, but it wouldn't open.

"It's locked," Bobby yelled.

"These are never locked. We use them all the time to go between floors. Probably stuck, warped by the impact," Marie said. "The whole building must have swayed twenty feet. I thought it was going to tip over."

They tried another door. It budged but would not open. Mike put his hand on the door. It felt warm but not hot. "Is there anything we can use to pry it open?"

Marie disappeared into the office area and returned with a long piece of metal that looked like it had been part of one of the modern art deco desks in a senior executive's office. Mike jammed it into the door space and leveraged the door. It budged slightly but remained stuck. Bobby and Marie added their weight to the lever. It moved again, then popped open, throwing them to the ground. A rush of heat, smoke, and stench enveloped them.

They cautiously stepped onto the emergency stairway landing, where thick darkness and smoke greeted them. Mike remembered his flashlight, pulled it out, and switched it on. It penetrated the thick darkness only about ten feet down the stairway.

"I don't know if we should try this?" Bobby said. "It looks pretty bad."

A group of other workers had gathered behind them. An older executive said, "We need to go up. It's closer. Rescue helicopters will be waiting."

"No!" Mike yelled over the noise. "You can't go up! The plane hit up there."

"Plane?" the executive said, laughing. "Who told you that?"

"We saw it come toward the building," Marie responded.

"It's the only way to get out. A lot of these people can't make it seventy floors down," the executive argued. "Follow me."

"Please, don't," Mike pleaded.

The others in the group followed the man up the stairway.

"They're all going to die," Mike said sadly.

"Mike," Marie said. "I would have probably followed them if it weren't for you."

A couple of people passed by, heading down. "Let's get going. It's gonna take a while," Bobby advised.

They passed more groups of people moving up the stairs. "You have to go down," Mike begged.

A businessman with gray hair snapped, "These people can't make it that far. We have to go up. Get out of my way, kid." He pushed Mike to the side and continued up.

"Are you sure we're going the right direction?" Marie said. "Won't there be people coming to help us get out?"

"It's the only way out," Bobby said and staggered, falling against the railing. "The whole building is going to collapse before help can get up here."

"Bobby, are you doing okay?" Mike said.

"Go as fast as you want. I can keep up," Bobby answered.

"Collapse...how?" Marie said sounding dazed.

"Don't know why or how, but it starts at the top and kind of pancakes to the ground," Bobby said. "The footage has been shown countless times and never stops being terrifying to watch."

They had just passed the fifty-fifth-floor landing when they felt, as much as heard, a tremendous boom and the building shook again. All three were knocked to the ground, and Mike rolled down a flight of steps to the next landing.

"That sounded like another explosion in our building," Marie yelled.

"Actually," Mike said. "It was a second jet hitting building two."

Marie looked at him strangely. "What's happening, Mike?"

"It's a systematic, well-planned attack on the United States, involving at least four hijacked commercial jets. By the end of the day it will be the worst attack since Pearl Harbor. We have only about an hour to get out before everyone left in here dies."

Marie looked at him seriously. "Thank you. I'm sure I would have followed my boss up or waited for help."

"You wouldn't have made it out," Mike said.

"I understand that now," Marie responded.

"We're not out of this yet." They got back to their feet and picked up speed.

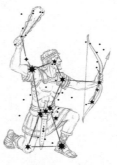

CHAPTER XXII

Collapse

Tim and Donna stood near the food cart on Liberty Street with a gathering crowd of people who were exiting the North Tower in a steady stream. Fire trucks and police cars arrived from every direction. Incredibly brave firemen jumped out, geared up, and went straight toward the buildings. He saw fear on many of their faces but was more impressed by their determination and sense of teamwork. It was clear their training and instincts had taken over, and they had an important calming effect on the crowd. He knew hundreds would be saved by these courageous first responders, many of whom would lose their own lives in the process.

They heard a stir in the crowd as people gazed skyward a second time. Many started pointing the way they did in Superman movies. But this time no comic book hero streaked across the sky. Tim and Donna couldn't take their eyes from the spectacle as a second jet approached the South Tower. Initially, it appeared that it would miss the building. It flew oddly, as if the pilot struggled with the controls. At almost the last moment, its wing dipped and it banked sharply. Tim instinctively raised his hands to protect his face as it struck the building slightly off center and seemed to disintegrate. Fire and pieces of the building and plane burst through the side, showering destruction on the plaza a second time in fifteen minutes.

People around him gasped, screamed, and cried. All was confusion, noise, and panic.

A police officer approached the crowd. "You need to clear this area so the fire units can get to work."

Tim addressed the officer. "You need to clear everyone out of the area for a couple of blocks. The buildings are going to come down."

"That kind of talk is not going to help. The buildings aren't coming down. Keep moving and don't cause a panic," the officer said in a cool manner. It seemed to Tim that the officer was breaking new emotional ground on a day beyond anything he had ever dreamed of or prepared for, but his training had also kicked in and he did his job without hesitation.

Tim feared for Mike and Bobby. He expected them to be back before the first impact and knew if they were still in the building it would be difficult getting out. He might need to use the star before they got out and hoped they would be holding theirs.

"Donna, we need to get as far away from here as we can. It's dangerous with all the falling debris, and trust me, it is going to become a death trap here in less than an hour."

Donna had a look of shock on her face when she pointed at the North Tower. "Tim, look at the buildings."

Tim followed her gaze and was immediately horrified. People were jumping from the upper floors, falling like rag dolls and hitting the plaza with loud thwacks. He turned away.

"Donna, I've heard about people jumping, but have never seen any of the footage."

Donna pulled Katherine toward her, turning her head from the gruesome scene. "I've seen enough, and Kathy shouldn't see any."

Tim's emotions were torn. He had told Mike and Bobby to meet him at the cart. "My friends aren't going to find us if we move, but it's too dangerous to stay here."

They began walking east on Liberty Street. Tim looked back and saw people streaming out of the buildings and congregating on the streets surrounding the World Trade Plaza. He shook his head. "They need to get away."

Donna didn't respond. She seemed to be in a daze, following him while staring blindly into the distance. Katherine wasn't moving at all, looking pale and trembling.

This is what being in shock must look like.

"Come on, guys. We can do this." Tim picked up Katherine. "You're gonna be okay, Kathy. I'm here to protect you."

They moved along the streets in a silent zombie-like mass. No one appeared to know where to go or what to do. Donna kept looking back at the burning buildings, unable to take her eyes off the otherworldly scene playing out before her. They turned north on Church Street and paralleled the plaza approaching St. Paul's cathedral. Tim saw a clock in a shop window. It read 9:15. He remembered the South Tower came down first.

World Trade number two and anyone left inside have only about thirty minutes to live.

He put his hand on the star in the shoulder bag to make sure it was still there.

Mike passed the twenty-fifth-floor signage. It was slower going the lower they got. The stairwells were heavily obstructed by an increasing number of people sitting or resting on the steps. In addition, a nearly continuous stream of firemen passed them going up the stairs. Each one was sweating and breathing heavily under the weight of their equipment. In spite of their struggles, they were positive, encouraging people to keep moving.

"It's taking too long," Mike said. "We've got to move faster."

They passed the twentieth floor and felt a tremor that grew and rushed toward them. Marie looked at Mike, panic in her voice. "It sounds like a train or another airplane."

The tremor increased to a pounding, shaking thrum, forcing them to grab the railing to keep from falling.

"Stay close or we'll lose each other," Mike yelled over the noise. Hysterical screams came from people in the stairwells. Mike felt the building move sideways and worried that it might be coming down. Thick, dark dust and smoke rose up the stairways, making it hard to breathe and turning the confined space into a claustrophobic nightmare. Mike could see his hand in front of his face but little else even with his flashlight.

"Marie, Bobby...you still with me?" he yelled.

Marie fell against Mike and cried. "This just keeps getting worse. What's happened now?"

"Building two just collapsed," Mike responded.

"But ours got hit first," Marie said, sounding panicky.

"Building two got hit lower down and had more weight above the impact area, so it buckled sooner. Both buildings had about a half-dozen floors blown out on impact and raging fires hot enough to melt metal."

Mike felt her body tremble against him. "We'll be okay if we just keep moving, but we've got to get out of here soon. Stay with me."

Tim and Donna were sitting on the grass at City Hall Park when they felt the rumble start. A tremor moved toward them like an out-of-control diesel truck with its air brakes on. They looked up to see building two suddenly buckle in the area where the plane struck. They watched in morbid awe as the building's floors pancaked, dropping straight down in about ten seconds. The collapse produced a tornado-like cloud of smoke and dust that sped along the man-made canyons like a flash flood turning day to night.

"Lay down and cover your face," Tim yelled. They all rolled over, and Donna and Katherine nuzzled their faces into Tim's side.

The storm hit with the force of a hurricane. The dust cloud filled with pieces of debris rushed over them, tearing and gouging their clothes and skin. It took about thirty seconds for the storm to pass over. When Tim raised his head, an inch-thick coating of dust covered everything, turning the scene into a moonscape. The park turned dark, as if there had been a sudden solar eclipse. Then he noticed a surreal snowfall of paper filling the air like an apocalyptic ticker-tape parade.

As they passed the tenth-floor landing, a rush of firefighters and people pressed down the stairway, threatening to trample those already there. The panic caused by the collapse of building two began higher in the North Tower and rushed downward in a tsunami of fear enveloping everyone in its path. Mike and Bobby were carried away in the dusky stairway, losing contact with Marie. It wasn't until they got to the lobby that they were able to pull out of the stampeding herd.

"Did she make it, or was she trampled?" Bobby said. "Should we look for her?"

"I can barely see anything in this dust," Mike said. "Let's keep moving, but keep your eyes sharp for her."

Mike and Bobby moved carefully through the treacherous obstacle course of broken glass, masonry, and debris that was the building one lobby. They exited the windowless doors and were greeted by a scene that looked more like the Arctic or Sahara than the center of Manhattan. The sun's dim light struggled to penetrate the thick air. Mike wondered if this was what it looked like on the storm-tortured surface of Venus.

They ran across the plaza, not knowing which direction they were headed. The ground was strewn with concrete, glass, metal, and bodies, all covered in a coating of thick dust. He suddenly felt sick and dry heaved several times. He could barely breathe and held his shirt over his mouth and nose. Neither Mike nor Bobby saw any trace of Marie.

"All this for nothing!" Bobby choked out the words as they moved away from the plaza.

"Unless she got trampled, she had to have gotten out," Mike said. "I hope she remembers what we told her and gets far enough away before the second building collapses."

"We may never know," Bobby said.

"Certainly not if we don't get out of here," Mike warned.

They stumbled south on Greenwich Street, not realizing they were going the opposite direction from where Tim waited. They turned east on Rector Street and south again on Broadway, still confused and disoriented, following others and hoping the crowd knew where to go.

Suddenly, Mike saw a large, black animal shape loom out of the darkness and uttered a pathetic choked-off scream from his dust-parched throat. His overtaxed mind jumped to the recent series of alien movies popular in theaters. He strained to see what was ahead, then laughed at his momentary fear.

"It's a statue of a huge bull."

"I've seen this before," Bobby said. "It's on all the tourist guides and is close to the park at the south end of Manhattan Island. Will that be safe?"

"Yeah, it's called Battery Park, and it should be far enough away."

They continued to Battery Park, discovering it also was covered with a coating of dust. They sat on a bench in the park and felt another rumble rolling toward them. They looked up and saw the huge antenna on top of building one suddenly slip from the sky as it too pancaked to the ground.

Mike knew the rescue operation would continue for days but few would be found. The stark truth was that those who got out survived, and the rest died. Mike braced for the storm of dust and debris he knew raced toward them. He and Bobby dove onto the grass and covered their heads.

"Don't you think it's time we should be holding the stars," Bobby yelled as the storm passed over.

Tim felt the fourth earthquake of the day.

"The other building is coming down," he said, emotionless as if he were pointing out that the sky was blue, which of course on this day it wasn't.

"My shop..." Donna started. "I would have been there."

"There's nothing left now," Tim said as the second dust storm of the day hit them with the same violence as the first. Mike held Katherine close, and they lay on the grass while it passed over. Afterward, he sat up and looked at himself, a yellowish-white ghost from head to toe.

"Thank you," Donna said, rising to sit next to him. "You saved our lives."

"Hey, you had a lot of faith in a crackpot tourist. That was just as important."

"You seemed pretty harmless. Too bad you're only three years old. I would enjoy hearing more about your crazy life."

"Will you be all right?" Tim said. "Can you get home?

"You can't leave!" Katherine said anxiously.

"It'll be a long walk," Donna answered. "But we can make it."

"Make sure you put something over your mouth and nose. This dust is very bad for the lungs."

"Will do," Donna said. "Thanks for the heads up."

"Yes, we need to be ready when Tim uses the star," Mike said.

Mike felt completely worn out from his seventy-second-story and ten-block race to safety. Bobby sat on the ground nursing his leg. "My adrenalin kept me from feeling this until now. Man, it really hurts."

He pulled up his pant leg, revealing a six-inch slice filled with clotted blood. His leg was smeared with black, dried blood that blended into a large black-and-blue bruise extending from his ankle to his knee.

"You'll be back home soon," Mike said. "Mom can take a look at your leg. But we better brush off, or they'll run us through a car wash instead."

They tried to brush the dust off, but it seemed caked onto their clothes and infused in their skin. As Mike brushed, he looked across the bleak landscape and saw dark figures moving toward him. "The Trackers are coming."

"Can't they take a break?" Bobby said. "Don't they know we've had kind of a tough day already?"

They heard a voice from the haze. "Today's a great day, boys. It's the start of somethin' that'll get us lots o' new recruits. Nothin' makes Trackers better than hate, and nothin' generates hate like war."

"Clynt's here. Grab your star," Mike said.

"They's gonna be so many of us that we's gonna get ya one way or t'other."

They held the stars tight, but nothing happened.

"I have to go," Tim said and removed the star from his bag. "I've stayed longer than I should have."

"Please stay," Katherine said.

"I wish I could, but there're things about these StarPassages you don't know," Tim said. "It will be very bad for me if I stay."

"Bad to be with mommy and me?" Katherine said.

"No, Kathy," Tim assured her. "That would be great. It's something else."

"Can I help in some way?" Donna said kindly.

"No, there are people that are stuck halfway between death and heaven. They did terrible things, like those behind today's attacks. They lived their lives full of hate and were consumed by anger and bitterness."

"They sound like the stuff of children's nightmares," Donna said.

"Actually, they kind of are," Tim said. "They're called Trackers and they are drawn to this star whenever it's used because they desire more than anything to have it for their own. It's the only way they can free themselves from their purgatory. If I stay much longer they'll show up. Those terrorists today were taught they'd be martyrs and go straight to some heavenly glory. But I know where people like that end up. Eternity as a Tracker is nothing like that."

"We'll never forget you," Donna said with a strange look in her eyes. "Maybe you can come back when you're older."

"I'd like that, too, I think. But the star makes those decisions. Sorry."

"Be careful. Don't let the Trackers get you," Katherine warned.

"Okay, I promise to be careful. Will you promise you'll use your life to do something good, Kathy?" Tim said.

Katherine put her arms around his neck. "I promise. I love you, Tim."

"I love you too. I'm really glad I met you, Kathy."

Donna leaned over and placed her dust-coated lips on his in a deep, heartfelt kiss. "Thank you."

On a day of stunning and shocking developments, this was the biggest surprise of all. He stammered and stumbled in response. "I...ah...need to get going."

Then he looked hard at Donna and Katherine. "I'll never forget you either."

Tim took the star by the three point and vanished, leaving Donna and Katherine with yet another story to add to a day full of tales that would forever change their lives.

The Trackers completely surrounded the bench. For some reason they held back.

They stopped. Is it because we have the stars? Mike thought. *Not likely.*

Clynt smiled. "Yer friend Tim seems to have forgotten about the star."

"He'll use it," Mike said in defiance.

"Get 'em, boys," Clynt ordered.

Iron hands closed around the arms of Mike and Bobby, and irresistible forces began to pry open their hands.

"Now would be a great time, Tim!" Mike yelled.

As he spoke, the world of dust and destruction faded. The bruising grip of the Trackers' hands lessened, then ceased altogether. His mind spun, and Mike shut his eyes tight. The silence surrounding him was a relief—almost like a hot shower after the end of a long day. Slowly, he opened his eyes and found himself lying in a cloud of dust back in his hospital room.

Mike looked up into Grandpa's eyes. "Never thought I'd say this, but it's nice to be back in the hospital."

"You look terrible," Grandpa said. "I'll take these clothes home for a good wash. You can have them back before therapy tomorrow. You need to take a shower before the nurses come in."

"Wait," Mike interrupted. "We need to call Martie and make sure Bobby and Tim made it okay."

Mike dialed and waited while the cell phone rang three times. Mike felt anxious as Martie picked up the phone. "Hello, Carsons."

"It's me."

"Hi Mike," she said. "You make it back all right?"

"Yeah, how about the guys?"

"They're here," Martie said cheerfully. "They're a dirty, dusty mess. I'm gonna have to deep clean my bedroom."

"I got a pretty good mess here too," Mike said. "Grandpa and I have some cleaning and probably some explaining to do to the nurses. See ya soon." He hung up the phone and breathed a sigh of relief.

Grandpa looked hard at Mike and raised his eyebrows. "You're going to have to tell me the whole story."

"As soon as I'm respectable again." Mike looked down at the filth on his clothing and now the sheets of his bed. They both smiled nervously, sharing unspoken knowledge that the thread to which they clung for life had never been thinner.

CHAPTER XXIII

The Therapist

ike endured lectures from both the floor nurse and the head nurse, neither of whom could figure out how the bed got so dirty. Fortunately, the nurses didn't come in to check while Grandpa helped Mike shower, stuff his dirty clothes into a garbage bag, and slip into his hospital gown. Only then did they press the call button and prepare for the worst.

When the nurse came in and saw the bed and Mike lounging on the couch, she gave them a scowl that should have set off the monitors on the entire floor. The lecture ended with a warning not ever to do whatever they did again. Finally, they were alone and almost laughed themselves sick.

Grandpa finally composed himself and said, "So tell me what happened."

"We appeared in the underground mall of the World Trade Center on September 11, 2001."

"Oh!" Grandpa said in surprise. "Was there some purpose?"

"I believe so," Mike answered cautiously. "Bobby and I were supposed to save Aunt Marie, but we don't know if we did."

Grandpa leaned forward. "But Marie survived 9-11."

"She's alive?"

"Yes, she is. Left the Investment Banking industry after about four years and moved out here. Got tired of the rat race I think. Her explanation was that she couldn't get over her anxiety of working in skyscrapers after the attacks. She joined an equity fund focused on the medical device industry and lives near the beach in Irvine. She says the change in lifestyle has been great."

"History has changed, Grandpa," Mike said. "You wouldn't remember because you weren't with us, but before we left, mom and dad would always talk about how wonderful Aunt Marie was and that the world lost a bright star on that terrible day."

"Interesting. I've heard your Aunt Marie tell the story several times. She always talks about the two nice boys that were visiting when the plane struck and how they helped her get out. She never said who they were or what happened, except that she was separated from them when they got near the bottom floors of the tower."

"Those two boys were Bobby and me. That's great to hear she made it. We did get separated and didn't know if she got out."

Grandpa's phone rang. He looked at it and then at Mike. "Funny, she's calling right now."

"Who?"

"Your Aunt Marie," Grandpa said. "Must be for you."

He handed the phone to Mike. "Hello, therapy wing, chief patient speaking."

"Mike is that you?" a woman's voice on the other end said.

"Yep, sure is," Mike said cheerily. "Is this my very *old* friend, Aunt Marie?"

"Something strange happened this afternoon," she said. "As I sat in my office I suddenly remembered that my dearest nephew was in the hospital and I hadn't even called."

Mike suddenly choked up and had difficulty controlling his

emotions. "I can't tell you how nice it is to hear your voice, Aunt Marie."

She fell silent for a moment. Mike thought he heard sniffles on the other end. "When did you get back from your trip?"

"You mean to New York City with Bobby?"

"Yeah, on that September day," she said carefully.

"About an hour ago," he said. "Just got cleaned up. It was a pretty messy business."

"I'm sorry I didn't come see you before," she said. "But it's like I just remembered something important."

"We just saved you today so history changed and your whole life has been lived where there was nothing before."

"That's a little hard to hear you say," Marie said.

"Sorry. I didn't mean to be insensitive."

"No, not insensitive. It's just...I guess I am so grateful... and embarrassed that I haven't come to see you."

"Not a problem," Mike said. "After all, it hasn't been very long since we were together." They both laughed awkwardly at the thought.

"I'll come over and visit soon," Marie said with emotion bursting into the conversation. "I owe you both my life."

"I'm glad it worked out," Mike said. "I'd love to talk all about it."

"I've never told anybody who the two boys were that saved my life. It didn't seem right."

"The family is becoming familiar with the StarPassage concept, so it's going to be fun for you to share the details."

"Thanks for understanding," Marie said. "I'll bring you lunch. How about lasagna? I've spent the last ten years trying to make it as good as your mom."

The next morning Mike wheeled himself into his therapy session with new enthusiasm. His opportunity to have a do-over during the passage to Faria Beach had given him new resolve. He intended to use that as a motivator starting today.

The 9-11 passage taught him that whatever directed the star was mindful of everyone and would not let him fail if he did his part. Grandpa brought his clean and pressed ODs early in the morning so he felt ready to go. The therapist greeted him with an odd look as he entered the room.

"You look like you're going to kill it this morning," she said.

"I'm ready for a tough workout today and a long run."

"Oh, we're running now are we?"

"Well, maybe an awkward, limping, lame walk kind of run." Mike couldn't keep from laughing.

"Let's get started then." She directed him to the parallel bars that stood on either side of an elongated treadmill.

Kathy helped Mike from the wheelchair, and he stepped onto the tread and began at his usual pace, which meant the conveyor belt barely moved. He mentioned he had some feeling and sensed a small amount of muscle and motor capability. Kathy pushed him until they were able to double the speed. He continued for ten minutes and felt fatigued, but refused to stop.

"Let's take a break," Kathy said, smiling. "You're making me tired."

Kathy helped Mike back into his wheelchair. He toweled off and leaned back. "That felt good."

"That looked pretty good too," Kathy said.

"Thanks for working me hard today."

"It's my job. I will work you as hard as you can or are willing."

"I need to rest for a few, but I'd like to go another round." Mike smiled, still breathing hard.

"I'll be back in a few minutes," Kathy said with a grin. "Don't take off."

"Take off?" Mike chuckled. "You mean run away? If I started running away now and you came back in ten minutes I wouldn't even make it to the hallway," he said, pointing at the door.

She laughed and disappeared into her office. Mike wheeled himself to a window and waited. He dozed off until he felt a tap on his shoulder.

"Mike, sorry to leave you hanging," Kathy said. "The paperwork keeps piling up."

"Not a problem," Mike responded. "I'm about ready to go at that pesky treadmill again. How about getting all the way up to half a mile per hour?"

Kathy hesitated as if a thought that kept slipping her mind had just resurfaced.

"I've been meaning to ask you something," Kathy said.

"Sure, go ahead."

"You look familiar. Have we met somewhere before?"

"Not unless you surf," Mike said cheerily.

"It's not that." She scratched her head. "Oh, well, it's going to drive me crazy until I figure it out."

"Don't go crazy until after the session, please."

Kathy laughed. "Okay, back to work."

Mike had just mounted the treadmill and taken his first step when Martie strolled in. "Hi, Mike. Looks like you're making progress. Must be all that outside exercise you're getting."

"What's up, Martie? You ride the bus over or something?"

"Nope. Tim brought me. He'll be up as soon as he finds a parking spot. It must be busy today."

"Yep, everyone wants to see my speed training."

"We wanted to check your progress, then we thought if we could get permission we'd take you out for some gourmet fast food."

"I'll go for that," Mike said. "Kathy, let's pick this up a little so I can show off my sprint."

"Will do, champ," Kathy said, adjusting the speed.

Mike felt the pace increase. "Good, that's a fast-enough crawl for now. Let's see how long I can keep up."

Tim appeared in the doorway and walked over to the treadmill, leaning on one of the rails. "Hey, Mike, you clean up real nice."

"Grandpa washed my clothes for me overnight," Mike said. "They were smelling kind of strong. The ODs probably could have walked the treadmill by themselves this morning."

"Forgot to shine your boots though," Tim pointed out. "Can't have that. I'll take them home and get it done for you this afternoon." The two friends laughed again.

Absorbed in the conversation, Mike didn't notice a change in Kathy until he turned toward her. "How about turning up..." Her empty stare stopped him cold. Her eyes were fixed on Tim as if he were a ghost. Then she looked at Mike, tried unsuccessfully to speak, teared up, and collapsed into a chair.

"Are you okay?" Martie asked.

"Did I do something wrong?" Mike said, concerned.

Still no response. Then slowly she raised her head and Mike saw tears and reddened eyes.

"I know where we met," Kathy said, choking back tears. "It was only for a few minutes, and I was very young."

Mike knew something important was happening but had no idea where this was going, so he continued walking. "You know where we met?"

"It didn't make sense until I saw him. Then the pieces fell into place," Kathy said.

"Saw who?" Mike said confused.

"Your friend," Kathy said, turning to address Tim. "Is your name Tim?"

Mike and Tim looked at each other blankly. Tim shrugged his shoulders then took a long hard look at Kathy. He squinted his eyes as if trying to place her somewhere in his memory. "It...can't be...Kathy, is that you?"

She dropped her clipboard and ran to him like a little girl, throwing her arms around him.

"Tim? I've tried to find you forever. But I only remembered your first name and that you were from Oxnard."

"And we only met yesterday," Tim said as she nestled her face in his shoulder.

"Yesterday?" she said.

"Yes, our little trip in time where we met only happened yesterday for me," Tim responded. "But history has been changed a lot for you I suspect."

"You saved our lives," Kathy said, stepping back and regaining some of her composure. "We might have died otherwise. Yeah, I'd say that's a pretty big change."

"How's Donna?" Tim asked.

"She's fine...still lives in New York. She's going to be so excited to hear we ran into each other."

"So you went into physical therapy, huh?"

"Yeah, I skipped some grades in an accelerated high school program but still have a couple of years left. Working as an intern right now. Mike's my lab rat." She smiled widely.

Mike enjoyed the reunion but felt his fatigue returning. He needed to rest, but didn't have the heart to interrupt their conversation.

"I don't know what to say," Tim confessed.

"No words are necessary," Kathy said. "I've been waiting to do this for a long time." She hugged him again, and before he could react, she gave him a long, deep kiss on the lips.

Mike felt thrilled for them both, but the speed of the treadmill began to overwhelm him. "Guys...a little help...please?"

Kathy lingered, and Tim didn't resist. She stepped back with color in her cheeks and looked around the room. "I hope I didn't embarrass you," she said in a husky voice. "I've had a crush on my 9-11 white knight since that day."

"Guys," Mike said again. "I'm happy for you both, but I'm about to do a face plant here."

"Oh, sorry," Kathy said and immediately turned off the treadmill. Tim and Kathy helped Mike to his wheelchair without taking their eyes off each other.

"Well," Mike said, looking back and forth between Kathy and Tim. "I suppose we'll need an extra seat at lunch."

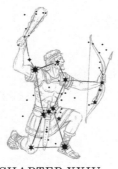

CHAPTER XXIV

Thieves and Spies

Donny was angry. It felt good. The world only wanted to use him. He wasn't going to let *them* stuff him into a nice neat mold.

He didn't know who *they* were who were against him. It wasn't about that anymore. He'd been cheated out of things he was entitled to. Right now he couldn't come up with a list, but he knew it was a long one. His life had been hijacked somewhere along the road from yesterday to now. He deserved anything he got because he had lost enough. How he got it didn't matter anymore.

"What I need is freedom, and I know how to get it now," he said to the four walls.

"You can have it all," Horst had promised. "Nobody tells us what to do here."

It sounded great to Donny. He didn't ask questions because he wasn't interested in detail. The Carson kids and the others he was watching represented the kinds of people he hated. He didn't know why he hated them. He just did. He had nothing.

Horst and Clynt had something. He didn't care what it was, but he wanted that *something* badly.

All I need to do is steal that stupid star and I'll get it all.

And he would do whatever it took to get it. His conscience gave one last gasp of warning and went silent. He was all in now.

Donny watched the Carson home almost every night. He didn't have to wait long. On Friday night, the parents were both gone for the evening. He smiled as the kids got in the car and drove away. Neither kid had the shoulder bag.

It's gotta be in the house this time.

He raced to the window before the car turned the corner. The window moved easily, still unlocked. He smiled—knew the drill this time. Shoes off, over the sill, into the living room, up the stairs, and search the house.

Horst and Clynt would be proud of him. He felt a greedy, lustful kind of sensation that was the closest he had ever gotten to happiness.

The star wasn't under the pillow or in the closet. His anger flared, and he ripped through the drawers and cupboards in Martie's room. Nothing.

"Where did she hide you? I know you're here," he said out loud.

Donny spent longer than he had planned in the house. Suddenly, a car pulled into the driveway. He sprinted to the stairs, bounded down them three steps at a time, dashed to the window, and pulled it shut just as the front door opened. He grabbed his shoes and fled.

"Thanks, that was a great treat," Martie said. "Gotta finish my math though."

"My pleasure, sis," Tim said happily. "Every good study session needs a chocolate shake break."

"See you after tonight's homework torture is over," Martie said, knowing math wasn't quite as difficult as she made it sound.

"No prob." Tim plopped onto an overstuffed kitchen chair, slurping his root beer float.

Martie climbed the stairs with a happy bounce. She turned the corner, entered her room, screamed, and ran to the top of the stairs. "Tim!"

Tim found her in her room. "What's wrong? It sounded like someone died."

"My room died," Martie cried. "Someone totally trashed it. Who does that?"

They looked around. "Is anything missing?" Tim asked.

"Hard to tell, but I don't think so," Martie replied angrily. They checked other rooms and found a few signs that things had been disturbed, but nothing like the disaster in Martie's room.

"Why would someone go after your room?" Tim said.

"I don't know," Martie said. "I don't have anything of value—" She stopped suddenly, and they looked at each other. At the same time, they said, "The star!"

"Where do you keep it?" Tim said.

"I started putting it under the mattress."

Tim lifted the mattress so it separated from the box springs, and Martie reached under, fishing around nervously. Finally, she pulled out the shoulder bag and flipped open the flap. "It's still here."

"We were only gone a few minutes, Martie. Someone must've been watching the house."

They both were breathing heavily as they sat on the bed. "Does anyone else, besides the Hernandez family, know about the star?" Tim said.

"Nobody. I haven't talked about it with anyone."

"Same here," Tim said.

"Someone knows," Martie said. "And they want it pretty bad."

"What about Clynt?"

"He can't come to the present time and get it," Martie said. "If he could he wouldn't need to chase us on passages."

"He's gotta be involved somehow. It's the only logical connection. Could he get someone to do it for him?"

"How would he do that?" Martie said.

"I heard him tell Dad once that, in the midst of his PTSD and mom's depression, they had called to him and the Trackers always came."

"That doesn't mean he can talk to them or tell them anything."

"Yeah, you're right. Doesn't make sense," Tim agreed. "But when the reasonable answers are excluded, you have to consider the crazy possibilities."

"Okay. We definitely have a real person trying to steal the star. What do we do?"

"Be aware of your surroundings," Tim said. "Has anyone been following or watching you? If you notice anything, let me know."

"How could you be so careless," Horst scolded him. "They will know! They will know!"

"I'll go back and get it tonight," Donny offered.

"Dummkopf!" Horst's voice stung. "They will take action to protect the star. They will be on their guard. You must wait until things settle down again."

The voice was silent for several minutes. Then Donny heard it again.

"We may have to find someone else to do this."

"No, please, I can do this. Give me another chance," Donny pleaded. Donny felt like a whipped dog. He cowered in the corner as his mind exploded with the Tracker's rage. "What do you want me to do? I'll make it up to you. I'll do anything."

The voices were silent again as if they were considering something new. Donny waited and his hate for the Carsons grew into an all-consuming rage.

It was all their fault. They'll cost me my new friends if I don't succeed this time. He pounded the floor with his fist.

"I can do this. Nothing will stop me," he said to the darkest corner of his room.

A quiet, wicked laugh sounded in his mind. "You'll need a weapon."

"I have a knife," Donny answered with relief.

"Do exactly as I tell you. This is your last chance."

Donny listened as if his life depended on it. He knew it just might.

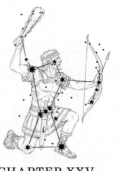

CHAPTER XXV

Of Faith and Worms

Tim had been floating around the house for a week. He was excited about his growing feelings for Kathy in a way he didn't quite understand. But he also felt torn between those feelings and his concern for Martie. He and Kathy were nearly inseparable when work and school weren't in the way. Kathy was two years older, but their shared experience had transcended the gap completely.

Tim made sure he spent time with Martie too. Neither of them had noticed anyone out of place, following, or hanging around. Tim felt life slide slowly back to normal.

Tim's parents invited Kathy for dinner.

Martie had also struggled. She felt her life had been violated in a very personal way by the trashing of her room. She gradually recovered but felt different somehow, a little more edgy. Kathy had become a welcome distraction, and Martie looked forward to the dinner.

Martie couldn't resist kidding Tim about his new girlfriend.

"She's not my girlfriend," Tim said.

His mom responded with a raised eyebrow. "She's certainly something, Tim."

Tim looked at his mom, speechless. He held his hands out palms up and shrugged.

Martie laughed out loud. It was fun to have Mom pile on with her.

"Dinner's almost ready," his mom added. "When did you say she got off work?"

"Regular hours don't quite explain her schedule," Tim said, seeming relieved that the topic had changed slightly. "Her last session ended about 5:30, but she has charts and paperwork to do so she guessed about 7:00."

"Good," Mom said. "That will give us just enough time to set the table if you help."

Martie realized that Mom's purpose was more than just to poke fun at Tim.

"Okay," Tim said. "Martie and I will both help."

The smirk from Tim let Martie know he felt he had just paid her back. They set the table for five and were just finishing when a knock came at the door.

"Got it," Martie said and turned to the door.

"No, you don't," Tim said, stepping in front of her. "I'll get it this time."

"Not your girlfriend, huh?" Martie said and giggled.

"None of that while Kathy is here, you got it," Tim said, pointing his finger at her in mock anger. Then they both burst out laughing.

"I'll be good," Martie promised.

"You're always a good girl. Just be good at that."

"Martie, will you get your dad please," Mom called from the kitchen. "He's in the study."

"Sure, just a minute," Martie said. "I don't want to miss the big entrance."

Tim set his hand on the doorknob and gave Martie one last warning look.

He opened the door, and Martie saw arms immediately wrap around Tim's neck and pull him out of view.

"I really missed you today," Kathy said.

Martie crossed her arms and grinned. "I guess the door is for you, huh?"

Kathy and Tim looked around the open door. Kathy was nodding her head and smiling, while Tim had a sheepish look as if he had no idea how to respond. "Yep, it's for Tim all right."

"Hi, Kathy, it's nice to see you," Martie said.

"Hello, Martie. How's it going? Take any trips to exotic places today?"

Martie shook her head. "Nope, the star's been pretty quiet lately."

"I'd sure like to take a look at this ornament that saved my life sometime," Kathy said.

"Sure," Martie said.

"How about after dinner," Mom said as she set a pitcher of ice water on the table.

"Dinner first sounds great. I'm starving," Kathy agreed. "It's been a long day."

"You've already seen the star, Kathy," Tim reminded her.

"Yeah, but I only saw it once a long time ago, and that was just for a second before you disappeared."

"It's upstairs," Martie said warmly. "We can check it out later."

Dad entered the dining room carrying a potato-and-ham casserole. Setting it on a hot pad in the center of the table, he said, "Kathy, I understand you're doing great work with our friend Mike."

"He is making good progress, but that's mostly because he has found a way to inspire his effort. Your family has played an important role in that according to Mike."

"I think the StarPassages have been the biggest influence," Tim said.

"Perhaps. But you guys have been there every step."

After Dad said grace, they dove in. Conversation revolved around passing plates and introductions for a few minutes before settling back into the discussion in which they had previously been engaged.

"How exactly does the star work?" Kathy asked.

"We really don't know," Martie said. "But it's no dumb object, that's for sure."

"Tim's told me how you came across the star, but the real question is why you ended up with it."

"Another unexplainable mystery," Natalie said. "It's been a wild ride and pretty scary at times, but we can't deny it's helped us a lot."

"The star picks who it will help, of course, but Tim and Martie do a pretty good job following its lead," Dad said proudly. "We've got a couple of great kids there."

Tim shook his head. "It was pretty tough to find the right person this time around. I never noticed before how many kids at school seem like they're struggling or lost."

"I noticed that too," Martie added. "There's such a cynical attitude toward life, the future, the government, the job market, just about everything."

"I've seen that in college also," Kathy agreed.

"Why do you think that is?" Jim asked.

"Not sure. It does seem that more kids are dealing with personal and family problems though."

"Family problems?" Natalie said as she poured water into her glass.

"I'm not saying their parents are terrible, but the demands seem so different now. Single parents like my mom do the best they can, but doing it alone is tough, especially when they work full time. The issues families have to deal with seem endless."

"What issues do you hear about the most?"

"There are loads of reasons. A society filled with people who see themselves as victims that are entitled to get whatever they want."

"How about kids lost in a constant effort to escape from reality," Tim added. "Drugs, virtual reality, gaming, social media, and a long list of self-absorbed behaviors drag them from fad to fad."

"That's all true, but unstable or broken home environments seem to have robbed them of the foundation necessary to build solid lives," Jim said. "Maybe this is what kids are missing and can't identify."

Kathy turned to face Jim. "You might have something there. Spiraling divorce rates and situations where there were never two parents to start with have got to be at the top of the list. Families seem to be breaking down for millions of different reasons."

"Or for no reason at all." Jim shook his head.

"It doesn't matter why. It puts kids at risk," Tim added.

Kathy continued. "Then there's the millions of kids who grow up in unstable family situations. Serial cohabitation where the partners keep changing is a fact of life for many."

"I see it at the community college also," Jim added.

"That means lots of kids have to figure life out on their own," Martie mumbled through a mouth full of potatoes.

"Or have nowhere to turn when stuff happens," Natalie said.

"Where do kids who don't have a solid family situation seek help?" Jim wondered.

"Their peers—sometimes those that are just as messed up or conflicted—or sometimes they have nowhere to turn at all and they escape through acting out to get attention or dropping out and giving up," Kathy said.

"What about turning to religion or God for support?" Natalie suggested. "That's always been in the discussion. I guess I'm a little surprised you haven't mentioned it."

"That's part of the problem. There's been a general slide away from belief in any kind of higher being that can do anything. It's like God is there, but he's more of a Greek or Roman myth doing His own thing and doesn't really have any power or a practical role in modern life."

Tim reached out and took Kathy's hand. "Kids our age are left without solid parental support or a foundation of faith. Without these they're forced to rely on themselves. That might work for a while, but it isn't enough to get them through tough times."

"Maybe I'm old and out of touch, but it reminds me of the life of a worm," Dad said with a smile.

"A worm?" Tim looked at him in confusion. "Should I be offended?"

"No, hear me out. Why do worms crawl out of their safe warm burrows onto the driveway when it rains only to dry up, get smashed, or eaten?"

Everyone chuckled at the unexpected twist in their serious conversation.

Natalie smirked. "This sounds a lot like one of your college lectures."

"Okay, Dad, I'll bite," Tim said, causing everyone to roll their eyes.

"Very good, Tim. But there is a serious and very applicable principle here."

Natalie winked at her husband. "I know you're dying to tell us, honey, so please go ahead."

"Worms breathe basically through their skin. When the soil is dry or only damp, it has a natural fifty-fifty mix of air and solid. But when it rains, the air pockets in the soil flood with water and the worms are forced to the surface to avoid drowning."

"Okay, that means they are on top of the dirt, not on the sidewalk," Kathy observed.

"Yes, that's the point. The real question is why they move from the soil onto the hard sidewalk," Jim said. "The answer is unclear because worms don't tend to give very good interviews."

Martie knew Dad was on a roll. He paused for effect then continued. "Here is where I must speculate somewhat. Worms have no higher reasoning, so they are driven by their sensory inputs. The saturation of the soil makes it hard for their basic senses to determine whether they are on water-flooded soil or pavement."

"Are you saying they do it because they don't know the difference?" Kathy said.

"Yes, that's a simple way to put it."

Martie suddenly became very interested in worms. "So how are worms and kids similar, Dad?"

"The story also relates to the struggles your peers are experiencing. Our senses are reliable only up to a point. They can be fooled or confused in many ways."

Kathy leaned forward in her chair. "That's right. Literature is full of studies where optical and other sensory illusions demonstrated such limitations."

"There are two important foundational resources everyone needs to overcome sensory limitations," Jim continued. "These are especially important to young people as they grow and develop. First, a solid foundational belief that there is a being that cares for them personally and that this being has a purpose for them in life that fits in with some larger plan. Implied in this belief is a requirement that there is some personal interactive communication that is possible with such a being. The stronger the conviction, the firmer the foundation.

"Secondly, a family unit where a mother and father are on the same page, working together to develop a secure and positive environment where children may grow and be guided through the rocks and shoals of this crazy world is essential."

"Unfortunately, you are telling us that there has been a breakdown of these two basic foundational resources in our kids' generation?" Mom added.

"Not with everyone," Tim said. "But there's a lot of it."

"Mr. Carson, what I hear you saying is that faith in a proactive and loving God and having a functioning basic family unit are the difference," Kathy asserted.

"Exactly. Too many kids are left to fend for themselves using their own senses and partially developed or even flawed understanding of the world. They are forced to make it up as they go or seek guidance from unreliable sources like equally limited peers, adults with agendas, or the Internet and cobble together their own view of the universe. You might say they are forced to be their own creator of the reality in which they live. Such a reality is inevitably based on diluted or twisted truth mingled with fable, pop culture, and limited reasoning."

"Even if it's a sincere effort," Natalie said. "It's not enough."

"I see it all the time." Kathy straightened in her chair. "Even students who are doing okay seem to have an emptiness in their lives that they have difficulty identifying. They feel like they've been robbed of something, but they don't know what. This can give place to cynicism and apathy. The result too often is anger or discouragement, which either lashes out or checks out."

"The fact that this generation has also been told they are entitled to complete and absolute fairness, equality, and success just makes it worse when it doesn't come sit in their lap," Jim said.

"There's a sense that something is owed. In reality we have been given a unique opportunity by being born in this country at this time in history where we are free to be whatever we choose and work hard to be."

"It's the *work hard* part that kids at the high school miss," Tim said. "I wish they could all see some of the things we've seen on our StarPassages. The sacrifices of people for generations like patriots and pioneers, immigrants and soldiers. People who have given everything so that the next generation might have something better. Sometimes I wonder if kids my age are willing to give anything, let alone risk everything."

Jim raised his glass. "And we live in that *better* time despite all its flaws. As a result, we become more and more like worms crawling from safety and security to certain death because we can't or refuse to tell the difference."

Natalie nodded in agreement. "It's not just young people. Our generation does it, too, and it's part of the problem."

"I see your point, Mr. Carson," Kathy said. "But I fall somewhere in the middle. I believe there is a higher being, but I don't consider myself religious. There are lots of people who feel the same. It's just that my generation doesn't like having to be squeezed into a specific pattern of rules and behavior. We want to do our own thing, not some church or government's version of it."

Tim smiled. "I see that too. It's almost like our generation would be more interested in God if He'd do it our way."

Martie smiled. "Like we know better than He does."

"So your generation is okay with the idea of a higher being as long as He's willing to change His rules to fit their expectations and behavior," Jim said. "I don't think it works that way."

"I know it makes no sense." Kathy nodded. "Maybe that's what you're seeing when you say our generation lives by its senses and can't tell the difference."

"The world seems so messed up," Tim said. "It's a pretty hard time for kids my age to have faith in much of anything. Being cynical and checking out seems easier."

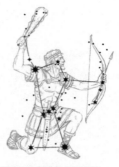

CHAPTER XXVI

The Martyr

Martie took Kathy up to her bedroom after dinner. She pulled the shoulder bag from under the mattress, removed the star, and laid it on the bed.

"So this is how Tim saved my life years ago?" Kathy said, shaking her head.

"Yeah, but to us it's days ago, not years."

"Right. It seems strange to think that in some alternate track of history I might be dead."

"But you're not and that's what matters," Martie responded brightly. "And look at all the people you're helping, including Mike."

Kathy's thoughts ran back to that terrible day. She was young and much of that day was a long, dark, blurry nightmare. But there were memories that kept shining over the years. Her mind fixed upon one of those moments, and she smiled.

"You must be thinking of something very happy. Your face just lit up like you walked from the shade into the sunlight."

"I was just thinking about what Tim said right before he disappeared."

"What's that?"

"He made me promise to do something good with my life. I've tried to do that."

"You are succeeding."

Kathy reached for the star, hesitated, and drew back her hand. "Is it safe?"

"Sure, go ahead," Martie assured her. "It's just an ornament most of the time."

Kathy reached out again, touched the star with her finger, and quickly pulled back, worried that it might make her disappear immediately. Nothing happened. She shot a questioning look at Martie.

"I told you, it's just an ornament most of the time. The only time it works is after it gives you a specific message, which appears right there." Martie pointed to the center of the star.

"It's pretty intimidating, though, knowing what it could do if it wanted."

"Hold your hands out and don't move."

Kathy extended her hands, palms up, side by side, and shut her eyes tight, nervous about what might happen. "I think it's easier not to know anything than to have heard all the stories at the dinner table tonight."

Martie laughed. "You know, you're right. Most of us have been completely ignorant when we took our first little trip. Don't worry. Nothing will happen. Keep your eyes closed."

Martie lifted the star and gently placed it in Kathy's hands. Kathy felt the cold metal. But she also noticed something else. "Did you feel that when you picked it up?"

"Feel what?"

"It tingles, like an electrical current is flowing through it."

"Never noticed that before." Martie put her hands back on top of the star so they both were holding above and below its center.

"Wait!" Martie sounded startled. "I feel something too. It's barely noticeable, but it's there."

Kathy opened her eyes. The feeling flowed over her body as if she had slipped into warm bathwater. She felt attracted to the star in some strange way she could not describe. "I like this. It makes me feel...I don't know...welcome."

"I'm all warm inside," Martie said. "Is that how you feel?"

"Yes, it is very seductive—almost addictive. It makes you want to keep holding it."

Martie removed her hands from the star. "Kathy, there's writing."

"Writing?"

"Yeah, on the star," Martie said. "It wasn't there when I hand-ed it to you a minute ago."

"Really? That's so cool," Kathy said. She leaned over and read the star's message.

"The journey ahead is for newly close friends, find a new meaning before reaching the end."

"I don't get that at all," Kathy said.

"The star can be a little tricky."

"What do you think?"

"That sounds like you and Tim," Martie said. "He's in the kitchen. I'll go get him."

"Why me and Tim?"

"You won't find that out until you get out there on the passage."

Martie disappeared, leaving Kathy alone with the star. She felt uncomfortable, as if she were in a cage with a wild animal. She sat, not knowing what to do, and watched the star closely. The writing disappeared as if it were water evap-orating on a hot summer day. An invisible hand wrote a new message in precise script in its place. She read, wondering what it meant.

Tim and Martie walked into the room mid-conversation. "...more writing on the star that sounds like you and Kathy are chosen this time."

"Let's have a look." Tim sat next to Kathy. "You know I have no patience with riddles."

"It's changed," Kathy said, feeling as if fog swirled in her head. She read the new message.

"At ten and two, hold the points tight, for rewards come after you've fought the good fight."

"This is a bit easier. Sounds like it knows what we were talking about at dinner," Tim said.

"And wants to add its perspective?" Kathy finished the thought.

"Well, let's get ready. Your dress is nice, Kathy, but probably not right for our trip."

"I can't go change at my place. That'll make it too late before we start."

"My clothes won't fit," Martie said. "But you're about Mom's size."

Kathy borrowed a pair of baggy denims, a USC sweatshirt, and pair of jogging shoes from Natalie. Then she met Tim in Martie's room. He wore faded cargo pants and a long-sleeved, black Under Armour shirt. Kathy noticed his hiking boots had a thick coating of dust. "Those have seen some action."

"Yeah, haven't cleaned them since 9-11," Tim responded as he slipped a pocket knife and flashlight in his front leg pocket and slung the bag for the star across his shoulders.

"Should I take this?" Kathy said, holding up her phone.

"Probably no service where we're going, but some of your other apps might work."

Her adrenalin pumped hard. Every sense surged to its peak, ready for a fight-flight response. "I'm ready, I think."

"Kathy, there are a couple of things you need to know before starting your first passage," Martie said. "The passage can be a little disorienting at first so keep calm. It won't last long. Tim will help you with the rest. Just keep holding onto the star unless he tells you not to."

Kathy shot a worried look at Tim. "It sounds like there's a lot I don't know about this."

Tim smiled warmly. "Yeah, it's like learning a new game. Sometimes it's better to play a practice round to learn the rules rather than to read through them."

"It sounds risky to do it that way. It's not like we're sitting at a table with a deck of cards."

"We're going to be okay. But you must be aware of one thing. Dangerous figures may appear. They're called Trackers and are drawn whenever the star is used. So keep your eyes sharp. If you see anything that looks like a horror movie— dark figures moving toward you, for example—let me know *immediately*."

"What aren't you telling me?" Kathy said, concerned.

"A lot, actually," Tim said. "But you needed to know about Trackers."

Martie nodded in agreement. "Trackers are people who have lived on this earth, but their lives were full of evil. When they die, they don't go to heaven or anything, so they're stuck in the past. They can move through history, but they can't return to the present time. They don't have the ability to interact with historical people, but they have physical power over real people like us."

"There must be thousands," Kathy said.

"Probably tens of thousands, but they are spread out through time and history. We've only seen a couple of dozen. But one is enough to ruin your day and your future," Tim cautioned.

"Trackers want that star worse than anything," Martie said. "They believe it will free them from their prison and allow them to enter our time, where they can take over real people's bodies and live again."

"Trackers are really bad," Tim added. "You can't ever let them touch you."

"Okay," Kathy said. The combination of her adrenalin spike and fear of the Trackers sent a tremble through her core, resisting her effort to maintain control.

"You're shaking," Tim said. "We don't have to do this now, or ever really."

"I'll be all right in a minute. It's a lot to take in all at once."

"Right. Let's sit for a moment and collect our thoughts."

They remained next to each other on the corner of Martie's bed. Natalie and Jim entered the room while they were talking.

"We'll be here waiting when you return," Mom said.

Tim and Kathy sat for another couple of minutes without speaking. Kathy waged an internal war between grabbing the star and walking away. Her mind slid back and forth, making arguments for both sides. Finally, she settled on one thought: *If the star's goal is to help and do good, then I have to follow.*

Kathy gazed into Tim's eyes. She tilted her head slightly as if it would help her see deep inside his mind.

Tim blinked. "Sorry, I feel like you are reading a page written on my soul. It's a little awkward."

"You're a good man, Tim," Kathy said. "I trust you. I always have."

For some reason the bond that had grown between them struck her as funny. She laughed. "I guess we better get this over with."

"What's so funny?" Tim said.

"It's just that I feel so connected to you...soul to soul. But it's weird because I was five and you were seventeen and now I'm almost twenty and you're still seventeen."

"I can relate to that. At least you've had fifteen years to adjust. For me, you gained those years almost overnight."

"That must be strange," Kathy offered.

"But I sure like you this way," Tim said, smiling with warmth. "Not complaining at all."

Kathy felt her anxiety ease. "You know just the right things to say. You always have."

"Well, I'll be eighteen in a couple of months."

"Right. That makes all the difference." She grinned.

"You ready then?"

"Yep, let's do this before I start overthinking it again."

They each held the star by the point as directed. They clasped their free hands also, which helped Kathy feel more secure. The colors around her began to run together, then fade. She let go of Tim's hand long enough to wave good-bye to Martie and immediately took Tim's hand again as she felt slightly dizzy.

Kathy became disoriented and worried she might get sick. Then something washed over her. "I feel that warmth from the star again. It calms my nerves."

"Me too. Hmm...never noticed that before," Tim said as the world around them went blank and gray.

"How long will it stay like this?"

"We should begin to see something come into focus soon."

Kathy expected to see trees, grass, or buildings, but their surroundings went darker, then pitch black. Her eyes fought to adjust. But there was no light to help them function.

"Would it be all right to use my flashlight app?"

"Sure," Tim said. "Can't stand here in the dark and learn anything."

She retrieved her cell phone and touched the screen with her thumb. It blinked on, no service. But the battery worked fine, and she accessed the flashlight app. The light revealed a half-circle, rounded ceiling curving down to the floor. She stood near one wall, reached out, and touched what appeared to be stone with a plaster covering. Tim flipped on his flashlight. They followed the narrow beam and turned a complete circle. The room was bare except for a small wooden desk, chair, and a cot in the corner, upon which sat a pile of rags. Kathy saw no windows at first, then upon closer inspection, she found a six-inch gap in one end of the room which led upward about two feet to a small, barred window.

"This looks like a prison cell," she said. "There's ancient graffiti all over the walls."

"There's a door at the other end," Tim added.

"I'd hate to be stuck in here," Kathy commented mostly to herself.

"Let's put the star in the shoulder bag and look around," Tim suggested.

Kathy let go of the point and was startled as Tim suddenly disappeared. Panic invaded her mind. "Tim, you there?"

Tim reappeared, closing the flap on the shoulder bag. "An important note. When you hold the star, you're invisible to the world. When you let go, you become visible."

"That little bit of information would have made the last ten seconds easier," Kathy said. "Let me know if something like that is going to happen again please. I only have so much adrenalin to burn."

She shuddered at the cold dampness of the cell. "This nasty place would make me sick in no time. It's freezing."

"Yes, one more rule you now know," Tim said kindly, as if a professor speaking to a new student. "You can't feel the air or weather when you hold the star, but you can when you let go. Also, even when you're invisible, you are still physical, so if a car runs you over, or if you step off a cliff or an animal attacks, you're gonna feel it."

"That means we could die," Kathy said with alarm.

"Yeah, StarPassages are dangerous for more reasons than just the Trackers."

She reached out to take Tim's free hand. "I'm glad you're here."

They moved together to inspect the door. Metal, probably iron, with a small, barred window blocked by a small latched door. She assumed it could be opened from the outside so someone could look into the room without opening the large door.

"It must be night, but even during the day this place would be gloomy and dark," Kathy said.

"It's the kind of place only a ghost hunter would love," Tim added.

She heard a noise from the corner. The creak of wooden slats or floor boards. They turned toward the sound in unison. The pile of rags on the small cot moved. Kathy jumped and let out an involuntary cry. The pile of rags moved again, and a pale white, almost ghostly, face appeared.

"Quisnam est illic," the ghost face said in a clear and concise male voice.

"What did you say?" Kathy said.

"English, it is pleasant to hear my native tongue instead of the Latin spoken by my inquisitors," the man said. "I see thou art not acquainted with Latin. I inquired as to thy identity. How hast thou come about this strange visitation? Are ye spirits? No human passes here."

"We are regular people," Kathy said.

"We were brought here by an ancient relic," Tim said. "We come from a future time."

"My inquisitors would burn thee for such a statement or perhaps even for thy strange usage of English," the man said. "Such hast been done for much less I suspect."

"Burn—you mean at the stake?" Kathy said horrified.

"That is the law," the man said calmly. "Thou wouldst first be questioned, proper charges would be prepared, and a judgment obtained in due course. There is a strict process, but thy fate would ultimately not be influenced. The outcome is preordained."

"Are you accused of something?" Kathy inquired.

"As to travel through time I cannot tell, but foreigners ye

must be. Are ye unaware of my plight, which is widely published by church and magistrates alike as a warning to engender fear in the common man?"

Kathy heard compassion in the man's voice that calmed her soul and lifted her spirit.

"May we ask your name?" Kathy said formally.

"Do ye not know me? I am William Tyndale at thy service," he responded and swung his legs, stood up, bowed slightly, then sat back on the edge of the cot. "I ask thy pardon. I may stand only briefly without support. My strength wanes in this damp cell with meager meals. But I do not complain. What I have is sufficient."

Tyndale looked at the strange pair. "Ye carry a curious torch. It giveth light without flame."

"It's called a flashlight in our day, although some still refer to it as a torch," Tim said.

"Does it not burn thy hand?"

"No, it does not operate by fire." Kathy tried to keep the explanation simple. "It works on a controlled current of minute amounts of what you might call lightning that makes metal glow, thus creating light."

"A fascinating concept," Tyndale said. "As with any torch, must it eventually grow dim?"

"Yes," Tim said. "But there are small containers of this lightning current that can be replaced like extra arrows in a quiver for a bow."

"You are an amazement." Tyndale rubbed his chin. "What manner of time ye must live in that the dress of men and women is alike and coarse."

"Styles have changed over the past five hundred years," Kathy said. "Although women often choose to wear dresses and gowns still."

"Five hundred years?"

"Yes, it is a long time and much has changed," Tim said. "I've heard of your name in our day but am unfamiliar with your history. Can you give us more understanding, please?"

"I am but a man who, like thee, wishes to shine a light in darkness. A light that doth not grow dim with time. A true light of the teachings of our Lord Jesus Christ, which have been obscured by the evil designs and careless stewardship of man. A light that hast been kept from commoners by the very stewards charged with its illumination."

"What is the year?" Tim inquired.

"It is the year of our Lord 1536, and a great awakening rolls across the land," Tyndale said. "Yet this awakening comes at a time when priests and kings are unified in one, and the one rules by fear, threat, and terror. The word of God is spoken in a tongue few understand and used to dominate and enslave. The great awakening of spirit will prevail. I have fulfilled my duty with all I have and will not see it."

"Why do you say that?" Tim said. "There's always hope."

"Well said and true," Tyndale responded. "Yet, my fate is decided. I am to be disgraced and burned on the morrow."

"What've you done to deserve such a fate?" Kathy said, feeling shock and concern.

"I have translated the word of God, as written in the Greek and Hebrew texts, into English. Such action is named heresy by the church. I hitherto have spoken against the errant doctrine taught. This too carries a deadly verdict, which has long been determined and justified by the instruments of such verdict."

"Perhaps we can get you out of here?" Tim suggested.

"Ye cannot set me free," Tyndale said. "For I am already free in the knowledge of my Lord and His atonement for every man's sins. I pray for the King of England, that his heart would be softened toward the work of translation, in which I have been long engaged, and that the common man may read in his own language."

"In our time, the English-language Bible is among the most printed and read books in history," Kathy said.

"It is the stone that rolls forth to fill the whole earth," Tyndale said, nodding his head. "Man's effort to stop the work of God cannot prevail. I am gratified to hear thy words."

"But there is much skepticism toward God," Kathy said. "Many believe He is distant, helpless, and uninterested in the people. Some place him alongside the fabled Greek and Roman deities created by tyrants or superstition to control and intimidate."

Tyndale's mouth turned up slightly in what looked like an attempt to smile. "Then I must thank God that my prayer is answered in part. I would tell thee to publish to thy time that evil men will use any tool to do their bidding; it matters not to the wicked the instrument's true purpose. The wolf would make itself appear as a sheep and walk among us. But that does not change the truth of God if used rightly. Fire remains fire, and its higher purpose unchanged though it may be used to kill or destroy."

Tyndale paused and drew in a deep breath, "Do not blame the tool for the acts of wicked men. The Bible has been used to justify terrible acts, which are an affront to our loving and benevolent God. He remains a God of hope, love, and compassion, and His words tell of that in every phrase. This is not changed though evil men use the sacred text to enslave or to create unrighteous dominion over their brothers. Do not fault the word of God or the true nature of Christianity. Evil is simply evil, regardless of the robes it attempts to wear."

"Many young people in our time choose to rebel against God with the idea that, if there is a God, He would not allow so many terrible things to happen and that churches simply use belief and faith to create fear and control the people," Kathy said.

"This is not different in my time," Tyndale responded. "Christ truly created an organization because he knew that working together and serving each other would be a blessing to the faith. The souls of many were brought to truth through such a divinely inspired earthly organization. Yet, evil men have corrupted it for their own purposes. The reformation that is now in process hopes to open the eyes of those who have been led astray and return us to true worship. Many before me have endured a martyr's death to see it through, and I suppose such a fate will continue for others."

Tyndale paused, seemingly deep in thought, then continued. "Regarding the nature of God and His interest in us, I can but say that He is close, loves His children dearly, and has provided His Word to guide us that we may return by that narrow gate and straight path to Him. I am certain that He hears the prayers of all, and His answers are available to any who humbly recognize His voice and hand."

"Is there anything else we can tell young people in our time?" Tim asked.

"If people in thy time truly are free to read as they wish and speak as they wish, then tell them not to make up their own religion as some have done in my day. They must turn to the Word, study it, and learn of the Author themselves, even the Lord their God. Those that seek Him will find Him. That is His promise and my purpose."

"Thank you," Kathy said.

"I believe it is time for us to go," Tim said.

"Godspeed, my young friends," Tyndale said. "I will speak words to thy time on the morrow. Should such survive, thou wilt know."

Tim removed the star from the shoulder bag and disappeared.

"I see thou art in possession of strange powers," Tyndale said. "It would raise fear among most. But I have felt of thy honest and open spirit. Be well and be faithful."

"We will try," Kathy said.

"A sincere desire and effort brings forth blessings," Tyndale stated as if he spoke something that was common knowledge. "It will bring thee close to Him, and His Grace shalt complete the process as only it can."

"I wish you well," Kathy said.

"I am well always, for my soul is at peace as all souls can be."

Kathy felt Tim guide her hand to a cold pointed surface. She immediately sensed the room and William Tyndale fading. Her last glimpse of the great reformer included his kindly smile and a nod of his head. Then all went gray.

They reappeared in Martie's room. "What happened?" Martie asked.

"We met a great man of faith," Kathy said. "We were able to question him about our world today and his in the past."

"It was interesting, given what we talked about at dinner," Tim added.

"His name is William Tyndale, and he gave his life to get the first complete English translation of the Bible into the hands of the people," Kathy said.

"We need to get to a computer," Tim said.

"Over here," Martie responded. "It's turned on and ready to go. Why do you need it?"

"I want to check Tyndale's last words," Tim said.

He sat down at the computer and typed, clicked a few times, then leaned forward and read. Kathy watched intently until Tim sat back and shook his head. "He did it. That's so cool."

"What did he say?"

"Here, have a seat and see for yourself."

"And read it so we can hear and share in the story," Natalie added.

Tim stood and stepped away from the computer so Kathy could sit down. She read silently. Finally, she leaned back in astonishment, rubbing her forehead. "It's amazing...and also very sad."

"What is it?" Natalie persisted. "Tell us."

Kathy read the words carefully. "History states that William Tyndale was executed by being tied to a stake, strangled, and then burned. Just before his execution, he is reported to have said, 'in a loud voice that was heard by many, *Lord! Open the King of England's eyes! And grant that thy words will be made manifest to all lands in their own language that they may come to thee and the understanding of thy word in all future times.'*"

"Tyndale said he would *speak words to our time* before he died," Tim said.

"He impressed me as a man who would stand by his word no matter what," Kathy said.

"He remained faithful to his promise," Jim said. "If you know the history of his life at all, you know him as a man who was so sincere, spiritual, and compassionate that even his jailers and adversaries, like Agrippa with Paul, were nearly converted. A great man raised up in a terribly wicked era. We should remember with gratitude men and women like him who, over the last five hundred years, made it possible for a free country to be established and thrive. As many have said, 'Freedom isn't Free.'"

CHAPTER XXVII

Kidnapped

Martie didn't like carrying the star with her, but felt more uncomfortable leaving it at home. She borrowed her dad's larger backpack he used for weekend maneuvers with the National Guard. It might draw some attention, but more attention was good, she decided.

Martie kept the backpack with her during school. She felt relieved when the final bell rang and trotted through the parking lot to meet her carpool ride home.

I've gotta find a new hiding place. I can't do this every day.

The evening passed uneventfully until shortly before nine. A dark, moonless night made the world outside her window pitch black. Her dad was teaching a late class at school, and Tim wore his headphones while doing homework in his room. Loud clanking sounds and music came from the kitchen, where her mom washed pots and pans.

Martie spent the evening in the kitchen doing homework, breaking only for dinner. She had not been up to her room since she first arrived home from school.

"Finally," she said and slammed her biology book closed. "I'm done, Mom. I'll be up in my room."

Natalie waved a rubber gloved hand in acknowledgement as Martie loaded her backpack and skipped up the stairs to her room. *It feels so good to be finished.* She had kept the star with her all evening, still feeling paranoid. She left the star in the backpack and put it under the mattress, thinking about the need for a better hiding place. She opened the door to the bathroom, approached the sink, and began to wash her hands and face. Martie hadn't noticed her bedroom door didn't open all the way to the wall.

Suddenly, a vague chill ran down her spine. Something seemed wrong. She turned, still drying her face, and strode back into her room. She stopped and looked around.

"Anyone here?" No answer.

Then she noticed her bed cover was messy. She scanned the room carefully. Seeing nothing, Martie moved to the bed and lifted up the mattress. The backpack and star were still there. *Don't be so paranoid, girl.* She sighed with relief, let the mattress drop back over the star, and bent to tuck in the sheets properly and straighten the quilt.

As she thrust the sheets under the bed, a sweaty hand covered her mouth and a knife immediately pressed against her neck. "Don't scream or move, you understand?"

Martie's mind exploded with adrenalin and fear. She shook uncontrollably, facing the window, only now realizing it was open a crack. She breathed deeply, trying to regain her composure, and nodded her head *yes* very slowly to avoid being cut.

"Get the star and ask it to take us somewhere."

"Where?" she whispered.

"Doesn't matter. Anywhere is good," the menacing voice said. "They'll find us."

"The Trackers?"

"The shadow people are my friends."

"Those are Trackers," Martie said in a low, controlled voice. "Whatever you think, they're not your friends."

Martie bent down carefully and retrieved the star from under the mattress. Her attacker continued to hold the knife to her neck.

"Just talk to the star, you hear me?"

"It doesn't work that way," Martie said.

"It better, or I'll have to take care of you and go out the window."

Martie pulled the star from the backpack, allowing the pack to drop on the bed. Unnoticed by the attacker, two small eight-pointed stars fell out of the center compartment, which had opened and dropped silently onto the carpeted floor. Martie kicked them under the bed, hoping someone would find them later.

"The star decides when and where," Martie said.

"It better decide *right now*," he snapped back. Martie didn't dare turn around to see his face.

She looked at the star as writing appeared. "There's some writing."

The pressure of the knife eased only slightly. "Read it."

Martie read:

"Take the star by two and four and suspend the rules, there are no more."

"What's that mean?" the guy said, sounding desperate and slightly unbalanced.

"It means the star will take us somewhere," Martie said, indicating the point at the two position. "You need to hold it by this point here."

"I'm going to let go of you. Don't try anything."

She turned to face a boy about Bobby's age. He stood taller than Bobby and had a dark, animal look.

"I don't think you'll like where we go," she said.

"Don't care. Just get us outta here." He took hold of the star with one hand and pressed the knife against Martie's cheek with the other, drawing a drop of blood.

Martie took the four point and shuddered involuntarily. A thought entered her mind as the world went gray. *This is going to be really bad for someone.*

CHAPTER XXVIII

The Arena

Martie's absence went unnoticed for ten minutes. Tim was finishing his homework when Natalie ascended the stairs to check on them. She saw his focus and decided not to disturb his concentration. She walked to Martie's room, surprised to find it empty and messy.

That's not like Martie to leave without saying anything, and certainly not with a messy bed.

She called out, "Martie." No answer. Natalie stepped into the hall.

"Martie." Still no answer.

She heard Tim respond, "Everything okay, Mom?"

She entered Tim's room. "Sorry to interrupt, but did Martie say anything to you before she left?"

"She's in her room, I think."

"No, she's gone," Mom said.

Tim suddenly looked alarmed and bounced to his feet. "That's not like her at all."

"I know."

Tim's eyes went wide. "The star!" He ran past his mom to Martie's room, found the backpack in the middle of Martie's bed, and held it up. "She carried the star in this all day, but it's empty now."

"Oh no! Where did she put it?"

"Under the mattress," Tim said as he rounded the bed and lifted the mattress.

Natalie walked to the open window. "That's strange."

Tim let the mattress drop. "Nothing." She felt alarms going off in her head as Tim said, "The star is gone."

The gray space around Donny began to come into focus. He felt sick to his stomach. "Whew! Glad that's over."

"It's only starting," Martie said. "That was the safe part."

The bright sunlight hurt his eyes as they took a moment to adjust. He put the knife in his pocket and shielded his vision with his free hand. He couldn't believe what he saw. "This is so cool."

They stood near the edge of a huge open stadium or arena, which rose several stories above them. He judged it to be about midday because the sun shone directly overhead. Donny kicked the ground, which caused dirt and sand to spray out in front of his toe. "Where are we?"

"This is some kind of ancient arena," Martie said. "There are thousands of spectators in the stands waiting for something to happen down here where we are."

"It looks like that big one in Rome, except it's new, not all beat up."

"The Colosseum," Martie said. "That's not good at all."

"The people have robes on," Donny observed.

"Remember, we are sometime in the past, and when you force the star, it usually doesn't end well," Martie warned.

"I didn't force anything," Donny said. "I'm just doing what my friends asked."

"What friends would those be?"

"The voices," Donny said as if it was something Martie should understand, "They come to me in the night in my room."

"Do the voices have names?"

"The one that talks the most is named Clynt, and the one who helped me learn some skills is called Horst."

"Those are Trackers!" Martie said, raising her voice. "You fool! You've been used by Trackers to get to the star."

Donny didn't know why the name Tracker should be so bad. He was confused. Why would the girl be so alarmed? "They made promises. They helped me."

"They told you whatever would get you to do what they wanted."

"No, they understand. They want to help."

"They told you to get the star, didn't they?"

"That's the idea," Donny said. "I did it. Now they will reward me."

"You may not like your reward."

Donny felt angry at this girl who thought she knew everything. "My reward is going to be awesome. They said I could have everything—freedom to do what they do."

Martie shook her head. "I'm sorry for you. But we can't worry about that right now. We've got to get out of here."

Donny heard a machinery-like noise from the other side of the arena. His gaze followed the noise, and he saw a large gate swinging open. It stopped and a group of about fifty people were herded into the arena by soldiers whose golden-colored armor and helmets reflected the sunlight. It was impressive and terrible at the same time.

He turned to run, but Martie held him back. "They can't see you as long as you hold onto the star."

Donny relaxed slightly and took a closer look at the people being herded into the arena. They wore rags in stark contrast to the soldiers' and spectators' fine apparel. Some had their hands tied. All of them shuffled as if they were worn down by poor food and worse treatment. They were herded into the center of the arena. As they came closer, Donny could see many had fresh or poorly healed injuries.

"They look totally thrashed," he said.

"Torture," Martie said. "Don't you know what the Romans used the Colosseum for?"

"Not really," Donny said. "Entertainment maybe?"

"Yes, particularly brutal and gory entertainment. If you're going to be involved with the star you better pay attention in history class."

"I don't care about that stuff. It has nothing to do with my life."

Martie smiled in a way that made Donny feel uncomfortable. "It does today. You're in history."

Donny's anger flared again. It was the only way he knew how to deal with someone who challenged him. "So what. We're in ancient Rome and we might see some people executed. Could be as cool as a zombie movie, and we have a front row seat. I can get into that."

"The problem is you might end up being part of *that*," Martie said sarcastically, sweeping her hand toward the people in the center of the arena. "You got us into a real mess, and we're going to need the star's help to get out of here. Stay away from the group until the star decides to take us back."

Donny warmed to the situation, and his fear began to be replaced by a buzz that he knew came with anticipation of the coolest movie he'd ever seen. "What do you think they're going to do?"

"Keep your eyes open," Martie said. "I'm no expert, but I've heard that the Romans were extremely resourceful at making a point."

"Okay, these people are the show for today. What do you think they've done?"

"Criminals, political prisoners, captured enemies, rebels, or even religious martyrs. Could be anything."

"You mean Christians?" Donny said mildly alarmed. "Weren't they fed to the lions?"

"My dad taught a seminar on that last fall. I remember him saying that historians have had a hard time finding examples of that in the Colosseum, but you can be sure people in this arena met their end with lots of different kinds of animals. That was a Roman favorite."

Their attention was drawn back to the soldiers.

"They're leaving," Donny said.

The soldiers retreated toward the large gate. It slowly swung on its screeching metal hinges as the last soldier exited. The doors slammed shut with a bang that echoed through the arena followed by the boom of an enormous cross beam falling into place. Some of the people in the center of the arena fell to their knees and bent over as if praying. The crowd cheered in anticipation of what would come next. Donny felt like cheering too. He couldn't wait.

"Whatever it is, we're gonna find out real soon," Martie said. She began backing toward the side wall of the arena, pulling Donny with her.

"Hey, we're not going to get a good view from there."

"Too bad. You gotta follow where I go."

Donny followed reluctantly until he felt his back against the wall.

There were more sounds of machinery. This time the sounds came from a dozen places around the edge of the arena. Donny and Martie could see smaller doors sliding up to reveal empty squares of darkness. The open doors remained mute to the secrets that lay within. The victims automatically pressed together like a heard of threatened animals awaiting their fate. Then the crowd cheered wildly.

"What's happening?" Donny said.

"Look," Martie said, pointing at the smaller doors. "Animals!"

A pair of large lions exited from the open door to their immediate left, causing Martie and Donny to involuntarily press backward against the wall.

Donny almost cheered with the crowd as several kinds of animals burst out of the small tunnels. In addition to the pair of female lions, at least one huge tiger and several packs of wild dogs issued from the black holes.

"Hey, these guys are good."

"Must be a system of cages behind the walls," Martie said.

The animals issued a variety of barks, growls, and roars. *They sound hungry.* Donny smiled. The defenseless people did one of two things simultaneously. Some broke and ran. These were the first victims. Most of them made it only a few steps before they were set upon by something hungry and deadly.

The others pressed closer together. This caused the animals to hesitate and circle. They would dart in after individuals, pulling them away from the crowd or wounding them. The human numbers dwindled. The animals became bolder as they seemed to realize their prey was defenseless. Ten minutes passed, and the crowd began to tire of the spectacle and boos were heard.

Martie covered her eyes and looked away. "It's taking too long. The real animals are in the stands. They see this as a sporting event. How does a civilization sink to this?"

In apparent response to the disapproving crowd, a man rose from a large gold throne and made a motion with both arms. Roman archers positioned around the first row of the arena stepped forward and nocked arrows in their bows. On a second signal, they loosed arrows into the remaining mass pressed into an ever-shrinking circle on the arena floor. Many of those still standing went down under the hail of arrows. Some ran and were immediately pounced upon by the animals. With the stalemate broken, the event ended quickly and the crowd talked and laughed as the animals were allowed to feed.

"Looks like halftime," Donny said cheerfully.

"You make me sick," Martie said. "So do they. Look how they're laughing and carrying on as if they had just witnessed a close football game."

Some of the animals lost interest in their former prey and began to wander around the arena. One of the female lions came within twenty feet of where Martie and Donny stood. The lion sniffed the ground, looked from side to side, sniffed the air, and lowered down onto its haunches, staring unblinking in their direction.

"What's that lion doing?" Donny asked. "It can't see us, right?"

"Uh oh! Some animals can sense our presence even if they can't see us," Martie said. "That lioness just picked up our scent."

"What? Our scent…it knows where we are?" Donny began breathing heavily.

"Move very slowly with me to the right," Martie said, keeping her eyes on the lion.

Donny began to panic. He had loved watching the show, but now it felt different. "We can't stay here! What do we do?"

"Hold onto the star," Martie warned. "It's our only hope. Have faith in the star and keep moving."

Donny froze. "Faith!" he yelled hysterically. "We're gonna die."

Martie began to see dark figures moving toward them. "The Trackers are here."

Donny heard a wicked laugh. "Gots you now. No place to run." He recognized Clynt's voice.

"Help me, Clynt. I did everything you wanted. Please help me."

"Oh, we's gonna help you right good, boy," Clynt said as the shadows moved closer.

"You're my friends," Donny cried. "I helped you!"

"You're gonna have our help forever, boy. Don't worry."

"I want to get outta here," Donny cried. "Get me outta here."

The lion tilted its head slightly, her stare never wavering from the spot where they stood. It hunched down further ready to spring.

"Donny, ol' boy, we's got your back forevermore, but today... heh...heh...you's on your own."

Donny felt a rush of hate directed at the Trackers. "You promised! You lied!"

"You got what you wanted, boy. Just another moment and you're mine."

The Trackers were close. Clynt looked at Martie. "Ya can't drop the star this time, girlie, less you wanna be a meal." A wave of dark laughter rolled toward them from the figures.

Donny's mind went blank with fear and rage that blended together to create a fatally insane moment. He let go of the star and ran.

Donny became visible. He felt the heat and smelled the stench of sweat and death. *I'm alive,* he thought for one brief moment.

The lion reacted immediately to the moving target, sprang, and pounced on him, tumbling in a cloud of dust before he took three steps. Donny heard the crowd cheer one last time before the lights winked out.

Martie had been frantically seeking a way out and found it. Escape through the nearest trap door was only fifteen feet to her left. As Donny broke one way, it drew the Trackers and the lion's attention. She sprinted the opposite direction for the door, still holding the star.

Clynt is right. I can't drop the star without suffering the same fate as Donny.

She screamed as icy cold hands brushed her clothes. Barely missing capture, she lunged for the trap door and scrambled inside.

The dark, musty air was heavy, probably with odors she was glad she couldn't smell. The ground felt soft and muddy but with what? She didn't want to know. She kept going. Her gymnast body raced in a half crawl along the tunnel. Martie heard Clynt's voice close behind.

"Come on, girlie. Don't make it so hard. We's gonna git ya anyways."

Still holding the star in one hand, she crawled through a low tunnel of metal cage-like bars. She rounded a corner and her head hit a dead end. The gate to the exit tunnel. She lay on her back frantically pushing the sliding gate upward with her hands. It was heavy, but it budged. Martie curled her body around and pushed with hands and feet together. It moved a little, then more.

The Trackers were only seconds away. She heard their labored breathing and could almost feel their foul breath. She slid under just as the closest Tracker reached out. The Trackers howled and screamed.

They'll have to backtrack. That'll give me a few minutes to work this out. They probably know all the shortcuts, so I better be quick.

Martie found herself in a large cage. She stood up and moved around the edges, feeling for a gate, hoping that it wasn't necessary to use a key to hold the animals. She found it on the far side of the cage and was relieved to discover the door held closed by only a round peg slid into a metal U. She popped it out and ran blindly down the stone-cut corridor lit by an occasional torch.

Breathing heavily, she stopped briefly to see if the star held a new message. It was too dark. She needed to get back to the sunlight so she could see if the star had new instructions. She was sure it wouldn't leave her to this fate. She rounded a bend and ran smack into a pair of arms that felt like an iron vise.

"Got ya," Clynt said. "Been wantin' to have you join us for a while now, youngin'."

"What will we do with her, Clynt?" said a Tracker with a slight accent.

"Well, Horst. I think we'll keep her with us for a while. See if somebody comes. I gots a little score to settle."

"How will you take me with you? You can't take me anywhere," Martie said. "I'm stuck here without the star."

"That's not entirely accurate, *fraulein*," Horst said. "If we have you in our grasp we can take you anywhere in history."

Martie felt scared and furious at the same time. "You've got the star. What more do you want."

Clynt looked at her, his yellow broken-tooth smile widening. "I wants the only thing that's any good in a Tracker's miserable life—revenge."

Martie felt his iron grip squeeze the air out of her lungs. She gasped for air as her world went dark.

CHAPTER XXIX

Missing Souls

Natalie called Jim, who rushed home from class, arriving about the same time as the police. The police asked questions, filed a report, promised they would do everything they could, but had no answers. The officer would only say it looked like a break-in and kidnapping.

Jim and Natalie were given phone numbers to call if they heard from any kidnappers. The family stared at each other, unable to discuss Martie's location until after the officers left. They sat in Martie's room as if being where it happened would give them insight.

"They can't do anything about it," Tim said. "Someone was here and made her use the star."

"Looks like the most reasonable explanation," Jim agreed.

"Reasonable," Natalie groaned. "Nothing about this is reasonable or logical."

"True enough," her husband said and put his arm around her. He guided Natalie to the edge of Martie's bed. "Have a seat. We need to figure out what we can do."

"We don't have the star," Tim said. "We can't do anything."

Natalie sat on the bed and curled her feet under the frame. "Ouch," she said. "Something sharp just jabbed me."

Jim dropped to his knees and bent over sideways. "Well... well...well." He reached under the bed.

"What is it, Jim?" Natalie said.

"The star was thinking ahead," Jim opened his hand. "Two Follow Stars."

"I guess there *is* something we can do," Tim said triumphantly.

"No telling where this will lead," Jim warned. "We better be ready."

"Who's going?" Natalie said.

"Probably Tim and me," Jim answered. "What do you think?"

"I can't lose all of you," Natalie pleaded.

"We'll get her back," Jim said and put his arm around her waist.

They left the two stars on the bed and got dressed as they had for previous passages. They returned to Martie's room, where Natalie waited. They wore boots, thick long-sleeved shirts, and jackets. Tim wore jeans and Jim his desert camo BDU pants. They each carried flashlights and sheath knives. Jim also had his personal issue sidearm holstered at his side—a 9mm Beretta M9A1 with a fifteen-round magazine and a spare mag in his BDU pocket.

"Why are you taking that?" Natalie asked. "It won't work on Trackers."

"They had to have help this time," Jim said sternly. "Not taking any chances."

"Bring her back, Jim," Natalie said.

"Don't worry. She's a handful. Martie may have them all whipped into shape before we get there." He forced a smile.

"Whoa," Natalie said. "The two Follow Stars just split into four."

"That's interesting," Jim said. "Do you have a magnifying glass?"

"One sec," Tim said and ran to his room. He returned with one and handed it to his dad. "What's that for?"

"Just a hunch," Jim said. He laid the stars side by side on the dresser and looked at them through the glass.

"See anything?" Natalie said, leaning over to get a better look.

"Take a look." Jim handed the magnifying glass to her.

"There are names in the center of each star. The names read *Jim, Tim, Bobby,* and *Chris.*"

"Do you think—?" Tim started.

"Yep. Natalie, can you get the other two stars to Bobby and his Grandpa Chris? The star seems to have a plan, but I feel like we should go now."

"Be careful, Jim. You know Clynt's got a particular hate for you."

"We'll be fine. See you soon." Jim kissed Natalie, then picked up the star with his name on it. Tim picked up his star and winked as they disappeared.

Jim's utility belt, holster, handgun, and extra magazine remained in the present time. They dropped to the ground just as Jim disappeared.

Near panic filled her movements. Natalie bent and picked them up, crying into empty space. "Jim, what have you gotten yourself into!"

Donny remembered the lion charging and being knocked to the ground but no more. Suddenly, he stood on a remote beach with jagged black outcroppings of ancient lava flows reaching down to the crashing waves. The ocean glistened like an emerald, rolling into perfect curls before they broke and surged toward his feet. Something large crashed into the ocean, spoiling the picture and sending a towering waterspout toward the sky. He looked behind him and saw the source.

A towering conical mountain dominated the island, spewing smoke and belching fire. The volcano's explosions ejected enormous pieces of rock, which Donny watched arc through the sky before crashing onto the beach or hitting the water with deafening explosions of violence. He was confused.

How did I get here? Did the star save me? The beach seemed deserted, and each impact of volcanic debris shook the ground like an earthquake. "I've gotta get outta here quick."

He ran along the beach looking for a canoe or row boat, anything to help him escape. He found nothing.

Donny looked at the volcano as reddish, liquid magma surged over its rim. He fell to his knees, buried his head in his hands, and screamed, "You sent me here. Now get me out before it's too late."

He heard a calm, familiar voice. "You're here 'cause you chose to join us, boy."

Donny looked up. "Clynt?"

"I promised I'd be takin' care of ya."

"I'm so glad to see you. Can you get me away from this?"

"Why would I do that?"

"Really? Look around. This place is a death trap."

"More like a trap for the already dead, boy." Clynt seemed to enjoy the play on words.

"What do you mean?"

"Yer dead, boy. Lunch for a lion, remember?"

Donny was shaken. "I'm...dead? What about heaven and all that stuff?"

"Heaven ain't part of yer future, boy. Yer future's with us. You gets to be a Tracker forever." Clynt gestured as numerous other shadowy figures materialized. There were figures dressed in every conceivable historical costume. "They's all come to welcome ya. We's yer family now."

A lava boulder the size of a minivan hit the ground next to Donny. Its impact threw him into the air. He screamed and braced for impact as he realized his body would land on the jagged lava rock. He hit with a fearsome thump. Donny expected it to be terribly painful, but he felt nothing. "Hey, that didn't hurt at all!"

"Yep, boy. Yer immortal. Nothing can hurt you anymore."

Donny smiled. "I could get into this."

"Ya got lots to learn, boy. But yer gonna be a good Tracker one day, and we gots nothin' but time here to get it right."

Martie woke up with a headache. She leaned against a cool rock wall and felt the sandy floor invade the creases in her fingers and toes. Her eyes focused on a faint light coming from somewhere around a rocky corner. Her shoulder felt stiff, and her ribs ached as if they were bruised or broken. The Tracker's embrace had left a mark for sure.

She stood and wavered, regained her balance, and moved toward the light. There were people on the ground, but they barely moved as she passed. Most were curled up into fetal balls, some rocking back and forth and mumbling incoherently.

This place is creepy, she thought as she rounded the corner. It remained dark except for a fire blazing in a rock ring near the entrance. She was in a cave. From the look of the rock walls, an ancient lava tube, probably near a beach because of the deep sandy floor.

Martie approached the fire. There were more people, and they seemed engaged in conversation, laughing and telling stories. She found a smallish rock and sat down just outside the ring to listen.

"Clynt has retrieved the star," a tall, slim man dressed in a business suit said.

"Aye, he has," said a man in an out-of-date sailor outfit. "Been a long time comin' it has."

"Tell me, what will he do with it now?" the businessman inquired.

"Goin' to the Present Time, he is," said the sailor. "If it be workin', we's all gonna join in."

"Where's Clynt?" Martie said.

The businessman turned. "Ah, the young lady. We owe you a debt of gratitude for bringing the star to us."

"I didn't do that," Martie protested. "He took it from me."

"Well, the manner of delivery matters little," the man said, smiling wickedly. "You will find Clynt outside over there." He pointed just outside the mouth of the cave to his right.

Martie rose and walked to the spot as directed. There were two men talking; one she knew, Clynt. She could identify the cowboy anywhere. The other wore a wool suit and matching cap.

"I see our guest is awake," Clynt said. "Girlie, meet Horst."

Clynt turned and immediately walked away down the beach.

"Good evening, Fraulein Carson," Horst said with an exaggerated bow. "But I believe we are already acquainted."

"Not sure...from where," Martie said.

"Oh, but I am confident you remember," Horst said. "Surely you have not forgotten the Britannic."

Recognition dawned on Martie. "You're one of the spies from the ship. You tried to sink it."

"Very good," Horst said, scowling. "I am here because of you and your family."

"You made your own choices," she said defiantly. "Don't blame me for the consequences."

Horst shook his head. "Quite right, but you did have some impact on the timing of the situation. That cannot be overlooked. You will pay dearly, young lady. You will pay your debts forever."

Martie had no interest in the conversation and changed the subject. "There were two of you. Where's your friend?"

"You passed him back there in the cave," Horst said sadly. "A heavy burden accompanies a Tracker's fate. It requires a strong will. Karl was weak. Weak Trackers do not die. They withdraw into themselves until there is nothing left but mumbling insanity in some dark corner of history. Many end up here in The Gall of Bitterness, their minds as lost as their souls."

"I'm sorry to hear that about Karl," Martie said, feeling compassion for their pathetic state. "What about the boy who helped you steal the star?"

"Donny has survived the initial shock better than most," Horst said. "He thinks it is a grand adventure today. But he is young and his will is fragile. Clynt likes his chances, but I'm not so sure. Time will decide."

"What about me?" Martie said.

"You are a different case, fraulein. You are a living soul. You cannot move between historical times by yourself. You must have a star of Orion or be in the grasp of a Tracker."

Horst paused, apparently for dramatic effect. He waved his hands toward the other Trackers, baring his teeth in the smile of an animal ready to pounce. "We will not be taking you anywhere, fraulein. I am afraid your fate is to stay here until you die of old age or an act of nature."

"My family will come for me," Martie announced.

"We hope so," Horst said, pleased. "We dearly hope so."

Clynt strolled up with Donny in tow. "Well, well, girlie. Horst, ya makin' the young lady comfy? Is she lookin' forward to her new life?"

"It has not completely sunken in yet, but her eyes have been opened," Horst said.

Clynt released a cold, wicked chuckle that made Martie recoil. "No need for bars 'ere, girlie."

A loud explosion sent a tremor through the cave. "What's that?" she said, alarmed.

"A very famous volcano. You may be gettin' to witness a little history. Of course, it'll be the last thing you witness." Clynt smiled.

"And just what does that mean?" Martie challenged.

"That my girl is Krakatoa and today is the 26th of August 1883." Clynt seemed pleased with himself.

"I've heard of Krakatoa," Martie said. "Wasn't it a volcano that blew up a long time ago?"

Clynt gestured to Horst. "Ya see, Horst, I told ya she's a smart one." He looked back into Martie's eyes and leaned in close. She nearly gagged at the smell of his putrid breath. "That explosion long ago, girlie, is gonna blow this island to the sky tomorrow morning."

Martie looked back and forth between Horst, Donny, and Clynt as if she were a trapped animal. "But we'll all die."

"Not us, girlie. Jus' you," Clynt said, and the other Trackers laughed. "We'll be needin' a new time in history for our Gall of Bitterness though."

"A new time?" Martie said.

"Ya see, girlie. We's gonna stay here in the cave, but we go back a few hundred years and start over. Ain't it beautiful?"

Martie edged toward panic. And yet in the midst of the terrible realization she looked at Donny. She caught a glimpse of remorse and pain that crossed Donny's face.

I need to get him alone and talk.

"Where's the star?" Martie said.

Clynt patted the saddlebag draped over his shoulder. "It's safe with me, girlie. Never gonna leave this ol' boy's side."

"Why haven't you used it yet?"

"Waitin' for the Follow Stars," Clynt said. "We was in yer room when Donny took ya. Saw 'em fall out. Yer dad's bringin' them to us."

"You see, fraulein, we look forward to meeting your father again, and you make wonderful bait," Horst said. "Then we will truly be able to enjoy the fruits of our labors."

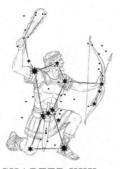

CHAPTER XXX

Desperate Acts

Martie felt unsafe on the beach with all the ejected debris from the volcano raining down. She hung around the opening and watched Donny. He followed Clynt around like a hungry dog. His expression looked angry, and she had not seen him speak. The Trackers began to gather around the campfire, but Donny sat alone on the outside of the ring.

She sidled up to him. "You don't have to put up with this. You can go anywhere in history."

"I want to be here," he responded meanly. "You don't understand."

"Maybe not," she said sympathetically. "But why do you want to be poisoned by these losers?"

"They're my friends," Donny objected. "My other life is what poisoned me."

"Really? Nobody cares about you or talks to you. You're invisible here."

"You don't get it," Donny said, raising his voice with fists clenched. Then he seemed to deflate and dropped his head. "It's all I've got now."

A new thought entered Martie's mind as if placed there by someone else. "Maybe you can earn a little redemption by doing something good."

"There's no redemption for a Tracker," Donny snapped. "This is forever. Clynt knows."

"Clynt lies," Martie said. "He's already lied to you, hasn't he?"

"Maybe," Donny said weakly.

"Why not try?" Martie said. "What could you possibly lose?"

He seemed to think about it for a moment. "What did you have in mind?"

"How about grabbing me and taking me somewhere else in history," Martie said.

"Where?"

"Are you kidding? Anywhere that won't kill me in the next few hours."

"I dunno. They'll know and they'll catch us," Donny said.

"So...what can they do to you?"

"They could banish me and shun me so I'd be alone forever," Donny said, anguish in his voice.

"Maybe there's more to the picture they're not telling you. What do you think happens to people who live good lives? Maybe there's another forever. It's got to be better than being a Tracker."

Donny looked almost hopeful.

He's taking the bait.

Neither of them had noticed Clynt and Horst approach in the darkness behind them.

"My young man," Horst said. "What is Fraulein Carson filling your head with?"

Donny reacted as if he had been struck. "I...I'm sorry...I mean...she told me I might not have to be a Tracker if..."

Clynt cut him off. "She don't know nothin', boy. She be tryin' to trick you into sneakin' her away."

"Go sit by the fire, Donny," Horst said. "We will take care of her so she won't bother you anymore."

Donny slunk off to the fire like a whipped dog.

"Why'd ya do that, girlie? Ya ain't getting' away from us. Yer only making him more likely to end curled up and mindless somewhere's in history."

"But there's got to be hope for everyone," Martie said boldly, feeling she had nothing left to lose.

"You are deluded by the myth of Present Time thinking," Horst said. "Those holding onto hope are quickest to lose their minds."

"And those all-powerful tyrants and dictators," Clynt chuckled.

"Tyrants and dictators?" Martie said. "You mean like Hitler or Stalin?"

"Yep, them's that thought they were so great and powerful in life. Them's that thought they could overthrow the world or God himself," Clynt said with satisfaction in his voice.

"They are unable to deal with their fall from life to having nothing," Horst said. "Such are simply bullies and cowards without their cheering or cowering crowds. There is no stage here for them to occupy. The descent to the life of a Tracker is simply too far, and their minds are broken."

"It be sad for the rest of us," Clynt added. "Their hate woulda made 'em great Trackers."

Clynt called two other Trackers over. "This one's causin' trouble. Tie her up in the cave 'til the others come."

Natalie called Bobby immediately following the disappearance of Jim and Tim. "Is Grandpa Chris with you?"

"Yes," Bobby responded. "What's going on? You sound worried."

"You both need to get to the hospital as soon as you can. I'll meet you in Mike's room. And bring some traveling clothes."

"Is it a StarPassage-related emergency?"

"Yes, but I don't have time to answer questions now," Natalie said, knowing they were in a race to save the lives of her family. "Just get there as fast as you can."

Fifteen minutes later, Natalie entered Mike's room, where Bobby and Grandpa Chris were already waiting.

"What's the big rush," Bobby said.

"We think Martie has been kidnapped and they used the star."

"Oh no," Mike said. "Do you think Trackers are involved?"

"Could be," Natalie said. "Four Follow Stars were left behind with the names of the intended users on them. Bobby and Grandpa Chris's names are on two of them. Jim and Tim took the other two and left about thirty minutes ago."

"We better get going then," Grandpa said.

"I brought you this," Natalie said, pulling a flashlight out of her purse and handing it to Bobby. "If you're going where the Trackers are, it's probably going to be dark."

"You might need this too," Mike said, pulling his great-grandfather's trench knife from the drawer.

"Thanks," Bobby said. "I know it means a lot to you."

"Don't lose it," Mike warned, then smiled. "It's an antique, kind of."

"Still looks new to me," Bobby said, smiling. "Looks like you just got it a week ago."

"How much do you know about what is going to happen?" Natalie inquired.

"Bobby and Mike have given me a pretty detailed rundown of what they have experienced," Grandpa said. "All we can do is get going and see what we see."

"Remember you need to keep the star in your hand," Natalie advised.

"Let's go. Where are the stars?" Bobby said.

Natalie took the stars from her pocket and handed them to Bobby and Grandpa Chris. Grandpa started to say something as his fingers closed around the star. Mike and Natalie were not able to tell what he said, but watched Grandpa's eyes grow wide as he immediately faded and disappeared.

"I hope they find her," Mike said.

"I'm worried about what else they'll find," Natalie countered.

Jim and Tim appeared at the opening of the cave on Krakatoa's beach. A fire burned brightly in a ring of rocks. Too late they realized a dozen dark figures surrounded the fire. The figures on the far side of the ring saw them immediately and cried out, pointing. The near figures turned and tackled Jim and Tim before their senses came into focus. They never had a chance to escape before they were in the Trackers' unforgiving grasp. They were bound and thrown into the cave with the other lost souls. They lay on the ground next to Martie in the near-pitch dark, the only light now the distant flicker from the campfire around the bend at the mouth of the cave.

"What happened," Martie said.

"We appeared right in the middle of them," her dad said. "They seemed to be expecting us and were ready."

"The whole thing was a trap," Martie said. "I'm so sorry."

"Not your fault, sis. Just bad timing," Tim said.

Martie looked at her dad. "I think Clynt is more obsessed with getting revenge on you than he is about getting the star."

"Do you have any idea what his next move is?"

"Don't think there is a next move, Dad. He told me this is

the volcano Krakatoa, and it's going to blow up in the morning, about three hours from now."

Jim's mind began to spiral downward. He fought the slide. "August 1883, the 27th I believe. That's very bad. The whole island simply disappeared and became dust in the atmosphere. There has to be a way out of here."

"Not likely without the star," Martie said. "They've got it now."

"There were two more Follow Stars," Tim said.

"That's right," Jim added. "Bobby and Grandpa Chris's names were on them. They could be arriving any time."

"I hope they don't get the same welcome you did."

"Clynt's not expecting them," he said. "But he may sense the stars when they arrive."

"Maybe their pull isn't strong enough to be noticed with everything else that's going on," Tim suggested. "He didn't even bother to take our stars yet."

"They're not going anywhere if the big star doesn't," Martie said.

"We can only wait and hope," Jim said as he continued to struggle with the ropes. "There will be an opportunity. We need to be ready. Keep trying to get these loose."

Clynt sat by the fire feeling as satisfied as he thought a Tracker could ever be. He still had the saddlebag over his shoulder. Horst was telling the story of the Britannic to the Trackers gathered around the fire.

"I see why it has brought you such satisfaction to apprehend these rascals from the Present Time," said a well-dressed British gentleman sitting next to Horst. "They have caused you no end of difficulty."

"That be a mighty big understatement," added a woman dressed in French peasant clothing from the 1700s.

"All that's left now is to watch 'em blown to the sky," Clynt said with evil glee. "Then we's gotta find a new time for The Gall so's we can welcome more Trackers. The Present Time must be gettin' pretty bad with all the new volunteers arriving."

The ground rumbled again. "Seems to be getting more violent with each tremor," Horst said.

"Ain't gonna be long now," Clynt said. "Then we tests out the stars."

Grandpa Chris and Bobby appeared on the beach about thirty yards from the cave entrance and the campfire where Clynt and Horst were talking. Grandpa fell to his knees. "I never could stand riding rollercoasters. Always made me sick."

"First time is tough," Bobby agreed. "I'm still not used to it."

"But this is my second time," Grandpa said. "The first time wasn't nearly this disorienting."

"Take a moment to get your balance back," Bobby said.

"Where are we?" Grandpa rose to his feet. "A beach somewhere."

The ground rumbled again, and the volcano ejected more huge boulders, some of which hit the beach close by. The shaking caused Grandpa to fall to the ground again.

"This is not a safe place to be," Grandpa said, regaining his feet. "We should take care of business and get home."

"Looks like a bunch of people over there by the fire," Bobby said. "Should we check it out?"

"Let's not let them see us yet," Grandpa said. "Can you tell if they're real people or Trackers from here?"

"The fire will blind them to what's in the dark, so we'll be able to get pretty close," Bobby advised. "But if they're Trackers they may sense that we're here anyway, so we should be careful."

"Let's not waste time then," Grandpa said. They moved along the edge of the jungle until they approached the cave's entrance. "There's no way without being spotted. The light of the fire will give us away for sure."

"What do we do now?" Bobby whispered.

"We wait for another earthquake or explosion as a diversion before attempting to sneak by."

They froze as one of the people sitting at the campfire straightened up and looked around. He wore a cowboy hat and six-gun in a holster. The cowboy hesitated, squinting into the darkness, then shook his head and returned his attention to the fire. The two travelers remained pressed against the rocks and listened to the conversation around the campfire, waiting for an opportunity.

"Can you tell if they're Trackers?" Grandpa said.

"Not sure," Bobby responded. "But I've heard Tim and Martie talk about the cowboy who is their leader and that might be him."

"Okay, we assume the worst," Grandpa concluded.

"Go and check on our guests, Horst," the cowboy said. "Don't want's 'em to feel we's in-hospitable."

The group around the campfire laughed as one of them stood and walked into the cave. He was gone for about a minute, then returned and sat again by the fire. "They seem to be enjoying the amenities. I informed them that room service would be a bit delayed, however." Raucous laughter erupted again but was interrupted by a massive earthquake.

"It feels like we're next to the railroad tracks with a freight train speeding toward us," Bobby said.

"Look. The beach is rippling like water," Grandpa said. "This might be our only chance."

The earthquake lasted almost a minute. Rocks tumbled from the mountain. The Trackers and the campfire were tossed around like toys on a trampoline. Bobby and Grandpa struggled to keep their feet and managed to slip into the dimly lit cave. They clung to the wall until the earthquake ended and their eyes adjusted from the bright campfire to the darkness.

Bobby led as they felt along the wall, moving ever deeper into the cave. There were bodies strewn along the sandy floor. They stumbled over them and fell more than once as they attempted to move deeper into the cave. The bodies moved, so they were alive, but they did not respond in any other way.

"There's life in these people but little else," Grandpa observed.

They arrived at a bend in the cave where it became nearly pitch dark. After turning the bend, Bobby switched on the flashlight. "I hope it's safe to use this now. They shouldn't be able to see it around the corner."

The cave shook again, and the travelers pressed against its walls. Several basketball-size rocks fell from the ceiling, landing on the bodies strewn haphazardly on the floor. Instead of the bone crushing thuds Bobby expected, the bodies simply vaporized and disappeared as the rocks hit.

"What's going on," Bobby said. "The bodies feel real, but they disappear as soon as the rocks hit them."

The two travelers stumbled on for another ten yards until they heard a familiar female voice. "Who's there? Trackers don't need a flashlight."

"Martie, that you?" Bobby answered. A face came into view.

"Bobby! How'd you find us?"

"Actually, there weren't a lot of places to look." His smile shone in the dim light. "You weren't sunning on the beach."

"Dad and Tim are here too," Martie said. "But I can't untie their ropes."

"This'll do it." Bobby retrieved the trench knife from his jacket pocket. "It'll just take a second."

He knelt down and sliced through the ropes like butter. "Great-Grandpa Robert sure had his knife sharpened to a fine edge."

Jim and Tim rubbed their wrists and ankles to get some circulation going. "Those Trackers tie a tight knot," Jim commented.

"Who are all these people laying around," Bobby said. "When the rocks hit them, they just disappear."

"They're Trackers who couldn't deal with their eternal prison," Tim answered. "But they can't die either. So most eventually go insane. They find a quiet corner of history, curl up, and disconnect from their horrible reality."

"Some of them had very different expectations. Horst told me those two over there were suicide bombers who expected to go immediately to heaven," Martie said. "That made their fate especially difficult to deal with."

"Yeah, I guess it would be kind of a shock for someone like that," Grandpa added.

"If the island weren't going to blow up and the Trackers didn't want to destroy us, it might be interesting to learn some of their histories," Jim said with a hint of sarcasm.

Martie pointed past Bobby. "The one just behind you in the dark robes is a priest from the Middle Ages who thought he did God's work during the inquisition by torturing and putting to death those who didn't conform to his beliefs."

"Like the ones that William Tyndale had to deal with," Tim observed. "I guess they discovered they were on the wrong team after all."

"This is what Clynt calls The Gall of Bitterness or just The Gall," Martie said. "It's kind of the home base for Trackers when they're not wandering around history. A lot of the hopeless Trackers must return here to die."

"Well, maybe not actually die, but as close to it as they can get," Tim added.

"What do we do next?" Bobby said.

"The only way out of here is to get the star," Jim said. "They didn't take our stars so all we need is the big one."

"I'll bet it's in that leather saddlebag Clynt has over his shoulder," Tim said. "He seems to keep that pretty close."

"He's at the mouth of the cave by the fire," Grandpa said.

"How many?" Jim said.

"Maybe a dozen," Grandpa answered.

"Taking on Clynt and the Trackers is not a good option, but it's all we've got," Bobby said.

As he spoke, Bobby felt an unearthly cold presence behind him. A voice came from the darkness. "You be downright clever boys," Clynt said. "Never knowed there was four o' them there Follow Stars."

Jim sprang to his feet and unsheathed his knife.

Clynt motioned and two Trackers grabbed Martie and held her tightly between them.

"Come on, ol' Jim," Clynt said. "You knows that ain't no good on a Tracker. Put it away and hand over the stars to Horst, or you gonna make us do somethin' hurtful."

Horst stepped forward and held out his hand, in which the travelers placed four small eight-pointed stars. Clynt held open the saddlebag flap, and Horst dropped the stars inside.

"You done me a great service, boys," Clynt said. "Now's I can takes four other Trackers with me to yer world while ya have a front row seat to watch the end of mine. Gonna be a good ol' time in town tonight." The gathering group of Trackers laughed.

Another tremendous earthquake shook the ground, causing everyone to lose their balance. Rocks fell from the ceiling, hitting three Trackers standing with Clynt, causing them to vaporize. One of the Trackers holding Martie disappeared as a rock crashed down, and another let go as he fell. The other Trackers, including Clynt, were tossed against the cave walls or hit the ground hard.

Clynt instinctively put both hands out to brace his fall, allowing the saddlebag to fly from his shoulder. It landed halfway between the Trackers and the travelers. Jim lunged at the saddlebag, snatching it up. The saddlebag flap came loose, spilling its contents on the ground as the earthquake doubled its intensity.

"Get 'em," howled Clynt.

The two nearest Trackers attempted to move toward the travelers but were both hit by falling rocks and disappeared in a dusty cloud. The travelers and Trackers alike were unable to get to their feet. Jim struggled to gather the stars. He found the large star and three of the Follow Stars and scrambled on all fours toward the travelers. He handed the small stars to Grandpa, Bobby, and Tim, then held out the larger star to Martie, who had crawled to his side.

"We have to be able to read the star to know where to hold it," Martie said.

"There's no time," Bobby yelled as the earthquake began to subside.

"Bobby, your flashlight," Grandpa said.

Bobby shined the light at the star and saw writing. But before anyone could react, they were set upon by angry Trackers and pinned roughly against the wall.

"Jus' where do you think you was gonna run to," Clynt said. "Ain't nowhere to go, ol' boy."

"What would you like us to do with them?" Horst inquired.

"Nothin'. They's doomed in a few minutes anyways," Clynt said.

Clynt reached out to take the star from Jim but was stopped by a brilliant white light that seemed to come from just behind Grandpa. The Trackers covered their eyes and cowered.

"This ain't your business," Clynt yelled at the light. "You gots no rights here."

The light glowed unaffected. The five travelers also shielded their eyes. Bobby was the first to see it. "There are two people standing in the middle of the light by Grandpa."

The figures of light moved forward, causing the Trackers to cower and pull back. Bobby noticed they did not walk; rather they seemed to float just above the ground. They stopped and stood between the Trackers and their prey. It appeared to Bobby that the light came from inside the robed figures. One moved toward Clynt, who remained the last Tracker standing. As the personage of light got closer, Clynt's knees buckled and he fell to the ground.

The travelers stood and moved backward into the cave as Bobby shined his flashlight on the star. He looked at Martie and laughed. "Guess I don't need this now. Got plenty of light."

None of the Trackers were able to respond other than to wail and thrash.

"Who are you?" Grandpa said.

A male voice came from the light. "Son, we promised we would walk at your side."

"Is that really you?" Grandpa said.

"Yes," came the voice of Leah in return. "You must be quick. We stand in the darkest of all dark places in time, The Gall of Bitterness. It is the heart of the Trackers' realm. The power of light cannot long persist in this place."

Bobby held up his star. "Look, they're glowing."

They all hesitated as if suspended in time.

The voice of Leah spoke. "As you have always expected, the star is not the source of its power. It is merely a vehicle within which a higher power wields a force for good. You are all part of that goodness."

The voice of Robert added, "It is the desire for unconditional goodness within you, in spite of your weaknesses, that allows the power of the tool to be wielded in your hands. Use it wisely, and it will be your guide. Use it unwisely, and it will be your undoing as it was for Donny."

Jim recovered and handed the large star to his daughter. "Martie, what does the star say?"

A sustained earthquake began again. The shaking became so violent that the cave itself seemed to bend and warp like a rubber tube. More rocks fell, vaporizing the priest and the two suicide bombers. The light from the personages wavered and began to fade.

Martie yelled as she read:

"Take hold of the star near ten and five, you'll return to your home and remain alive."

Bobby let go of the star in his pocket. He wanted to make sure everyone got safely out. Jim and Martie immediately grabbed the star by the points as directed. Bobby watched as they faded, followed by Tim and Grandpa.

"We made it," Bobby said, relieved.

The cave around him echoed with crashing rocks, blended with the wails of damned souls as the Trackers voiced their frustration at being thwarted again. He closed his fingers around the star. The world lost focus, but not before he was shaken by an enormous sound—the loudest sound ever heard in recorded history. The sound of an island ceasing to exist in one cataclysmic explosion. And that was only the beginning of the terror that followed.

Clynt had never been so furious. He stared into the darkness. "I'll gets my revenge. I never stops 'til I sees yer doom, *Carsons*."

The cowboy pounded the sand, his rage turning immediately to bitter hate as he struggled to stand. Trackers all around him were being vaporized or simply fading to escape Krakatoa's explosive destruction.

As the last of the hateful travelers disappeared, Clynt heard and felt the earth groan from its core, a deep thrumming rumble that rose as if climbing from the darkest depths, pulling with it the very hounds of hell threatening to split the world in two. Clynt fell to the sand again. His fingers dug deep as if tearing at the very heart of Jim Carson. Then his hand closed around a metallic object partially buried in the sandy cavern floor. His smile went wide as he lifted it to his shadowed face.

"A Follow Star!"

He straightened and reached his hands toward the roof of the cave in exaltation. "I'm comin' for y'all."

He slowly faded and began his journey as the island ceased to exist. His path took him through history and space...to the Present Time.

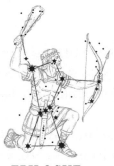

Rules of the Present Time

A figure crouched in the shadows, watching. He felt the sea breeze chill his skin, raising goosebumps. The sensation surprised him. It charged him with energy he had not felt in a hundred years. The object of his interest was a New England style shingle home across the narrow beach community road. He knew the house well, had been within its walls many times before. Invitations were extended, and he had always dutifully responded. But no such invitations had come for months. Today, for the first time, he needed no invitation. A smile stretched his wind-weathered face.

Clynt felt excited and anxious at the same time. *Am I mortal now?* He had been there for several hours waiting for the right moment. Initially, the new rules caught him off guard.

The first surprise that greeted him was physical. Clynt disappeared from The Gall as the cave collapsed. He felt awe as the world faded to gray, then came slowly back into focus. He felt exalted by the strange surroundings in the alley where he now stood. Something felt immediately different, a good, human

kind of feeling. The Follow Star slipped through his right hand
to the ground. "What?"

Clynt bent casually to pick it up. His fingers passed through
the star as if they were mist. He howled in anger and stabbed
at the star again and again. *I'm partly physical. The breeze tells
me that much.* A realization slowly dawned on him. He had only
crossed partway over the bridge to being fully physical. Then
a thought formed and he froze, looked up slowly, and smiled at
the house across the street.

"That's what I needs. It's right there."

He knew what he had to do. "Them's the rules of the star, and
I've gotta play by them rules."

He needed to inhabit a human vessel to have a real life. He
wasn't yet sure exactly how that worked, but he had chosen the
vessel. Tim Carson seemed the perfect candidate, and it would
be sweet revenge. He laughed at the thought of introducing himself to the family through their own son. "It's perfect."

He shook his head. "Ya shoulda expected it. No excuse for bein'
caught unawares. Gotta learn the rules. First time for everythin'."

There were visitors at the home, and he watched as Tim
walked a young girl to her car, a light green four-door Jeep parked
at the curb. They held hands and hugged awkwardly before she
got in and drove off. Tim stood there for a moment watching as
she rounded the corner.

"I see," Clynt said. "There's a lady in your life, eh? It jus' gets
better and better. Y'all's gonna wish ya'd never been born."

He waited another hour until the last lights blinked out at
the Carson home.

"It's time and I's comin' for ya, boy."

Clynt left the alley and started across the street. A two-door
sedan with only one working headlamp sped around the corner.
Clynt froze, unable to get out of the way. He instinctively raised

his hands to his face for protection. The sedan's tires squealed, leaving a patch of rubber on the road as the driver speed shifted and accelerated toward him. He flinched as the car made contact, but he felt nothing. It sped through him as if he were light fog. He saw three teenage boys laughing and pumping their fists out the window as the sedan's taped-over taillights disappeared into the darkness.

Clynt bent over to catch his breath, his heart racing. He pumped his fist like he had seen the teenagers do and said, "Rule number two. Nothin' can touch me."

He reached for the front door, but the knob slipped through his fingers as had the star. Then the experience with the speeding car struck him. He reached his hand further. It easily penetrated the door as if he were a ghost. Clynt hadn't enjoyed anything this much in a long time. He leaned into the door and felt no resistance as he moved through the woodgrains to the other side.

Standing in the entryway, he listened in the dark. Nothing. He confidently walked up the stairs. As he made a walking motion, he felt nothing underfoot. He seemed to float a fraction of an inch above the steps. Clynt stopped moving his legs to see what happened. His forward motion immediately ceased, and he hovered above the step. He chuckled as he looked at his feet.

"I s'pose I gots to make like I'm walkin' to move."

He knew the house and glided more than walked to Tim's closed door, passing through it into the bedroom. He entered quietly, still concerned that he didn't know all the Present Time rules. Tim lay in a deep sleep on the bed in front of him. Clynt could hardly contain his excitement.

Can he hear me or see me?

He stood at the foot of the bed, wondering what to do next and not daring to make a sound. Another delicious thought occurred to him. *If I can walk through doors and folks can't see me, then*

maybe I can jus' lay down, push the old soul out, and be takin'
its place.

Clynt smiled wide, baring his yellow crooked teeth. He could
no longer contain himself and laughed out loud. His voice made
a long, chilling echo that would have frozen the soul of any who
heard, but no living soul could. He stepped back, waiting. Tim
didn't stir and Clynt knew this rule was in his favor too.

"If ya can't see me and ya can't hear me, ya ain't gonna stop
me. Get ready for the ride o' yer life, boy. I'm takin' over."

Acknowledgments

Any work of literature endures a long uncertain childhood. It cannot come of age without giants who walk beside it to guide, inspire, and support the difficult fits and starts of progress. So, too, has been the continuing development of the StarPassage series.

I must begin by expressing my deepest gratitude to Bill, Tamara, Kit, Crystal, Andy, Bev, and the excellent staff of professionals associated with Deep River Books. This especially includes my editor Barbara Scott. Their kindness and patient direction has made this work possible and enhanced the result. Guiding an author along the path to a great work is a delicate balance. In my case it has been accomplished with firm and clear direction while allowing the work to remain in my voice. It is an art they practice to perfection.

The same is true of my good friends at PR by the Book. They have unwaveringly waded into the marketing arena to assist in wisely directing this often-ignorant Don Quixote away from tilting at windmills and into the modern world of social media, blog tours, and appearances. You have made a tremendous difference.

I also wish to extend appreciation to my growing following of fans and readers. It is for you that I do this, and I dearly appreciate the comments, blog reviews, feedback, and encouragement.

My greatest joy is meeting with and being edified by your stories of how my books have inspired and uplifted. Because of you, there is much more excitement to come.

I cannot write without careful review and advice. I appreciate the contributions to this work provided by Karin and Todd Cook, Creighton and Lisa Rider, Win and Becky Jones, Lt. Col. John Burbidge (Ret.) and Alan Peterson, Travis and Shaunna Burbidge, Shauntae Browning, and Devin Thorpe. Thank you for putting up with fragments of thoughts, ideas, and constant retelling of stories. Do not doubt the influence of your input.

Finally, there is no author and no book without the daily inspiration, encouragement, and unconditional love from my dear sweetheart, Leah. You are the hand that reached into my darkest moment and led me into the bright noonday sun of life. You have walked hand-in-hand with me, living a life exemplified by our dear Savior and Lord. It is an overwhelming blessing from our Heavenly Father that I am fortunate enough to travel the narrow path with such an elect lady at my side. Thank you.

Reader Assists

The Stars of Orion:

Star of Passage—Large 8-point star
Follow Stars—Small 8-point stars
Stars of Tongues—Small 4-point stars
Star of Sight—Small 6-point star

Rules for StarPassage

1. Hold onto the star. It keeps you from being seen or heard.
2. Always check the star for new writings.
3. Read the writings carefully and follow them exactly.
4. While holding onto the star, you don't feel weather or temperature.
5. Invisible doesn't mean not physical, so **watch out for** stuff.
6. You return when the purpose of the **StarPassage** is done.
7. Beware. Anything you do may change history.
8. You don't get to choose your StarPassage. The star or something else does.
9. Watch out for the dark figures. They can see you and want the star. They call themselves Trackers.
10. The dark figures move slower that we do but have a strong grip and can use anything, including weapons, that exist in their time.

11. They appear to be in every past time and can move between them. But for some reason, they cannot come to the present. They call our time the Present Time.

12. There are multiple silver relics of which the star seems to be the most important. The dark figures seek them all and believe that with them they can enter the Present Time. They call the relics Orion's Belt.

13. Trackers can't influence history or interact with historical figures. They can only observe.

14. Whenever the Star of Passage is used, it will draw Trackers to it.

15. Trackers can physically interact with anyone from the Present Time or any historical individual that possesses one of the stars.

16. There are at least six stars: The large eight-pointed Star of Passage, two or more small eight-pointed Follow Stars, two small four-pointed Stars of Tongues, and one small six-pointed Star of Sight.

17. The Star of Passage will allow the Trackers to come to the Present Time where they believe they will have power to possess the bodies of people and control their minds and acts.

18. People in the Present Time draw Trackers when they are discouraged or depressed, etc. If people look backward, they can be pulled into the realm of the Trackers and be lost. But we have the power always to turn our backs.

19. Trackers may be able to hypnotize you with their voice.

20. Animals can sense your presence even if you are invisible.

21. Severe handicaps we have in the present time may be nonexistent on a passage.

Referenced Quote

Quote from former President Theodore Roosevelt, an excerpt from a talk entitled "Citizenship in a Republic" delivered on April 23, 1910, at the Sorbonne in Paris, France.

THE MAN IN THE ARENA

"It is not the critic who counts; not the man who points out how the strong man stumbles, or where the doer of deeds could have done them better. The credit belongs to the man who is actually in the arena, whose face is marred by dust and sweat and blood; who strives valiantly; who errs, who comes short again and again ... who knows great enthusiasms, the great devotions; who spends himself in a worthy cause; who at the best knows ... the triumph of high achievement, and who at the worst, if he fails, at least fails while daring greatly, so that his place shall never be with those cold and timid souls who neither know victory nor defeat."

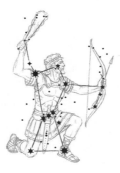

References

Ambrose, Stephen E. *D-Day June 6, 1944: The Climactic Battle of World War II* (Touchstone-Simon & Schuster, 1994).

Astor, Gerald. *June 6, 1944: The Voices of D-Day* (Dell Publishing-Random House, Inc., 1944).

Burgett, Donald R. *Currahee! A Screaming Eagle at Normandy* (Dell Publishing, 1967).

"Colosseum & Christian Martyrs," http://www.tribunesand triumphs.org/colosseum/colosseum-christian-martyrs.htm.

The Colosseum in Rome, http://home.comcast.net/~burokerl /colosseum.htm.

"Curiosities: After rains, why do worms crawl out onto the pavement and 'commit suicide'?" (University of Wisconsin-Madison News June 29, 2007) http://news.wisc.edu/13900.

Koskimaki, George E. *D-Day with the Screaming Eagles* (Random House - Presidio Press, 1970).

101st Airborne Division, *Combat Chronicle*, http:// www.501stpir.com/101st_airborne_history/101stabn_history.html.

Rider, Creighton and Lisa, Salt Lake City, Utah, Team Leaders, Creighton's Riders-Saints To Sinners Relay Race. Personal interviews, August 2015.

The Almanac of Theodore Roosevelt, http://www.theodore-roosevelt.com/trsorbonnespeech.html.

The National Commission on Terrorist Attacks Upon the United States, *The 9/11 Commission Report: The Attack from Planning to Aftermath—Authorized Text* (W. W. Norton & Company, 2011, 2nd Edition).

"This Day in History, August 27, 1883, Krakatoa Erupts," http://www.history.com/this-day-in-history/krakatoa-erupts.

Teems, David. *Tyndale: The Man who Gave God an English Voice* (Thomas Nelson, Inc. 2012).

"Map of the Mall at the World Trade Center," *Wikipedia*, https://en.wikipedia.org/wiki/Westfield_World_Trade_Center#/media/File:Map_of_the_Mall_at_the_World_Trade_Center.svg.

"Timeline for the Day of the September 11 Attacks," *Wikipedia*, https://en.wikipedia.org/wiki/Timeline_for_the_day_of_the_September_11_attacks.

"William Tyndale," *Wikipedia*, https://en.wikipedia.org/wiki/William_Tyndale.

Winchester, Simon. *Krakatoa: The Day the World Exploded—August 27, 1883* (HarperCollins Publishers, 2003).

Other Books by Clark Rich Burbidge

Gold Medal Award Winning Current Trilogy:

StarPassage: Book One—*The Relic*

Fiction: Gold Medal Award Winning Young Adult Trilogy:

Giants in the Land: Book One—*The Way of Things*
Giants in the Land: Book Two—*The Prodigals*
Giants in the Land: Book Three—*The Cavern of Promise*

Fiction: Gold Medal Award-Winning Family Christmas Story:

A Piece of Silver: A Story of Christ

Non-Fiction:

*Life on the Narrow Path: A Mountain Biker's Guide to Spiritual
Growth in Troubled Times*

See how the award-winning
StarPassage trilogy began...

StarPassage

CLARK RICH BURBIDGE

Also check out the the award-winning
Giants in the Land trilogy...

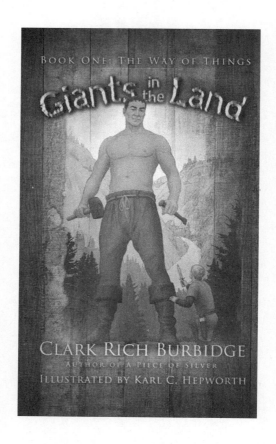

BOOK TWO: THE PRODIGALS

Giants in the Land

CLARK RICH

AUTHOR OF A PI

ILLUSTRATED BY K

BOOK THREE: THE CAVERN OF PROMISE

Giants in the Land

CLARK RICH BURBIDGE
AUTHOR OF A PIECE OF SILVER
ILLUSTRATED BY KARL C. HEPWORTH